Irish Tales

from the
Otherworld

GHOSTS, FAIRIES
& EVIL SPIRITS

BOB CURRAN

POOLBEG

Published 2008
by Poolbeg Press Ltd.
123 Grange Hill, Baldoyle,
Dublin 13, Ireland
Email: poolbeg@poolbeg.com

Typeset by Type Design in Caslon 10.6/14.5
Printed by
Litografia Rosés S.A., Spain

www.poolbeg.com

About the Author

Dr Bob Curran was born and raised in a remote area of County Down, Northern Ireland. Much of his early life was spent listening to the tales of the country people around his grandmother's fire and this has given him an ear for and a love of a good story. Leaving school at an early age, he firstly became a gravedigger – working in the isolated mountain cemeteries – and later a lorry driver. He has held a succession of jobs including musician, journalist and hospital worker. He has also lived in a number of countries including the United States, Morocco and Holland. After going to University as a mature student, he graduated with a Ph.D. in educational psychology and an honours degree in history and worked for many years as a teacher. He now works for a variety of employers, including the Northern Ireland Community Relations Unit and a number of cultural bodies to whom he acts as advisor on cultural matters. He is the author of many books, which have been translated into a number of languages including Japanese, Spanish, French, Italian and Hungarian. Throughout his career he has always listened to the tales of the Irish country people, which have formed the basis of this book. He currently lives in County Derry with his wife and young family.

Acknowledgements

I would like to acknowledge the kindness, hospitality and co-operation that I have been shown in the compiling of this book. In many areas of Ireland I was made most welcome by the storytellers who were willing to share their tales with me. This is really their book. I would also like to thank Brian Langan and the staff at Poolbeg Press for their hard work in bringing these tales together in the format which you see in front of you.

To my wife Mary and to Michael and Jennifer
for all their help, support and patience throughout
the writing of this book

Contents

Sheehogues and Other Horrors

The Dark Art

A Personal Tale

Introduction

In Ireland, the supernatural is usually never all that far away. It lies sleeping beneath a seemingly peaceful and beautiful landscape, just beyond our vision but ready to emerge when we least expect it or when we inadvertently stir it to life. Of course, it is nothing like we expect it to be. Those of us who believe in a world of gambolling spirits, merry and mischievous leprechauns and weeping banshees are in for something of a shock, as are those who see Ireland as a place of timeless mysticism and wonderful insights that have been passed down the centuries to the present day. Such an impression has been fostered by countless books of Irish fairy stories and fanciful films such as *Darby O' Gill and the Little People*, and it is altogether wrong. Ireland is *not* a land of playful pixies and singing spirits; rather it is a place where ancient and bloody gods once ruled, where children were often sacrificed by gore-stained druids to satisfy the voracious appetites of dark deities, and where, in later times, fearful outrages and atrocities were committed against the poor and the innocent by military forces and rackrenting landlords. Many of these fierce gods still lurk somewhere in the shadows and the horrors of the past have certainly left their mark on the landscape.

For many Irish people – particularly in rural areas – there was a shadowy and gloomy realm that lay all around them, just outside human sight and comprehension, where such things are well remembered. This was a world of fairies, witches, sheehogues (neither ghost nor fairy but containing elements of both) and uneasy spirits. Here too dwelt those ancestral gods which had once stalked the countryside and which still sometimes exerted a baleful influence on those mortals who had come to live there. This was known as the Otherworld – an ill-defined place which often impinged upon the day-to-day existence of the human sphere. There were places, it was said, where the two worlds merged, places such as old forts, mounds or ruins and which were knowingly counted as "bad places" or as "fairy haunted" by local people. They were spots where people might be snatched away by the creatures that dwelt there or where strange and fearful sights might be seen as eerie beings who have crossed over into our world. The Otherworld, and places associated with it, was therefore a place to be avoided if possible.

Of course, there were those in country areas who might well traffic with this shadowy domain, whether for personal gain or for spite against their neighbours. These were the practitioners of the dark arts and those who were "in with the fairies". They were usually viewed with fear and suspicion by those who lived around them.

Stories concerning fairy-haunted places, the restless dead, the evil spirits and the dark people who were connected to them, have made their way into the folklore of many communities. In rural areas there is usually some person who can tell an old tale about a place or person of dubious repute. Many of these stories have been handed down across the generations and, though perhaps never widely told, are still part of the local lore. This is the secret knowledge of the countryside, preserved in the old stories, to which only a few privileged souls are privy.

My own grandfather was one of those privileged people. He had spent at least part of his working life as a labourer in the South Armagh border region between Louth and Monaghan, where tales of such things were rife. Nor was he a man given to drama or exaggeration, for all his stories were told in the same slow country fashion that held the kernel of truth. As a small child, sitting at his knee, I listened with awe and wonder to the stories he told – tales, a number from his own experience, which hinted at ancient gods and wandering spirits still fearfully present in the areas where he had worked. It was from him that I learned that fairies were not jolly little fellows at all but hostile and malignant beings who frequently sought to do mankind harm; that ghosts and spirits often stalked the midnight roads, seeking to draw those whom they met away with them into the Afterlife; and that there were those who could cure an injury but could also kill with a glance. That dark knowledge has stayed with me long after my grandfather has gone.

"I remember one time," he said, sitting back in his chair, "there were fields a few miles from where we lived owned by a man who I worked for. In one of them was the stump of an oul' church which had a very bad name in the locality. It was mostly a ruin, only a couple of walls standing and a bit of an oul' bell tower. It was so old that most people had even forgotten when it had last been used or even what it had been called. It stood right in the middle of the field and the farmer who owned the place used to graze his cattle all around it. But like I said, it had a very bad name on it – it was said to be haunted and was a gathering place for the fairies that came there in order to do mischief. There were the carved faces of angels or children high up on the broken walls and there was always rubbish and branches of trees and things lying around just inside the archway of what had once been the door. It had been a grand place in its time, all right. The stonework of the oul' place was covered in ivy and creepers and the farmer was always frightened that the cattle would wander into the place, eat the ivy and take sick and die. So he sent me in with a scythe and a billhook to clear the place up and take away all the growth. I worked there for two or three days, cutting and scything all round the walls and out into the field. It was a lonely job all right, and not many would have taken on, because of the stories about the place, but I was young and easy and had no fear of fairies or ghosts.

"But late in the evening, when the sun was going down and the shadows were lengthening and moving across the fields, I could sometimes feel the hairs rising on the back of my neck and I suddenly felt very cold. The broken faces of the stone angels, up high on the walls, seemed to be watching me as I cleared away bushes and stuff that was growing on the walls and in the inside of the tower. I felt just a tiny bit afraid.

"Although it was a church, there were no graves about the ruin, although I think that a couple of times I did strike an old whitish-looking stone buried in the grass with the end of my scythe. Set into one of the walls, however, was a big iron door, that had been painted green at some point but was now all covered in rust. It was fixed with a big padlock that was so rusted you'd never have got it open and it had almost become part of the wall itself. It was said to lead into the tomb of some great local family whose people had been laid to rest there. Nobody could agree on their name – some said it was this name, some said that it was another – but it couldn't have been a very big crypt, just a badly overgrown vault that was fixed onto the side of the church. Well, it was late in the evening of the second day and I was cutting away some ivy that hung down close to the door, when I heard a sound. It was a woman crying – sobbing as if her heart would break – and although I could hear it quite clearly, it seemed to come from far away.

"I thought it might be a tinker woman, for there were tinkers camped by the side of the road a little farther along, and I went to the old ruined archway of the church. I stood looking out across the fields that were turning gold in the declining sun, but I saw nothing. And when I stepped back into the ruin, I could hear the crying more plainly. Then I knew: it was coming from behind the big iron door that led into the oul' tomb. I went and put my ear to the ironwork and, sure enough, I could hear the woman crying far away. Her voice had a strange echoey tone to it and I suppose this added to the idea that it came from a great distance. Even so, I could hear her very plain. From time to time she would give a wee sobbing gasp – 'Oh! Oh!' – and then she would start crying again. I've never heard anybody so miserable. I looked all around me but all I saw were the empty faces of angels carved into the stone of the building and an old stone cross, half buried in the ground close to my feet. But as I listened, the sound seemed to draw farther away until it was gone altogether, but I knew that I'd heard it.

"Was it a ghost? There were some that would've said that it was some poor spirit, caught in the stone, continually weeping over some sorrow that had been long forgotten by the rest of the world, but I don't know. I never did find out what it was, but that was my work over for the day. In the morning when I went back, I put my ear to the door and I heard nothing. There was no sound in that oul' place save the cawing of crows in the trees nearby. I never told anybody about it – not even the farmer I was working for – but that day finished me in the fields. Maybe it was a ghost of some kind, maybe it was no more than my own imagination, but I doubt if I'll ever know, for the old church has been pulled down long since and whatever lay in that tomb is either reburied or scattered to the wind."

I think that, perhaps more than any other of his tales – and there were many – that story frightened me the most. Maybe it did so because it had the ring of truth about it and because it hinted at old sorrows and secrets lurking beneath the surface of the familiar world that I knew. It hinted at the Otherworld. And perhaps it has set the tone for this book.

You are about to enter a world of hostile fairies, dark spectres and dangerous *sí ógs* or sheehogues (not quite fairy, not quite ghost, but embodying elements of both). This is the world that my grandfather told me about in his stories and that other storytellers I've since met have known about. Here too are those who dealt with the shadowy beings and who followed dark ways which sometimes even jeopardised their very communities. Each tale exemplifies the mysterious and sometimes deadly world that lies behind the façade of the existence that we take very much for granted.

These stories come from all over Ireland. They are the authentic voice of the country people, coming from a variety of sources. Following on from my grandfather's story of the hidden, weeping woman, as I grew up I began to travel along the back roads of a vanishing countryside, catching the last of these old stories before their tellers died. These are stories that I gathered over the years – in pubs in County Offaly; at fairs in County Louth; or sitting beside a peat fire in some lonely cottage in North Antrim. The tellers were an odd assortment too, from old mountainy men and women to polished doctors and housekeepers. None of the stories has ever been published before and even though I've made some stylistic adjustments, they are pretty much repeated in the same way that they were told to me. In all cases, I have permission to share them with you, although I've been requested to change a few details in some cases. This is a testament to the storytellers of Ireland, who were (and are) without peer in their craft. This book is dedicated to them.

Here is the tale of a phantom maid who committed a dreadful sin, endlessly wandering the corridors of a great house in County Roscommon, carrying the evidence of her shame with her; of a lonely woman in the Slieve Bloom Mountains in County Offaly who tries to gain the affections of the man she craves in an ancient and terrible way; of a hill farmer from County Kerry who marries a tinker woman only to find that she is in truth the embodiment of an ancient evil that has haunted the land for years; of a husband who tries to restore his wife's wits, which have been taken by the fairies, and makes a dreadful mistake. And what is that shadow moving in the yard – is it simply a trick of the sun or something far more dangerous?

All of these tales reveal the arcane and hidden knowledge of Ireland which has been handed down since the earliest days. So step with us now across the boundaries of our own comfortable reality as we travel across Ireland in search of the sometimes elusive creatures of the Otherworld. And tread carefully, for they may be much closer than you imagine!

The Fairies

I THE WEAVER OF DERRYORK

COUNTY DERRY

Throughout the Irish countryside, humans and fairies occasionally made bad neighbours. Because their lifestyles were often very different, the two sometimes annoyed each other, either by their general conduct or by their daily habits. For example, fairies often had specific paths across fields and through glens along which they travelled to and from their abodes without variation and which they regarded as their own personal roads, exclusive to themselves. Humans insensitively crossed these paths without permission, trampling across fairy routes and providing a danger to the fairy kind, who often travelled invisibly. Even worse, humans sometimes had the temerity to build their own houses on the line of such paths, thus obstructing them and rendering them useless to the fairy kind. There were, however, certain people in the countryside who knew the locations of these tracks and could be consulted before any building took place. This was not always done and often as not the fairies would take revenge on those who came to live in such dwellings.

1

On the Fermanagh/Cavan border, for example, close to the famous Marble Arch caves, a number of ruined houses stand in a small glen. The hamlet of about six or seven houses, which also included a shop, was raised on the direct line of a fairy path, cutting off the fairies from a small lake beyond, which was considered special to them. As a result, the community never prospered due to the supernatural intervention of the fairy kind. According to the great South Fermanagh storyteller and raconteur, the late George Sheridan, there was nothing but "illness and bankruptcy" amongst the people who lived there and when the shop finally closed, the remainder of the people simply moved away. It was, he said, a salutary lesson to those who crossed the fairies and who obstructed their paths. When crossing the actual glen, he advised, one should always say either "Good day" or more appropriately "By your leave" in order to ward off ill-fortune.

But it was not only the crossing of unseen paths that led to tension between humans and fairies. It was once the custom in many rural households to throw out "the water of the day" before retiring. This might be the water in which plates and cups were washed; in which potatoes had been washed; or, more commonly, in which feet had been washed before going to bed. It was usually thrown from the door of the house and into the nearest bush. However, it might also drench some invisible fairy who happened to be passing by the door at the time, naturally causing distress and annoyance. There are a number of stories of women who have been neglectful in throwing out the "feet water" and who have reaped some supernatural consequences. In one case, in County Sligo, a strange creature – often given as a black lamb – came into a house every night, lay down in front of the fire and died, causing a noxious stink throughout the building. The corpse was removed but every night for a month the same thing occurred and at last a priest had to be brought in to exorcise the building and the visitations stopped. It was considered that this was the result of dirty "feet water" drenching an invisible passer-by. To prevent such hauntings, it was advisable to utter a charm as the water was being thrown out. A common one was simply to say "Hugitha Ugitha Iskey Sullogh" (Away, away, dirty water) as the action was being performed. This acted as a charm and as a warning to anything which happened to be going past.

Because some fairies chose to live underground, water offered another problem. On Rathlin Island, a family was disturbed one night when a fairy man came knocking on their door. He asked them to stop teeming (washing) potatoes at their back door as the water was running into his house below and was threatening his wife and children. Some sort of resolution was eventually reached in this respect.

But the annoyance was not only one way. Fairies could also irritate humans with their thoughtless behaviour, especially if they congregated in large numbers. Fairies kept different hours to mortals, enjoyed parties and often had little regard for human property. Some of these problems are highlighted in the following tale from the townland of Derryork, near the village of Dungiven in North Derry.

The townlands of Derryork and Gelvin were supposed to be badly fairy-haunted and the fairies there seemed unusually aggressive. The 1835 Ordnance Survey Memoirs of the area detail interviews with an old woman and her daughter, both of whom sported purple marks on their thighs where they had been struck by "fairy bolts" fired by belligerent fairies as they passed them by. Several farmers of the region also reported cows and sheep injured by fairy activity. This version of the tale is attributed to Denis McCready, an elderly seanchaí, who lived near the Gelvin Water in the late nineteenth/early twentieth centuries.

In the townland of Derryork on the other side of the Gelvin there was a house standing – a long, low dark stone place that stood by the side of a path that led up to an old earthen fort in a field beyond. It was a good solid house but few people wanted to live there because the old fort behind it was supposed to be haunted by the fairies and, after dark, their screams, shouts and roars could be heard drifting across the Gelvin and into the countryside beyond until the early hours of the morning. They said a man had lived in the house after it was built but he didn't stay long because of the noise and because the fairies would play tricks on him when they had a mind to. In the end, he upped and left and the house stood empty for a time.

After a year or so, however, a weaver called Joseph McPherson came to live there with his wife and daughter. The house suited Joe for it had a grand front room where he could set up his loom, with a smaller room off it where he could store his cloth and his materials. It had a fairly big yard out the back that he could use for setting out his materials and finished work. All in all, it suited him grand. And even better, the landlord, Peter McCloskey, gave it to him for a low rent because of its bad reputation. The old fort in the field behind didn't concern Joe greatly for he was a Protestant and had no great belief in fairy powers.

For a few nights all was well – Joe settled in well to the house by the lane, as if he'd always lived there, setting up his loom in the front room where he could look out over the countryside as he was working and storing his bits and pieces in the little side-room. At night everything was quiet and the only sound that drifted across the fields was the occasional bark of a young fox or the sob of an owl among the trees – all was peaceful and Joe and his family got several good nights' sleep.

It was not to last, however. After a week had passed they were wakened one night to the sounds of shouting, shrieking and singing. When he went to the window to see what it was, Joe McPherson saw that the old earthen fort was bright and alive with light. Shadows were going back and forth from it across the fields and even as he stood there, he could hear the sound of fiddles scraping and glasses chinking. There was also the sound of laughter and of voices raised drunkenly in song. It was the Good Folk at their revels but it was an awful racket.

"I declare," said Joe to his wife, "none of us will get a wink of sleep while that din goes on. I'm for going up to the fort and telling them to be quiet." But his wife laid a restraining hand on his arm. She was a Catholic woman, strange and dark, from the Kilhoyle mountain country where the fairies are as thick as ticks on a blanket and she knew the dangers of dealing with them directly.

"Leave them be, Joe my jewel," she told him. "No good will come of your going up there and they'll pay you no heed. Let them have their party for the night and maybe all will be better tomorrow." And so the weaver stayed where he was and waited for his fairy neighbours to be quiet.

The party continued until about five o'clock in the morning with the sound of music and dancing drifting down to the cottage. Neither Joe nor his wife nor daughter were able to close their eyes for long, for there were lights in the sky over the old fort, and it was their brilliance as much as the noise that kept them awake. About half-past five, the cock crew and the sounds in the fort ceased. Everybody in the McPherson house was all but exhausted and, even though he had a number of orders to fill, the weaver was far too tired to put a hand to his loom for the rest of the day. He hoped that was the end of it.

But as darkness fell, lights flickered on in the ancient fort and the music started up again. The fairies were getting ready for another grand night of revelry. Glasses clinked, voices shouted and the sound of fiddles, fifes and bodhrans drifted down to Joe McPherson's window. He looked out, the eyes standing in his head for want of sleep, and saw the shadows coming and going in the fields around the fort.

"Faith," he said. "I'm going up there and make them be quiet, for I'll not put in another night like the last one."

Once again his wife tried to restrain him. "You'll only harm yourself by dealing directly with them, for they have ways that none of us understands," she pleaded. "We can put up with it for another night if we have to." But the weaver was not to be turned. Shrugging off her hand, he marched out of the door and up the laneway to the field. There he stood in front of the old fort which was now alive with lights and merriment.

"In the Name of God, cease your racket," he shouted loudly. "There are Christian people trying to sleep in the house below and cannot do so for your din. By all that's holy I urge you to be quiet." For an instant the music stopped and the night was still. The wind stirred the dark trees and bushes on the high earthen edges of the fort. Then a voice answered. It was deep and hollow and seemed to resonate in the air – like a man speaking from the depths of a bell.

"Who interrupts our sport?" it asked hollowly. "Is it Joseph McPherson, the weaver that lives in the cottage below?" The night felt suddenly colder and Joe shivered a little at being so readily recognised.

"It is," he replied, swallowing loudly.

The voice from the fort paused for a moment. "Come forward then, Joe, and into the fort and join our revelry, for we have no wish to offend you." Afraid to disobey, Joe took a few steps forward and entered the earthen walls of the old fort. Instantly the countryside around him was gone and he stood in the middle of a grand, columned hall which seemed to stretch away into the distance. And it seemed to be packed to capacity with all sorts of fairies – some were stately and gracious-looking while others seemed to be low and deformed. Everyone was of varying size: some were as tall as himself; others no bigger than a two-year-old child. All of them were engaged in all manner of pleasures and sport – drinking, dancing and wagering. And all around were casks of wine, beer and poteen, and tables that were literally groaning with foods of all kinds. Several of the fairies beckoned him forward and motioned him to join in, which Joe, despite his tiredness, did with a will.

"Isn't this a grand place?" says he to himself. "I'll wager that the gentry of the area – the Hamiltons and the Ogilbys – don't enjoy themselves as well as this." And he sat back to drink his fill and listen to the grand music.

Once again, the party lasted until cock-crow and as the first rooster opened its beak, the whole assembly melted away as if they'd never been there in the first place and Joe found himself lying among the grass in the middle of the old fort, with the morning dew on his coat. He got up and went back down to the cottage where his wife and daughter were anxiously waiting. He told them that he had spent all night with the fairies and assured them that there would be no further trouble.

And so it was for a couple of nights. The old fort lay dark and no sounds of merriment drifted down to the weaver's house. Joe and his family enjoyed their sleep and each day Joe was at his loom, filling in all the orders that he'd received, for he had a great reputation in the countryside.

Less than a week later, however, Joe's wife looked out of the window across the fields and saw lights starting up again in the fort. Hardly had she called to Joe to come and look than they heard the sound of fiddles and drinking coming from the place and they knew that they were in for another night of partying. They were both at their wits' end but there was worse to come. As the merriment got under way, the great brassy voice boomed across the fields and could be plainly heard in the house.

"Come up to the fort, Joseph McPherson, and join in our sport, for we have a mind to make you our guest once again."

Joe stood frozen to the spot, terrified by the fearful invitation.

"Pay them no heed, my jewel," his wife advised. "It's probably some sort of trick of the fairy kind. Once they get you into the fort, you might never get out again."

But the temper had risen in the weaver. "By God, I'll go," he snapped back, "for we'll get no peace down here for the rest of the night. And when I'm up there, I'll tell these creatures what I think of them." And he stormed out of the house and up the lane, for the temper was greatly on him.

But when he actually got to the fort, his fury had cooled a little and a creeping fear had begun to take hold of him. Although there were lights flickering within the place, the bushes and trees about it were very dark and odd shadows came and went between them. He thought that he saw little figures scuttling along the top of the earthen walls and then vanishing again and he was aware of small, sharp, bright eyes steadfastly watching him. His heart was fairly stopping within him but nevertheless he stepped forward to the mouth of the fort.

"I am come as you asked," he shouted. "And I've come to tell you to cease your racket and to give me and my family some peace." If the fairies in the fort had heard his request, they gave no sign.

"Welcome, Joseph McPherson," boomed the voice. "A thousand welcomes to you. It is our desire that you should join with us in our sport. Come forward, for we are bound for the deserts of Africa and we would wish you to come with us." Now Joe had no wish to go to Africa or anywhere else for that matter. All he wanted to do was to go home to his bed but he had grown afraid of the fairies and was fearful of disobeying them. So he took a couple of steps forward into the fort.

Instantly, he was snapped up in a great roaring wind – like a whirlwind – which carried him up into the sky. Higher and higher it carried him until it seemed that it was taking him up towards the very stars themselves. He was buffeted around, becoming more and more terrified as the minutes passed. And all around him, shadows came and went in the maelstrom and he knew that these were the fairies and they were taking him to Africa. The wind took him even higher.

"In the Name of God!" he shouted. "Are you going to carry me into Heaven itself?" At the mention of the Holy Name the wind ceased and the weaver found himself falling back to the ground. As he tumbled from a great height, he feared that he might injure himself but, as luck would have it, he landed on a bag of lime which a neighbour had left below a bush, several fields from his house. Badly bruised and shaken, he made his way home where his wife tended to him, using special ways that she had learned in the Kilhoyle mountain country, so that although he was stiff, he wasn't hurt.

It would be safe to say that Joe didn't sleep a wink that night. And in the early morning, just before cock-crow and as the first rays of the sun were lighting up the fields, the fairies returned. They settled back into the old fort like a mighty wind, disturbing birds sleeping in the trees. Then everything was quiet once more but all that day Joe McPherson was fit for nothing. He wasn't able to work at his loom, let alone sort out his cloths and materials and for most of the day he dozed whilst his wife looked on at him worriedly. She had used all the arts that she had learned in Kilhoyle but she had no idea what to do about the fairies.

And the next night there were lights in the old fort once more. Shadows came and went across the surrounding fields and the sound of distant music started up. Sitting in his kitchen, Joe heard the sound of the great brassy voice calling him again.

"Come up, Joseph McPherson, and join us in our revels. We are bound for the coasts of Spain this night and we would wish you to come with us." This time, Joe sat where he was and though the voice called several times, he didn't go. Soon after, he saw some of the fairies emerge like a great cloud from the fort and head off over the fields, probably to the Spanish coast, but the music and drinking still seemed to continue and went on all through the night. Once again, nobody got a wink of sleep.

Joe's work was falling badly behind and his customers were calling at the house and finding that the work that they had ordered wasn't done. Most of the time Joe lay sleeping and this didn't do much for his grand reputation in the countryside. And it seemed that the fairies had also taken against him for refusing to go with them to Spain. Now they partied every night up in the fort, keeping everybody in the house up until cock-crow and indeed they seemed to be a bit bolder.

One evening Joe looked out into his yard and there were a group of fairies sitting at the far end of it, a great flagon of poteen between them, fiddling and wagering away as if they were up in the fort. Angrily, he made to go out to them but his wife caught his arm once more.

"Leave them be," she advised, "for we don't know what powers they might have and what sort of revenge they might take on you if you spoke sharply to them." So Joe stayed where he was and the fairies partied all night at the end of his yard and up in the fort as though it was the middle of the day. Nobody slept at all. The next night, just as it was growing dark, they gathered half-way up the yard and partied once more until cock-crow, when they returned to the fort.

The night after that, Joe looked out and saw them gathering under his window.

"By God, they'll soon be in the house," he declared. "But I know what I'll do. I'll fetch a clergyman, for no fairy can stand against a man of the cloth." His wife reminded him that Peter McCloskey had once brought a priest to the place but that even the holy man had made little difference. Joe, however, waved her caution away. "I'll bring a Protestant minister about the place, for one Protestant clergyman is worth half-a-dozen Catholic priests." His wife said nothing.

And so Joe brought the local Protestant minister to the cottage. At first the good man was reluctant to come but Joe insisted that as a man of God, he should exorcise the fairies from his home. So he came up from the Manse, his Bible under his arm. And what a sight greeted him as he entered the house, for the great room where Joe kept his loom was full of fairies. They had climbed up on the shelves, where they sat drinking and smoking long clay pipes; they hung from the beams of the loom, spilling drink as they did so; they played cards across the cloth that Joe had made, splashing and dribbling poteen on it as they did so. They were everywhere, playing their fiddles and rolling their dice, and every bit of space in the room was covered with them.

The minister made his way to the centre of the room and instructed Joe to bring him an iron knife from the kitchen. Joe did so and joined the holy man in the middle of the room. Standing in the midst of the fairies, the clergyman began to read from the Bible whilst Joe made threatening jabs in their general direction with the blade of the knife. Because it was made of iron, none of the fairies dared approach it, although they danced back, jeering wildly, every time he darted at them. And behind him the minister continued to read from the Bible as loudly as he could to get above the din they were making. But it all did no good. Some of the fairies simply retreated into the next room where Joe had his cloth stored and proceed to spill poteen and laugh whilst others hung from the beam of the loom and made rude noises. They started pelting Joe and the clergyman with stones and with some of Joe's old shoes and bits and pieces they found about the room, laughing and screeching uproariously as they did so. Despite all his readings from the good book, in the end the clergyman was forced to flee out into the yard, declaring that he would not go back into the house for a fortune.

The fairies continued to party in the house all night, whilst Joe and his family camped outside. The whole thing was getting far beyond a joke and was now a great nuisance to them. From the fort in the field, the great voice boomed down, expressing regret that the fairies' invitation to the weaver had been so indifferently rebuffed. It informed them that if it had not been for Joe McPherson's "leaves and lances" (a reference to the pages of the Bible and to the iron knife), he could have dined with them in the "Lowlands of Holland" that very night. The weaver was, however, defeated and paid it no heed, but his wife had a vague plan in the back of her mind.

"Over in Kilhoyle," she said, "I heard old people say that if you give up a life of one of your own, the fairies will leave you alone. There was a trick that the people used to use to get rid of them. They would promise them their next unborn child, even though they had no intention of having any more." She paused. "Look at you and me, my jewel, we're far too old to have any more children. I'm nearly past the child-bearing age. If we promised them our next child, they might leave us alone."

By this time, Joe didn't know what to do and would grasp at any straw in order to get rid of the fairies. "Very well," he answered. "I'll go up to the fort now and make them that offer." And so saying, he marched up the lane and into the field. There he stood in front of the earthen walls of the fort and cried out: "Those of you within, listen to me. It is Joseph McPherson of Derryork that speaks to you. If you torment me and my family no more, I will pledge to you the next child that is born to me and my wife. It is the most precious thing that I can offer you, but I will do it if you will leave us in peace." He waited as the wind began to rise and the branches and bushes around the old fort began to move fitfully. Shadows shifted within the fort.

Then at last the brassy voice answered: "Your pledge is accepted, Joseph McPherson. Go back to your home and you will be troubled no further." Everything fell silent once more and the only sound that the weaver heard was the bark of a dog on a distant farm, the sound carrying in the stillness of the evening.

And that was the way of it. For a good number of years, Joseph McPherson and his family lived in the low house beside the lane that led up to the old fort and he was never troubled. His business prospered for he was a good worker and his family was able to put a bit of money by. In time he forgot about the pledge that he'd made to the fairies in the fort; in fact, he forgot about the fairies altogether, for they never annoyed him.

Years after, despite her advanced years, his wife became pregnant again and gave birth to a healthy baby boy who was the apple of his father's eye. All seemed to be well but when the little boy was about two years old, he mysteriously managed to smother himself among some cushions whilst his father was working at the loom. It was then that Joe McPherson suddenly remembered the pledge that he had made at the old fort, years before, and his heart broke within him.

The tragedy was too much for them all to bear and, in the end, the weaver and his family left Derryork and set sail on a ship from Coleraine to St John's, Newfoundland, there to start a new life, and were never heard of again. The house by the lane stood empty until the roof fell in and the wind blew in the windows and the damp rotted the doors away. Soon everyone in the area had even forgotten Joseph McPherson's name or that he had even lived there. But from time to time – even to this day – people still talk of the lights in the old fort and of the sounds of merriment and drinking that drift down from it of an evening across the twilit lands beyond the Gelvin.

* * *

Note: This tale may indeed have some basis in fact. The 1835 passenger lists from the port of Coleraine do indeed show a Joseph McPherson (McPhearson) from the townland of Derryork, near Limavady, who took passage for St John's, Newfoundland, with his wife and daughter, around the summer of that year. However, it should be noted that he may have been one of a number of people from the area who were emigrating due to a linen slump – triggered by English taxation – in the Dungiven and Limavady areas. Nevertheless there are still a number of "fairy forts" in the area

15

and some people around Gelvin suggest that the fairies are still active there. Maybe there is some element of truth in the story after all.

2

THE RABBITS' ROCK

County Sligo

Fairies were usually a brooding presence in the Irish landscape. In many cases, Irish people went in terror of the "Other Sort", avoiding places where they might be or even trying not to refer to them at all. (The "Good People" were said to object to the name "fairies" which they, for some reason, considered derogatory. Therefore few country people used the terminology.)

If fairies took exception to an individual (and many of them did, sometimes for the most trivial of reasons), they could, at the very least, cause misfortune, and at the worst, death. But what was feared most was abduction. It was believed that they would carry away certain people on the slightest whim, sometimes not returning them until many years later – if at all. Irish folklore is littered with tales of those who have been carried away, to return perhaps seven years after, often still wearing the clothes that they had on when they were "taken". Children were especially at risk and many rural tales concern infants being taken or lured away. Adults too might be abducted and, in many cases, they did not come back and were doomed to spend the rest of their lives in the fairy realm. In places like Tipperary and Kerry, several stories were to be found concerning local individuals who were supposed to be held by the "Others" under hills and below mounds and raths close to where they were abducted, for it was believed that the fairies did not travel all that far with their captives. On certain nights of the year these individuals might be seen by people who knew them, appearing like ghosts, crying and pleading piteously to be released from the fairy world. Few, however, knew how to do so.

Nor was it necessary for the "abductee" to be actually taken away from his or her surroundings by the fairies. People sometimes simply changed, lost their wits, or became incredibly withdrawn. It was then said that their "essence" had been captured by the fairies and that it was being held somewhere else. Thus whilst they were physically present, their soul or mind had been removed by the Good Folk. This may have been used to explain an individual's mental or nervous breakdown and hinted at the power of the fairies over humans. This, indeed, is the origin of the well-known expression "away with the fairies".

Although it was difficult to "retrieve" such people from fairy captivity, it was not impossible. There was certain lore in the countryside which suggested how individuals might be returned or freed but it was very often a complicated process to do so and might only be achieved at certain times of the year when fairy magic might be at its weakest. Even then, it was not all that successful, for people who returned from the fairy world were often changed – dreamy, listless and unfocused. Sometimes, they would try to return to the unseen fairy realm from which they had been "saved" and one "abduction" might be followed by another. Their behaviour often paralleled that of today's alleged alien abductees – abduction by aliens from space seems to have replaced abduction by fairies in the modern mind.

The following story comes from the Ox Mountain region of County Sligo and deals with the "reclamation" of one of the fairy abductees. It was told by an old man, Patrick Duffy, who came from Coolaney on the edge of the Mountains but variations of the same story are to be found in several parts of Ireland.

There was a man called Anthony Mullaney living at one time near the village of Tullaghan down near the coast, in the Ox Mountains. He was a small farmer, working a holding on the slopes of the mountains and by all accounts he was a decent and civil man. As well he should be, for his wife was the sister of the priest in Innishcrone and her family was very strict. They wouldn't have tolerated Anthony Mullaney as their relative if he hadn't been decent and sober in his ways. The couple had no children but lived in a small, neat cottage up on the side of the hill above the village.

Tullaghan is a strange place that is steeped in very ancient lore and legend. There is a famous well there which is still called the Hawk's Well or some such name to this very day. In old, old stories they say that Gamh, a servant of an ancient king called Eremon, was beheaded there for some reason and that his head was thrown into the well. Ever after, the water had a bitter taste at certain times. Another old story said that Caorthanach (the Mother of Devils), the last demon that even the Blessed Patrick couldn't drive out of Ireland, came down to drink there at night, when it was dark, and that her spittle poisoned the water, making it taste strange. But everybody knew that the lands around Tullaghan, up into the Ox Mountains, were badly fairy-haunted. It was said that fairies hid behind every rock and every bush, waiting to carry the unwary away.

Now as I said, Anthony Mullaney's wife – I think that she might have been called Kathleen, but I'm not sure – was a sister to the priest in Innishcrone and I think that she had a cousin another priest in Kilcloud and this gave the fairies a particular interest in her. The Good People take a great interest in those who come from holy families and often try to lure them away into evil. So with two relatives in the clergy (and maybe more) Anthony Mullaney's wife drew them like a beacon and they were determined to get her.

One evening, she was walking along a pathway that led up above Tullaghan and up to the Hawk's Well. She had been gathering bilberries from the bushes in order to make jam and was not all that careful where she went. It was here that the fairies came on her and took her. How they did it nobody knew but when she came back to her own place, a good number of hours later, she was a changed woman. When she had left home she was a fine, brisk, sharp woman, as befitted the sister of a priest, but when she came back again, she was a dreamy, lazy creature who seldom spoke. She moped about the house like an old dog and did nothing – no work, no cleaning, nothing. And, as the days passed, she grew steadily worse, gradually withdrawing from everything. In the end, all she would do was to sit in a corner of the kitchen, moaning softly to herself and groaning loudly when anyone spoke to her or asked after her. Either that or bare her teeth like an animal. She wouldn't wash nor cook and she had to be lifted and laid and put to bed.

Anthony Mullaney was at his wits' end. He wasn't really sure what had happened to his wife and so he sent for her brother over in Innishcrone. The priest came with his black coat and Bible under his arm and looked at her. When he was there she simply groaned all the louder and snapped at him like a dog when he came too close. The fairies have that sort of way about them with priests – they have no great love of the Cloth.

"There is something not natural here," said the priest, "Something that might lie in the spirit world. I will have to think further about this." That's always the way of it with priests. They never act right away when they're faced with something that they're not sure of, but always need time to pray and reflect. And so he went back to Innishcrone to think about the matter and to consult his Holy Commentaries.

In the meantime Kathleen Mullaney grew even worse. As soon as the sun went down, the fairies drew close to the house and began to scream and shriek in the most alarming manner, their voices high and shrill like the cries of young foxes or curlews and Anthony's wife would answer them with screams of her own, just as shrill and piercing. And when he walked up in the hills, Anthony could hear the fairies calling to him in their shrieking voices from every hidden hollow and from behind every rock and bush and he knew full well that they were being answered from his own house. And he didn't know what to do about it.

The priest returned from Innishcrone with his books under his arm. He arrived in a great hurry late in the day, just as the sun was beginning to set.

"I was right," said he grandly. "There is fairy work here. My sister's wits have been taken by the Good People and they have left her a husk, as you see before you. They have struck her because she is the sister of a priest and has a cousin a priest as well. She must be exorcised from their influence and her wits returned to her." He spoke with great certainty and authority and Anthony Mullaney knew better than to argue with him. "Go and prepare the kitchen now and I will pray for her deliverance." Priests are always great at praying. And so the kitchen of the cottage was swept and cleaned and all the while the woman sat in the corner and groaned. And then the priest came in with his stole about him and his cassock buttoned up to the neck, and the scent of incense on his hands. With him he brought several old books, full of prayers and ritual, that he spread out on the kitchen table.

The priest prayed – he prayed hard and he prayed formally, without emotion, even though this was his own sister. He prayed in Latin, he prayed in Irish and he prayed a bit of the time in English. He prayed until the sweat stood on his forehead. He prayed for the forgiveness of any sin that his sister had committed and which had drawn the fairies to her; he prayed that she would be kept safe and that her wits would be returned to her; he prayed that the fairies would leave her alone thereafter and that she would be free of the fairy taint. And whilst he prayed, the fairies drew close to the house in the gloom and shrieked and screamed and tapped on the darkened windows with their long fingernails. And Kathleen Mullaney answered them with screams of her own. Eventually, the sounds outside fell away and with a loud groan, the woman collapsed into what appeared to be a sound slumber.

"There!" said the priest. "The exorcism is done and she is at rest now. When she comes to herself, her wits will have returned to her. That is the power of prayer. That is the power of the Lord!" And with that he closed his ancient books of prayers and rituals and departed into the night. As he went there were a few shrieks from hidden places in the darkness but the fairies never bothered with him. It seemed that all would be well now.

But it wasn't. For when the woman woke up again, she was as bad as ever. In fact, she was twice as bad as she'd been before. She roared and screamed and tried to bite her husband and for every one of her shouts, the fairies in the hills around answered her. None of the priest's prayers or holy incantations seemed to have worked. There was no point in sending for him again, even though he was her brother. Besides, Anthony Mullraney had another plan.

Away in the Ox Mountains beyond Tullaghan, he'd heard of a woman living who had knowledge of the fairies and their ways. She lived alone and some people said that she was "fairy touched" and wandering in the head but all agreed that she had great power and great knowledge about her. He name was Grey Ellen and none knew her last name. She had been carried away by the fairies when a child and had lived amongst them for more than seven years and had got to know their habits and weaknesses. The time had marked her but she was still consulted by the country people who were "fairy-ridden". It was to her that Anthony Mullaney thought of going for he now had no faith in the power of priests. So he put on his best brogues and went striding up into the Ox Mountains.

He travelled along lonely trails, through narrow valleys and along the banks of streams. He walked for miles around the edges of bogs and he climbed steep slopes where the loose scree had slipped down and almost barred his way.

The place where Grey Ellen lived was no more than a small hut, made out of stones and mud and set at the upper end of a glen between frowning cliffs. It was thatched with leaves and rushes and as Anthony Mullaney drew close to it, he saw a thin trail of blue smoke rising above it which told him that the strange woman was at home. Knocking on the doorpost, he looked inside.

Grey Ellen sat on a low stool in front of a fire of rushes and twigs, smoking her pipe and stirring something in the black pot which bubbled and seethed among the ashes. The hut was almost bare, for there was little furniture, only a few old chests with ragged blankets thrown over them and a low makeshift bed – no more than a straw mattress – in one corner. All around hung bunches of dried flowers and plants that the odd woman had gathered on the mountain. The only light came from a lantern that hung from a pole in the centre of the earthen floor. Grey Ellen barely looked up when Anthony Mullaney came round her door.

"I knew that you were coming," she told him in a thin, far-away voice. "For I heard the fairies crying in the glen below. It was them that told me." She was very thin, her arms little more than sticks as she stirred the pot, the grey hair that gave her her name hung down about her narrow face in long, greasy cords. She wore what looked like an old coat that had once been green or blue but that was now so shabby and dirty that you couldn't make out the true colour of it. As she stirred the pot with a long stick her eyes had a certain dreamy quality about them as if they might be fixed on sights that were far away.

"I know why you've come," she continued. "This is a bad time of year for the fairies, for they're greatly agitated and at their worst mischief. They steal away children and sometimes injure or take away the wits of good Christians. I know that your wife is "fairy-touched" and this is because she is the sister of a priest and that the fairies have taken a spite against her because of it. They've muddled her mind so that she can't think right and wanders about like a dead thing." Anthony Mullaney was astounded that she knew so much about his circumstances but then Grey Ellen was supposed to have great powers that she'd been given by the fairies themselves.

"What should I do about her?" he asked. "Her brother, the priest came and read over her from his holy books and commentaries but it made no difference. She slept for a while but when she woke she was as bad as ever and the fairies came round the house, shrieking and tapping on the window-panes to stir her up." Grey Ellen nodded and spat into the fire. Something stirred and moved in the shadows of the hut – a cat, or a large rat, perhaps?

"The clergy are useless in these sorts of things," she answered. "They hide behind their religion and the Church. The fairies know of no such things – nor are they truly bound by them – for they were here long before the Christians came and their ways are far older than those of any Church or priest. All the chanting and praying has no effect on them at all." She gave the pot another stir. "But you can get your wife back and restore her to her full wits if that is your wish."

"It is my wish indeed," said Anthony Mullaney. "Tell me what I have to do."

There was silence in the hut for a moment and dark, unseen thing scurried and whispered in the corners.

"You can't recover her right away," Grey Ellen told him, "for such people can only be brought back from the fairy world at certain times when the fairy power is weakest. On the night of the next full moon, which is very close now, you must go up onto the southeastern slope of Tullaghan Hill, where the servant of Eremon was beheaded, to a place called the Rabbits' Rock. Do you know it?" Anthony Mullaney said that he did, although he knew it under another name. It was a place where rabbits gathered in the shade of a large rock, to escape the heat of the sun. "Go there then and take with you an iron knife that has been dipped in well-water. Go just before midnight and wait. Keep close to the Rock itself and don't make a sound or sudden motion or the fairies will know that you are there and will take revenge on you. Around the stroke of twelve you will see a number of horsemen riding up the hillside towards the Rock. These are the fairy kind who use the spot as a gathering place. Look between the first two horsemen and you will see your wife riding on a pure white horse and tied to the riders on either side of her by a silver rope. She will not see you nor recognise you for her mind is still with the fairies. Stay where you are and do not make any movement or cry out until they are almost beside you, then run forward and cut the silver rope on both sides using the iron knife that has been dipped in well-water. Once the rope has been cut, the spell that binds her to the fairies is broken. But they may still have a hold over her so you must lift her down from the horse and run with her as fast as you can. For the fairies will throw bolts and lances after you, any of which if they hit you will take away your own wits and powers." She spat into the fire and the spittle sizzled and hissed on the edge of the ashes. "There is one other thing that I must tell you and it is most important. In all the time you are at the Rabbits' Rock until your wife is freed and back in your own house, you must not say a word or she will be lost to you forever." She poked the fire with her stick and said no more.

Anthony Mullaney looked fixedly at her. "And what happens if I should fail?" he asked softly.

Grey Ellen laughed and it was not a pleasant sound to hear, for it was like the sharp cackle of a bird on the mountainside. "You had better pray that you don't. If you think that you might fail, then it's best to leave your wife as she is, for the fairies will take their revenge on you and that revenge will be sore. If you are lucky, they will only take your wits from you but it's possible that they will take your life – aye, and take it slowly and painfully – and then have their amusement with your soul. Will you go to the Rabbits' Rock then, Anthony Mullaney?"

The man drew himself up to his full height in front of the old woman. "I still want my wife back as she was," he declared. "And I'll go to the Rabbits' Rock if I have to in order to fetch her home." Outside in the glen, he thought that he heard the fairies screaming and wailing and the blood grew cold in his veins.

Grey Ellen nodded. She fumbled inside her dirty coat and drew something out. "You are either very brave or very foolish," she told him. "Few mortals ever cross the fairies. But if you are in difficulties, take this." And she handed him something that looked like a small stone that had been sharpened into a point . . . In the firelight it glinted like metal and Anthony Mullaney had never seen anything like it. As he took it from her and held it up to the light, he thought that he saw the vague tracery of some sort of spidery writing across the broadest part of it. "This is a fairy bolt," went on the old woman, "but it is one with special powers. If you get into trouble with the fairies, throw this at them. It is marked with a special spell, and they should not be able to harm you if it hits them. But be warned – the effects of the spell will only last for a few minutes and then the fairies will be more angry than ever. And more dangerous. But it might buy you time to get away from them."

Anthony Mullaney took the stone from her. It seemed a little warm to the touch. "It is the magic that is in it," explained Grey Ellen as if she could read his thoughts. "It is far more powerful than the mutterings of any priest or bishop. Or the words to be found in any of the books that they carry. Use it only if you have to for its powers will not last long. I'm giving it to you because I like your spirit. The fairies can be very dangerous and it's not many that would have the heart to stand up to them. Take it with my blessing and go, for I'm very tired. It's getting very dark and the fairies are getting restless down below the glen". And she seemed to sink back into her own thoughts as if he was no longer there.

Anthony Mullaney turned and, leaving the narrow hut, walked back down the glen, hearing the faint cries of the fairies from their hidden places among the rocks.

He didn't tell the priest – his wife's brother – that he'd been up in the Ox Mountains or that he'd visited Grey Ellen, for the cleric might have something to say about consorting with such people. He simply waited for the next full moon to come around when he would go up to the Rabbits' Rock. And it was not long until it did so.

As the sun started to dip in the sky, he took an iron knife and went to a well near his house. Dipping the blade in the cold water, he made sure that it was spotlessly clean. Then, putting it in his pocket and making sure that he had the fairy bolt under his shirt, he set out for the Rock.

The Rabbit's Rock was about halfway up Tullaghan Hill, a great finger of stone about twice the size of a grown man, pointing up into the sky and tucked away into a kind of dip in the land. This made it a dark and shadowy place where things seemed to come and go that had neither shape nor form. It was a place where wild animals sometimes went for shelter but which humans avoided. Some of the older people of the locality said that it was fairy-haunted.

It was very late in the evening and the daylight was just starting to fade when Anthony Mullaney reached it. Even as he drew close to it, he could feel the air getting slightly colder but he walked on up to the rock itself. In its shadow, he waited to see what might happen. The air grew even colder as the sun went down and darkness crept up Tullaghan Hill, but Anthony Mullaney stayed on. A bird called away in the valley below him and something small ran across the ground in front of him, although he couldn't see what it was. Still he stood where he was, the knife in his hand, never making a sound. He waited and waited and the night grew colder and colder. Nothing happened and apart from the occasional call of an owl or a fox, there was no sound. He was thinking of walking back down the hill and going home again when he thought that he saw a movement away down the slope. There were dark shapes riding up the hill towards the Rabbits' Rock and they seemed to be those of tall men on horseback. There was a group of them – about six or seven – and they rode very slowly indeed. Anthony Mullaney waited, praying that the moon would come out from behind a cloud and show him what was farther down the hill. And come out it did and it filled the hillside with a yellow light so that he could see what was coming up towards him.

He had been right: there were about six or seven tall people – he could not tell whether they were men or women – mounted on dark horses and dressed in dark, flowing old-fashioned clothes. Their horses stepped very high and moved very slowly. It was almost as if they were riding through treacle. The faces of the riders, in so much as he could see them, were very pale, almost to the point of being chalk-white. In fact they looked almost like skulls – long and thin. They wore heavy cloaks coloured black and dark green and red, which hung on them like old sacks. The hands that held the horses' bridle and reins were long, thin and pale and had nails like bird's claws. Some of them wore veils across their faces, like the lacy veil of a bride, but this did nothing to hide their terrible faces in the moonlight. The very sight of them made Anthony Mullaney want to cry out in sheer fright, but he remembered what Grey Ellen had told him and kept quiet.

As the awful shapes drew nearer, Anthony saw that there was one among them that wasn't a fairy, even though the horse she sat on moved as slowly as the others. In the moonlight, he recognised his own wife, sitting in the middle of the dark fairy shapes. She seemed to be bound to two of them by a long silver rope, just as Grey Ellen had said, and she looked very woebegone and down at heart. She rode with her eyes downcast and fixed on the ground beneath her, like a prisoner that has given up all hope of escape. Anthony Mullaney's heart went out to her from the shadow of the Rabbits' Rock but he still waited as the terrible procession drew closer.

Eventually they drew almost level with the Rock, but still he waited. Then as Kathleen came forward, he raised the iron knife that had been dipped in the well-water and ran forward. The silver rope was hanging down between the dark horses and this was what he had his eye on. With a twist of his wrist, he cut at one rope, surprised at how easily it parted. The dark horses reared and the riders raised their hands in anger. Their mouths opened, showing rows of sharp teeth and their shrieks and screams filled the air all around the Rabbits' Rock. Running round to the other side, quicker than a rabbit himself, Anthony Mullaney cut the other rope and made to pull his wife down from the saddle of the horse. A fairy struck out at him with a big cudgel, spiked at one end, but missed. The screams grew louder and pained his ears but he lifted his wife down from the horse.

As soon as her feet touched the ground, recognition returned to Kathleen's dead eyes and she knew who he was. She would have said something but he motioned her to be silent and run. And they did. Down the slope they went towards the seashore below while the fairies wheeled and danced about, their horses pawing at the air. As Anthony and his wife ran, things rattled off the ground around them and he knew that these were the fairy bolts and if one of them hit either him or her they were finished. Half-turning, he brought out his own bolt – the one that Grey Ellen had given him – and threw it back at them. As soon as it touched the ground, it roared up in a great fountain of fire, sending the fairies and their horses falling back.

But one broke away and came galloping after them, swinging the great cudgel that had spikes all over its end. It had nearly drawn level with them when Anthony Mullaney pushed his wife forward to avoid the swinging weapon.

"Get down!" he shouted. Then he realised what he had done, for the whole scene faded away before him as if it been no more than smoke and his wife with it. He was alone on the bare slope of Tullaghan Hill just below the Rabbits' Rock, and there wasn't a soul near him – neither human nor fairy. From all the hidden places round about, he heard the screams and cries of the fairy kind and it seemed to him that they were shouting in triumph.

And so he went home, back to his own place. He went home alone. He came in to find Kathleen lying on the bed as if in a swoon. She had been able to go about before – however imperfectly – but now she just lay there, like a log in the fireplace. She made no move or anything. He put her into the bed and sent for her brother that was the priest in Innishcrone. He came quickly enough but there was nothing that he could do for her.

And that was the way of it. She was not dead but she might as well have been, for she made no movement afterward. She simply lay in bed all the time and wasted away. And Anthony Mullaney looked after her for she was his wife and the sister of a priest. But from that day until she died, there was never a flicker in her eye, nor a word or sound on her lips. And at night Anthony would sit by her bed while she slept and the fairies cried and screamed in the valleys and among the trees between his house and the Ox Mountains. And sometimes, he thought that he heard the voice of his wife amongst their calls, weeping and pleading, crying maybe, for a salvation that would never come. Wasn't that a terrible burden for any man?

* * *

Note: Anthony Mullaney seems to have been very unlucky. In many cases, the captive is saved from the clutches of the fairies and returns home unharmed and well. Had he not spoken, this would have most probably been the outcome. However, in many parts of Ireland, the notion of silence is paramount when dealing with the supernatural (see also "The Dumb Supper" in this collection). The breaking of the "no noise" rule, either by speaking, dropping something or making some other sound, will most certainly invalidate all that is good and any helpful magic. Words and sounds, it is assumed, had some sort of negating supernatural power of their own which would thwart all best efforts of humans to deal with fairy powers. Variations of this tale (mostly with more positive outcomes) are to be found in other parts of Ireland, including a celebrated one from the slopes of Benbradagh Mountain near Limavady, County Derry, serving to demonstrate the widely perceived interaction between humans and the fairy kind.

3

THE FAIRY MAN'S SERVANT

County Antrim

In the minds and imaginations of many country people, fairies largely lived and behaved as they themselves did. They owned land, they harvested crops, they kept livestock and they carried on their lives in an understandable and recognisable way. They were invisible neighbours, after all. It was even believed in some parts that the fairies frequently interacted with humankind in order to conduct their affairs. For instance, at harvest time, they might take on human labour to help bring in the crops and there were stories of labourers who had been spirited away into the Otherworld for several days to work in the fairy fields. This, of course, provided a ready explanation for why certain individuals "disappeared" at a busy time of the season when there was work to be done!

Fairies often behaved like human masters, or so it was generally believed. They would take on a labourer for a certain time (maybe a day or a week or so) and would give them their shelter and food in a fairy house, before returning them to the mortal world. Sometimes they would pay them, sometimes they would not. Some fairies were said to be surly and bad-tempered towards their human employees; others to be kind and generous; but of course this reflected the general experience of the labouring man. There were good and bad employers in the mortal world and, generally, their fairy counterparts mirrored this. Even the way in which they acquired their workers was strikingly similar to the conduct of employers in the mortal world.

It was widely believed that, like mortal farmers, fairies attended the hiring fairs which were once common all across Ireland and where prospective employees came to be hired out to local farmers, passing invisibly through the human throng, their eyes alert for a prospective worker of pleasing aspect and quality. When they spied such a person they would make themselves visible to him or her and state their business. The worker would then be free to accompany them into the fairy world for a fixed period. If they chose not to go, all memory concerning the encounter would be wiped from their minds through fairy magic. There were some who had attended the hiring fairs who later claimed to have been in the fairy world for many years, labouring on fairy farms there, but who were really able to show no evidence of having been there. In most tales, the money that they received from their fairy employers turned into leaves or ashes as soon as they returned to the mortal world. Thus, they often received no real benefit from their employment in the Otherworld. But where were these fairy fields and fairy farms and why had nobody, other than those who went there, ever experienced them?

Off the coast of North Antrim, just above Ballycastle, an island was said to lie, somewhere between the mainland and Rathlin Island. So strong was the belief in this place that it appeared on old maps and sea charts of the area as the Green Isle or the Shamrock Isle. This was believed to be a fairy place which appeared in our world only once every seven years (although it was said that the pure in heart could see it all the time). From this island, fairies would come ashore to the local hiring fairs, to bring back employees to work for them until seven years had passed and the place reappeared once more. Indeed, there were numerous stories throughout the Glens of Antrim of people who had gone to work there.

The following is the most famous of these tales and at one time was widely known throughout the Glens. It was told by the great Rathlin Island storyteller, Rose McCurdy, who was actually born in Glenshesk and who claimed to know the woman involved personally.

There was a woman living over in Glenshesk – I knew her well – who had lived on the fairy island between Rathlin and the Ballycastle coast for seven years when she was a girl. She had been a housekeeper to a fairy man there and he had hired her at the fair in Ballycastle well before the First World War. There were two fairs in the year – one in the spring and one in the autumn – where people were hired out usually for about six or nine months to farmers from the Glens to help with the sowing and the harvests. They said that during the autumn fair, the fairies came to Ballycastle and took people back with them to the Green Isle to work. These servants were not taken on like other workers but were hired for seven years until the island itself came round again into our world. Most of those at the fairs couldn't see the fairies unless they were being hired by them or unless they had special powers.

This girl came from Glenshesk, from a very big family in a poor house, away up at the throat of the Glen. Her mother was dead and her father was never well and there was a crowd of them in a small cottage, all tripping over each other and fighting and arguing among themselves. And because the father couldn't work there was never much money. A couple of her sisters worked over in Ballycastle but they never brought in much and the family was always struggling to get by. In the end, the girl decided that she would make her own way; she would go to the hiring fair and offer herself up as a housekeeper and maybe make a pound or two for herself.

So she went to Ballycastle at the time of the autumn fair and it was a very busy place indeed for there were plenty giving themselves to be hired. There was a great trade in cattle, horses and "shelties" (Rathlin sheep) as well, so everything was fairly busy. The girl took up a stand at the corner of Ann Street and the Diamond where the main market was going on and waited. People were hired round her, mainly to farmers from away up in the Glens, but few came near her and she thought that she'd wasted her time and wasn't going to be hired at all.

It was late in the afternoon and nearly everybody had been hired but none of the farmers had come near her and only one or two had even spoken to her. Then all at once, a strange man in a grand, long green coat down to his knees appeared out of the crowd. He was tall and thin – as tall as anybody at the fair – with a long, pointy face and with a tall black hat, the like of which she had never seen before, perched on his head. He looked around the fair with dark and darting eyes, staring here and there and then at the girl in front of him.

"Are you for the hirin'?" he asked.

"I am," she said.

He considered her reply for a moment. "And are you willin' to work anywhere, even far away from your friends an' family for a whole seven years? For that's what I'm offerin' you. Now are you willin' to take my offer or will I look somewhere else?" He looked closely at her and she saw that although he was fairly good-looking, his skin was deathly pale. And there was a sort of earnestness in his voice and manner – the way that he cocked his head a little to the side like a bird; the way he stared at her with his queer, bright eyes. She thought for a minute about the offer and then she thought of her father's narrow, crowded house up in the Glen and the squalor and poverty of her life.

"Will you be good to me?" she asked. "For I've heard that some masters can be very hard and cruel and if I were to go with you for seven years I mightn't be able to stick it."

He thought for a moment. "I'll be as good to you as any other master," he answered. "What I want is a housekeeper. Your duties will be light an' I'll never ask you to do anything that you cannot do. But I must have your answer now, for the sun's goin' down an' I must be back at my house before too long."

She thought a minute longer. "I'll go with you," she answered finally. He took her hand and led her from the fair down to Milltown at the back of the Diamond where he had a horse and cart and he motioned her to climb up. Whipping up the horse, he took her out to the very edge of Ballycastle.

"Where are we going?" she asked him. "Where is your house?"

But he held up a long, thin finger against his lips. "You'll

39

see," he replied. "But first I must make a strange request. I must ask you to let me put a hood over your head until we get to my house. The road up there is difficult an' I wouldn't want you to be frightened by it. Do you consent to this?" The girl said that she did and so the man put a small velvet hood over her head as she sat on the cart.

Almost at once there was the sound of rushing wind and the cart seemed to jump forward. The hood had been on only a second before he lifted it off again and they were in front of a large, grey stone house with a slate roof. It was a grand enough dwelling, sturdy and well appointed, with lights burning in the sconces on each side of the heavy wooden front door. The windows were large and let in plenty of light and shrubs and flowers grew around the bottom of the steps that led up to it. The girl looked around her.

As they had come out of Ballycastle, a light evening mist had been starting to form in the hollows of the hills but now she saw that it had turned into a thick fog which hung everywhere around her and she couldn't see where she was at all. She might be in the Glens, she thought, but she might be somewhere else – she just wasn't sure. All she could see was the grand farmhouse in front of her.

"I live here alone," said her master getting down. "So, as my housekeeper, you will have the run of this entire place. If you need anything – anything at all – you must ask me for it and I'll get it for you." He helped her down from the cart and brought her into the house.

It was a grand farmhouse with a great entrance hall. In the room beyond, a fire was burning, though the girl wasn't sure who had lit it if there was nobody there. Even with its brightness, she thought the place was very odd Although the flames burned cheerily enough, they seemed to give off little heat. But the house was bigger – much bigger than any she'd known before – and it was comfortably furnished, all of which was well suited to her tastes. She thought that she would get on well in such a place. But as she looked out through the window, she saw that the mist hadn't lifted; nor had it the following morning nor the day after that. She could see nothing through it except the shapes of trees. And when she wandered out, intending to take a walk, no matter what direction she took, she always finished up at the front door of the house again. On her walks, she passed the outlines of trees but when she reached out to touch them, they seemed to draw back further into the mist. Slowly it began to dawn on her that this might be a fairy place – perhaps she was on the Green Isle, the fairy land that appeared every seven years – and that her master was probably one of the fairy kind.

And there she lived for the next seven years. She had the run of the big roomy house and there wasn't a room that was closed to her. She lived comfortably enough and the work was fairly light – some dusting, sweeping, setting fires and a bit of cookery, though she noticed that her master ate very little of what she made. And he was very good to her; whatever she asked for in the morning he would usually have for her by evening. She wanted for nothing. Few servants could have asked for more.

There was, however, one drawback to it all: she was very lonely. In all the seven years she lived with him, she saw no other living soul except her master. The fog around the house never once lifted in all that time and when she walked into it trying to find a town or a village where there were other people, she found herself walking to the front of the house again or else walking in circles. On all of her walks, she met nobody. At times, she thought that she heard voices in the mists and called back to them but nobody answered. She would then return to the big cold house with its comfortable but desolate rooms to resume her lonely existence. Nor did she see much of her master, for he kept himself to himself in some of the upper rooms or, when she was in bed, in the kitchen below. For long periods, he was away and so she had the place completely to herself.

On several occasions, late at night and when she was in bed, she thought that she heard voices down in the kitchen – sounds of argument and laughing – and she knew that her master might be entertaining others of the fairy kind. Sometimes, she went to the head of the stairs and, peering round the banister-post, looked down into the dark below. From the kitchen she could see lights and shadows moving; some of them didn't seem to be all that human. Badly frightened, she stayed where she was – her master had forbidden her to come down anyway when he had guests – and went back to bed. The next morning, the fairy man was as pleasant to her as ever. In all the seven years that she was there, he never uttered a cross word to her and if she wanted a new dress or new shoes, she always had them. But he was not a great conversationalist and the talk between them was very little and this only made her all the more lonely.

As she wandered through the big, cold farmhouse, she began to think more and more of her father's cottage up in Glenshesk. It had been crowded, sure enough, and there had been fights and arguments but there were always people coming and going and always a great sense of everyday life. And there'd always been company, both from her own family and from neighbours. It now seemed far better than the cold silence of the fairy island. And, as time went on, she began to look on her former life more and more fondly.

At the end of the seven years, her master called her to him.

"You've been with me now for seven years," he said, "and our agreement is at an end. You've been a good servant and I should be sorry to lose you. However, I can offer you a choice. Engage with me and stay here for another seven years if you wish but if your mind is set on going home, then I'll not stop you."

The girl thought about it for a moment and remembered all the times that she'd been lonely in the great rambling farmhouse and how she hadn't seen anybody but her master in all that time. Her mind was made up.

"You've been a very good and kind master to me," she told him, "and I can find no fault with you. But it's lonely here in this place and if it's all the same to you, I'll go back to my family in Glenshesk."

He nodded slowly. "If that's your wish," he answered, "I'll not hinder you. But I must tell you one thing. If you ever see me again, you must ignore me and let on that you haven't seen me or it'll be the worse for you. Promise me that." And the girl gave him her word. "Now," says he, "we must be going to your home."

Out at the front of the house, the horse and cart waited for them. The fairy man helped her up onto the cart. Around them the thick mist, which had hung over the place for seven years, lapped around the edges of the farmhouse.

"Now," he said, "I have to put the hood over your head as I did when I brought you here. This is so that you will not be frightened by the journey that we're about to take." And she let him place the hood on her head and there was a sound like rushing wind and the cart seemed to move forward slightly. Hardly a second had passed when he lifted the hood again and she was on the outskirts of Ballycastle.

"There," says he, "now you are home and our time together is ended. But remember your promise – should you ever meet me again, you must not let on that you even see me." And he helped her down. She stood straightening herself on the road with her back to him and when she turned to say goodbye to him, he was gone. There was nothing there and she was alone on the road.

She made her way back to her family in Glenshesk and they were right glad to see her and welcomed her home. But her father's cottage had got even more crowded over the seven years that she'd been away. Two of her sisters had got married and had brought their husbands home to live with them and a couple more had given birth. There was hardly room for them all and they were just as poor as ever. There were arguments, fights and children crying and the girl herself had to sleep on a straw mattress in the corner of the kitchen because there was no real room for her. It was very different from the big roomy house on the fairy island.

Soon any money she'd brought back with her was gone and her sisters were whining and complaining. The noise and poverty of the place was dreadful and the girl found herself wishing that she was back on the Green Isle with her fairy master. As the situation in her father's cottage became too much for her, she resolved to go back to the autumn fair and see if she could strike up again with the fairy man. After all, he had offered her another seven years on the island and she was now beginning to regret that she hadn't taken them!

On the day of the hiring fair, she made her way to Ballycastle and stood once again at the corner of Ann Street and the Diamond with the others who were there to be hired. And as the day was ending, she saw the fairy man again. He was walking through the throng in his shirt sleeves with the long green coat thrown over his arm. She ran across the Diamond towards him and grabbed him by the shoulder. He swung round on her viciously.

"Don't you remember me?" she asked, a little bit taken aback. "I worked for you on the Green Isle for seven years. You said that I was a good worker and I was wondering if you'd take me back again." But with an oath, he lifted the coat from his arm and struck her across the face with the sleeve of it.

"I told you never to let on you saw me," he snapped, "and neither you will again!" And from that day until the day she died, the girl was stone blind. I mind her well as an old woman, and she still had to be helped everywhere that she went. That's what comes from dealing with the fairies.

* * *

Note: This story was at one time widely known all across the Glens of Antrim and many people, still alive, claim to have known the woman concerned, although most give her different surnames. According to Rose McCurdy she was still alive in Glenshesk in the 1950s – albeit as an extremely old woman – and was reputedly interviewed by Michael J. Murphy, a renowned collector for the Irish Folklore Commission, in 1957. There is also said to be an interview with her, recorded for radio, somewhere in the BBC archive in Belfast, although nobody has so far been able to trace it. The father of Kevin McGarry, the current Tourism Officer for Moyle District Council, in which the Glens of Antrim lie, claims to have known the woman extremely well and stated that her experiences on the Green Isle were completely true.

4 THE FAIRY SHILLING

County Donegal

It was usually highly inadvisable for humans to have anything to do with the fairies or to interact with them in any way, no matter how innocently. At best, fairies were to be regarded as tricky, unreliable creatures; at worst as agents of the Devil, always eager to entrap human souls at the behest of their Infernal Master. It was well to avoid them or, if this proved impossible, to ignore all of their advances.

Fairies, it was believed, were always trying to ensnare humans to their own will and the slightest acknowledgement of them would enable them to do this. Consequently, one must never speak to a fairy, answer a direct question from one or show any of them kindness. An old tale from County Armagh tells of a young man who was spirited away inside a fairy hill after giving one a light for its pipe. He was never seen again and his disappearance was connected directly to his kindly action.

George Barnett, the celebrated storyteller of County Tyrone, told a story that he'd heard from his mother concerning two sisters who lived in Lavey, South Derry. On their way to bring cattle from a wood near their home, they had to cross a field which was considered to be badly fairy-haunted. The elder sister drew slightly ahead and as the younger one strove to catch up with her a fairy stepped out from behind a bush and asked, "Would ye like a tune on the fiddle?" Knowing that the fairies were trying to draw her into their power, the girl walked on without answering. A little farther along another fairy stepped out from behind a tree and asked, "Would ye like a tune on the fife?" Although her heart was stopping within her, the girl kept on without answering and a little further along, a third fairy stepped out from behind a big standing stone and asked, "Would ye like a tune on the bodhran?" – whereupon she fainted and her sister had to come back and carry her home. According to George Barnett, she never enjoyed good health afterwards and later left the country to go to America.

If one should avoid speaking to fairies, then to accept money from them was extremely unwise, since to do so could damn one's immortal soul. In any case, fairy money usually turned to leaves or cow dung as soon as the fairy departed or when it was exposed to direct sunlight. The Godly therefore tended to shun the fairies and their riches for more wholesome pleasures. But some did not and some received fairy money inadvertently.

This story comes from the Malin area of Donegal, right up on the very north coast of the country and a number of variations of it exist. The following version was told by Cathal Boyle, an elderly storyteller from the region.

Just beyond the Malin Crossroads up into the Glen, there was a man living one time and his name was Paddy O'Gadhra. He was a decent, honest man and well known in the countryside for his goodness to his neighbours. Paddy had never married and lived alone in a tidy little cottage well up in the Glen, where he farmed a bit of land.

One evening, he had some business in Malinmore and was coming home by way of the Crossroads. It was late in the evening and the day was darkening down. A few stars were out and a fat moon was nipping out and in between the clouds. Paddy quickened his step as he wanted to pass the Cross before nightfall. Crossroads were dangerous places after nightfall, for ghosts and fairies sometimes hung about them, waiting to prey on lonely travellers.

As he approached Malin Cross, his heart nearly failed him, for there was someone – or *something* – there. A shadow moved in the gloom just where the roads crossed and as he drew nearer, Paddy saw that it was a small woman in dark clothes, her head wrapped in a shawl. She was sitting by the very edge of the road and close beside her was a large wicker basket. As he drew level with her, Paddy wished her a "good night" and made to go on, but at the sound of his voice, she lifted her basket and fell into step beside him, walking into the Malin Glen.

As they walked, Paddy, being a civil man, tried to make

conversation with his strange companion but she never answered him a word. He noticed that the basket she was carrying appeared to be very heavy and that she was struggling as she walked.

"Give me your basket," he said, "an' I'll carry it a piece for you." So she gave him the basket and, to his surprise, he found that it was as light as a feather and that he could carry it quite easily. They walked on in silence with the moon now coming out from behind the clouds and flooding the countryside with a pale light. Now that she'd got rid of her basket, the woman stepped out fairly quickly and Paddy almost had to run to keep up with her.

At length they came to the end of the lane which ran up into the Glen past Paddy's house. He turned to the woman, meaning to hand back her basket.

"I'll have to leave you here," he said, "for I'm going on up into the Malin Glen. I'll give you back your basket." The woman, however, never slowed her step but spoke to him for the first time.

"Hold onto it," she answered, "for I'm going up into the Glen myself. I am lodging with Jimmy Jeck who lives up there. I have business in these parts and Jimmy Jeck has agreed to give me a bed for the night."

Now this astonished Paddy. Jimmy Jeck was his neighbour and lived a little way above him at the very head of the Glen. The two men were good friends and Jimmy Jeck had never mentioned that he had anyone coming to stay with him, least of all a woman. All the same, Paddy carried the woman's basket further into the Malin Glen.

Soon they reached Paddy's own gateway and this is where he set the basket down.

"I'll have to leave you here," he said, "for this is my home."

She reached into the pocket of her apron. "Are you a drinking man?" she asked him.

"Well," said Paddy, "when I am in a pub or shebeen, I can take a pint of stout or a sup of whiskey as well as the next man." The woman reached him an old shilling, which somehow still sparkled in the moonlight.

"This is for your trouble," she said. "When you are in a pub, have a drink and think of me." And with that she lifted her basket and walked on into the Malin Glen towards Jimmy Jeck's house.

For a long time Paddy stood there looking at the old coin in the palm of his hand. He had never seen a shilling like it. It was certainly very old, for it was worn round the edges; there seemed to be an inscription there but he couldn't read it because it was badly worn away with use. And yet, it seemed to glow with some sort of inner brilliance that reflected the moonlight around it. At last, he slid the coin into his pocket and went indoors.

That night Paddy couldn't sleep, nor could he even settle in bed. The strange woman kept invading his thoughts. Who was she? What was her business in the Malin Glen and why hadn't Jimmy Jeck mentioned her to him? It was all very mysterious. Lying in his bed, he made up his mind to go and see his neighbour the following morning and ask him about his curious guest.

Jimmy Jeck was out sweeping his yard the next morning when Paddy called up to see him. He asked Jimmy straight away about his visitor of the night before.

"Damn your eyes," said Jimmy Jeck. "There's no woman here and no woman called up with me last night. I was in the house on my own until I went to bed. The two men looked at each other. It was growing stranger by the minute. And it was to become stranger yet."

Paddy was worried that the woman he had helped with her basket might be a fairy. The thought frightened him a little but he put it to the back of his mind and tried to get on with everyday life. He had a message to do at the Post Office in Malinmore and when he was there, he bought a twist of tobacco for his pipe. And as he paid for it over the counter, he reached into his pocket and brought out the old shilling that the strange woman had given him. He used this to pay for the tobacco, receiving a handful of change in return.

On the way home, however, he had occasion to put his hand into his pocket again and count his change. To his astonishment, there in the middle of it was the old shilling with the odd, worn writing around the edges that he couldn't read. The late afternoon sun caught it, making it glow with an eerie light. It was the same coin that he'd used in the Post Office, of that he was sure, and it had somehow returned to him. It was a magic coin – maybe something to do with the fairies.

And that was the way of it. Every time Paddy was in a shop or a pub or a shebeen and he used the old coin, it would return magically to his pocket and would bring the change of it with it. Soon Paddy's pockets were jingling but the thought of it gave him no peace. Paddy O'Gadhra was a religious man who never missed Mass of a Sunday and the thought of having some fairy thing about him unsettled him. At times he thought of putting the old coin in the Church poor box but he somehow couldn't bring himself to do it. Who knows what might happen, he told himself. And anyway, he never wanted for anything as long as he had the fairy shilling about him. It was a tempting thing. He thought about using it to wager or to buy grand things that he wouldn't normally afford and he knew that the coin was exerting some kind of spell over him, luring him away from righteousness. He had been a simple man before but now he had grand ideas and it was all the work of the fairies.

In the end, his conscience got the better of him. This was certainly a fairy thing and it had been simply put in his way to lead him into the paths of wickedness and to damn his own soul. He decided to take it to the priest in Malinmore and tell him the tale.

When he heard about it, the priest took the story extremely seriously.

"Let me see the coin," he said and Paddy brought it out and laid it on the priest's hand. At once the holy man dropped it as though it were a hot coal, fresh from the fire. It lay on the table between the two of them. Paddy gazed at the other for he could handle the old coin with no hurt but obviously the priest, being a holy man, could not.

"This is without a doubt a fairy thing," said the priest solemnly, "and something that has been forged in the fires of Hell to waylay the Godly. It must be exorcised." And he went to his robing room and put on his religious vestments and stole and came back with a Bible. Opening the Holy Word, he instructed Paddy to lay the coin on its pages. Then he said a few words in Latin and made the sign of the Cross over it and the coin faded away like a drop of rainwater, as though it had never existed at all.

Paddy O'Gadhra had a lucky escape sure enough, for who knows the depths of wickedness that the old coin might have led him into? The priest instructed him to attend Mass every day for a month to ensure that there was no further fairy taint about him and he was glad to do so. And at night when he walked up from Malinmore, he always felt a bit of a chill as he approached Malin Cross, for perhaps the fairy woman might be waiting there. But if she was he never saw her again. But he had a very lucky escape all right.

* * *

Note: Stories like this were once common all over many parts of Ireland and many of them did not always have such a satisfactory outcome. In some of them, the protagonists die in rather horrible circumstances as a direct result of accepting fairy money. However, in the above tale Paddy O'Gadhra accepts the shilling unwittingly and as the result of performing a kind act which, presumably, stands to him as far as the outcome is concerned.

5 THE HOPE OF SALVATION

COUNTY DOWN

When people in the countryside talked about the fairies, one question in particular concerned them: did fairies die? Was this the reason for the apparent absence of the Good Folk in many rural areas? Were they simply dying out? And if they did die, would they get into Heaven as mortals did or did they simply fade away like the mist on a river? The question of whether or not the fairy kind had souls perplexed many rural thinkers and sometimes even the country clergy. The general consensus of opinion was that they did not and this meant that they could not enjoy God's direct blessing, nor could they hope to see Paradise. When their time on earth (which was far longer than the human span) finished, they simply dissolved to dust and blew away in the wind.

This difference between humans and fairies often led to hostility and resentment on the part of the Good People, particularly as God seemed, rather wickedly, to accentuate it. At Hallowe'en, for example, He was believed to command the fairies to gather up all the human souls that had died within the past year and to escort them to the Gates of Paradise which they (the fairies) were themselves not allowed to enter. This was the "fairy funeral" which moved along the winter roads and to meet with it was an ill omen, for the fairies were especially belligerent and might take a traveller whom they encountered with them into the Beyond.

Of course, this did not stop fairies from trying to gain souls, either for themselves or, more usually, for their children. There are some stories of fairies trying to buy the souls from dying people by promising to look after their families supernaturally after their demise, but more usually fairy women married human men in order that their offspring might have a soul and so enter Heaven. Nevertheless, such an option was also conditional on the infant being accepted by the Church through the act of baptism. Priests in rural communities would sometimes refuse to baptise a child, fearing it was the offspring of a human and fairy union.

For many years, in a corner of a field between Hilltown and Rathfriland in County Down, an old cracked baptismal font lay, almost completely covered by briar and weed. Local legend said that this font had once stood in a chapel in a remote area of the Mourne Mountains and had been used to baptise the children of the parish. During Mass one Sunday, there was a loud banging on the chapel doors and when they were opened, there was a fairy woman standing there with an infant in her arms. She called upon the human father (who was one of the congregation) to acknowledge the infant and upon the priest to baptise it in the Name of God. That way her child would be assured of Paradise. The named father, however, refused to acknowledge the fairy child and without his acknowledgement, the priest refused to baptise it. In anger, the fairy woman fired a bolt through the chapel door, hitting the baptismal font and cracking it down one side. If her child was not good enough to be baptised in it, she declared, no other child would enjoy *its blessing. Outraged, the priest ordered the font to be removed from the chapel and dumped in a field a good way away. It had been contaminated by the fairies, after all. The font lay for many years, with the country people even afraid to touch it, until it was removed to facilitate the building of a house. But the debate about fairies and souls still continued across the country.*

The following story, also from County Down, reflects this concern and considers whether the fairies would eventually see Heaven for themselves. It was collected in the 1950s from the great storyteller of the Mourne Mountains, W.J. Fitzpatrick.

J ust beyond Moneydarragh School on the road that runs down to Bryansford, there was an old priest living long years ago. He had formerly been the parish priest in Closkelt or Ballyronan but was now retired and had been given a little house to live in. Nevertheless, he was still widely known throughout the countryside as Priest O'Hagan and he was much loved everywhere. Even though he no longer practised, the country people still came to his house to ask him on matters that affected them and with problems that they had. And nobody was ever turned away, for, no matter who his callers might be, the old priest listened to them sympathetically and with great kindness. Catholic and Protestant, he advised them both, and made no difference.

In the garden at the back of the house, however, there was a great standing stone, a little above the height of a grown man. It was an old pagan thing that had existed since

Celtic times and, in the evening sun, it sometimes cast strange and broken shadows. Some people queried whether such an ancient and ungodly thing should actually stand at the back of a house in which a priest lived but it did not seem to worry Priest O'Hagan. And there were those who said that the old priest was such a holy man that no evil influence from the stone would affect him.

As the Priest O'Hagan grew older, he became more infirm and so he got a local man called Ned to do work about the house. Every day, Ned would come round to the priest's house and fix anything that was broken, paint anything that needed painting, work at the vegetable patch and cut the grass. However, he was careful not to stay overlong in the back garden of an evening, for he feared the great standing stone there. It was a pagan thing and who knew what powers it might have? So he tended to give it a wide berth, especially in the evening.

Late one afternoon, however, he was clearing up in the garden after cutting the grass. The sun was going down in the sky and all around the big stone cast queer shadows which made Ned feel a little uneasy. But, he reassured himself, the priest was in the house having a bite to eat and nothing could happen to him with the holy man close by. Nevertheless, he was still ill at ease.

Suddenly, Ned became aware that he was being watched and, turning quickly, he saw a figure standing in the shadow of the stone. Although his heart was stopping, he took one step forward and he saw that it was a little man, no taller than a two-year-old child, close against the stone itself. He had a long skirty coat on him that brushed the ground when he moved and an old wide-brimmed hat that was pulled well down over his face so that Ned couldn't really see what he looked like. All the same, he was sure of two eyes that watched him intently from under the brim. Ned froze, for he knew that this was one of the Good People, come to speak to him.

"What . . . What is it that you want?" he asked, the words nearly sticking in his throat with the fright. The little man moved farther out into the brassy late afternoon sunlight.

"Are you the priest's servant?" he enquired in a strange high-pitched voice.

"I am," replied Ned, his own voice still failing.

Although the little man had stepped forward, his face still stayed in deep shadow and Ned couldn't make it out at all.

"Then I want you to ask your master a question for me," said the other. "Will you do this?"

Ned nodded slowly. "I will and gladly," he answered. "But you can ask him yourself, for he's finishing his supper in the house beyond and he has never turned away anybody yet." But the little man shook his head and seemed to take a step backwards.

"I fear the collar that is about his neck and what it represents," he admitted. "And there is an odour of sanctity about him which is not settling to me or my kind. Therefore I want you to ask him a question on behalf of both me and my people."

"Ask it then," said Ned, "and I will see what he says." He was frightened to disobey the other for fear of what he might do to him. The fairy merged with the shadows of the stone once more.

"Ask him this, then," he said, his voice sounding hollower the more he spoke. "Is there any hope of salvation for me? Will I see Paradise? Ask him that and I will return and hear his answer at the same time and in the same place tomorrow night. Be waiting for me here."

"I will," said Ned, still trembling. At that moment, a bird, swinging on a briar nearby, began to ease its throat in the evening and Ned turned at its sound. When he looked again, the little man had gone and there was nobody by the stone.

Ned went into the house to find that Priest O'Hagan had finished his supper, had poured himself a whiskey and was lighting his pipe.

"Ah, Ned," the old man greeted him. "Have you finished up for the night? Sit down and have a glass with me before you turn for home." That was the sort of him, for he was kindliness personified. But Ned, still troubled by the encounter in the garden, waved the kindly invitation away. He told the Priest O'Hagan what had happened behind the house and of the little man's question.

"And he will return tomorrow evening for your answer," he finished, his voice fairly trembling. Now another priest might have baulked at the question, on hearing that it was from the fairies, but the Priest O'Hagan pondered it for a long time. He wanted to give an answer if he could.

"I don't rightly know," he replied at length. "But tell him this when he comes. If he has but one drop of Adam's blood within his veins, he has as much hope of Salvation and of seeing Paradise as any other man. Our Lord died on the Cross to redeem Adam's children from their sin and if anyone has the smallest speck of the blood within him, he will be included in that." And he drew thoughtfully on his pipe and would say no more. Ned was vastly troubled but it was the only answer that the saintly old man would give him.

The next evening, he was working in the back garden once more, putting in some flowers, close to the old stone. Once again, the sun was going down and odd shadows were chasing each other across the fields in its final rays. As he was planting a rose in the corner of the garden, Ned became aware of a faint sound behind him. Turning, he saw the little man once more, standing in the shadow of the stone just as he had done on the previous evening. Ned straightened up.

"Well?" queried the other. "Did you ask him?"

"I did," said Ned "and I have his answer for you."

The fairy moved closer but Ned still couldn't see his face, which lay in the shadow of the brim of the hat.

"What did he say? Will we see Paradise?"

Ned swallowed. "He said that he didn't truly know. But he did say that if you had but one drop of the blood of Adam in your veins, then you had as much chance of Salvation and of seeing Paradise as any man. Our Lord died for Adam's children and if you have but one spot of the blood within you, He will extend His Grace to you."

For a moment there was silence as the little man considered the words in the darkness below the stone.

"And is that all he said?" he asked.

Again Ned swallowed. "It is," he replied truthfully.

Then the little man hunkered down where he stood, drawing his skirty coat about him, and began to wail. "Och anee anee!" And it seemed to Ned that it was not one voice that cried but a thousand altogether, and the sound was so sad and so pitiful that it would have broken your heart to hear it. "Och anee anee!" And the suddenness and sharpness of the cry made a big hare start up in the field which ran down to the back of the garden, sending it bounding away into the distance. Instinctively, Ned followed it with his eyes and when he looked back, the little man was gone once more. All he saw was the large stone, casting queer and broken shadows in the late evening sun.

* * *

Note: The theme of this story is very well known in many parts of Ireland and a number of variants of it exist. The most famous is told by the great Limerick storyteller Kate Ahern and concerns a priest in Galway who encountered a troop of fairies at a bridge when riding home one night. They asked him the same question regarding Paradise and he gave them a somewhat similar answer to Priest O'Hagan. The answer caused great distress in the fairy throng. Given the general spread of this specific story, the spiritual status of the fairy kind seems to have been of some concern to the country people and perhaps this was a general way in which fairies might be compared to humans. In the minds of the country people, this gave them both their identity and their place in the world.

Ghosts and the Supernatural

6

GRÁINNE DALY'S WEDDING

Counties Armagh / Monaghan

When, as a child, I asked my grandfather to tell me "a scary story", he would always tell me the tale of Gráinne Daly's wedding. My grandfather had come from the country area around Jonesborough in South Armagh and he always claimed that he'd heard the story from a priest and that it was true. The events which it details, he said, occurred a hundred years or so before he was born but the tradition had been handed down through the clergy in the region through the generations. However, it was noticeable that every time he told the story, its location shifted slightly through Armagh and Louth. This, of course, did not take away the sheer terror of the story as far as I was concerned.

For the ancient Irish, the dead simply didn't go away. They could, if they so desired, come back to interact with the living in various ways. They could come back in order to warn, advise, admonish or convey secrets to the living or to fulfil tasks which they had left uncompleted in life. And those who did return to the world of the living were not always the insubstantial phantoms of the Victorian imagination. Rather they were corporeal figures who could make their presence felt in actual and substantial ways. They could, for example, eat meals, perform physical task, engage in family or communal entertainment as they had done in life and, in some cases, even claim their conjugal rights. Indeed, there are a number of stories from all over rural Ireland of dead husbands coming back from the grave on occasion to lie with their widows in the martial bed. Marriage, or indeed lust, it seems, may have transcended even the grave.

There are a few stories concerning living people who have married corpses. Some have done it deliberately – an old story from County Tyrone tells of a girl who married her lover who had tragically died before the wedding – but others have done so unwittingly. A story from County Limerick, for example, tells of a bridegroom, killed on his way to the wedding, who turned up at the church anyway in a "phantom" carriage in which he took his bride away to some unknown destination.

The story of Gráinne Daly contains elements of true horror – the desperate, unmarried girl, anxious to make a life for herself and her mother, and the shadowy evil of the stranger who comes to their door asking for her hand in wedlock. Although it is a long time since I first heard it from my grandfather, the terror of the story has never quite left me. Is it a true story? I'd be very frightened to think so!

There's a narrow road that runs down from Keady in Armagh towards Castleblayney in County Monaghan. A lonely road it is too, running through bogs and empty countryside with few houses along its length. And it was even lonelier in times that are past. The land was poor and the huts along the way were badly scattered and were the places where only herdsmen and turf-cutters lived. It was a road that few people ventured along; only one or two during the day and fewer at night.

Gráinne Daly lived with her widowed mother in a low, mean cabin at the side of this road. Her father had been a hedger and turf-cutter but was long since dead and now her mother got by as best she could. Mrs Daly was a seamstress by trade and she sewed a few things for whatever gentry lived round about and kept hens, selling the eggs at the markets. But they were still very poor and the cabin where they lived was isolated with not many opportunities for making money.

It would be nice to say that Gráinne was a great beauty who would eventually make a fine marriage which would solve all their problems, but she wasn't. In fact she was extremely plain. Her nose was too big and was set in the middle of an undistinguished face with a wide and generous mouth full of crooked teeth. She dressed very dowdily for neither her mother nor herself had the money to buy fine clothing. She was not in terribly good health and had a slight limp, as one of her legs was slightly longer than the other. But she was a kind-hearted and willing girl who had worked off and on as a scullery maid for some of the gentry. It was hoped that at one time she *would* get married, perhaps to some farmer who might have a little bit of land, but as time passed and she grew older that looked less and less likely.

Certainly there were dances in the countryside run by the priests which young men and young women from the area attended and Gráinne sometimes went along to these. Other, more attractive girls were often gathered up by potential husbands but none came near Gráinne. She was not even asked to dance – not that she could dance very well with her shortened leg. In the end she stopped going to the country dances altogether and consigned herself to the life of a spinster, living with her mother beside the lonely road.

One night, however, long after the lamps had been lit and set in the window, Gráinne and her mother were together in the cottage. Mrs Daly was doing some sewing and Gráinne herself was dozing a little in front of the fire before going to bed. Suddenly, from the road outside, both of them heard a noise – the steady clip-clop of a horse coming from the direction of Castleblayney and drawing near to the house.

"It's late for a traveller to be on this road," said Mrs Daly. "Maybe it's someone who's got lost and is looking for somewhere to lodge for the night." And as she spoke, the horse appeared to draw level with the house and came to a stop. "Maybe he's stopped here to ask directions." There were more sounds from outside, then someone struck the door – a series of loud, ringing blows.

"Should we answer it?" asked Gráinne in fright. "There might be robbers skulking about at this late hour." She had heard the stories of highwaymen who supposedly prowled the lonely roads locally in search of any loot that they could steal. Her mother, however, got up and went over to the door.

"It is simply some lost wanderer," she replied, "and we must show them Christian hospitality. If you show charity to your neighbours, nothing can harm you." And she pulled the bolts on the door and opened it.

Outside it was not completely dark but the light was very poor. A few stars sparkled in the sky as the last rays of the sun fell beyond the horizon. Mrs Daly couldn't really make out the figure who stood in front of her house, for he seemed to be little more than a huge and menacing shadow. He was dressed in a very old-fashioned style – knee britches and a heavy dark travelling cloak, which he had wrapped around him against the wind and which was fastened about his throat with a large, ugly brooch. But what caught her eye was the great wide-brimmed hat, long out of fashion, which threw most of his face into darkness. Yet she was conscious of his eyes, which glinted like evil jewels under the brim of his hat. As she opened the door, he stretched out a hand, cased in a metal gauntlet, to greet her.

"Is this the home of Gráinne Daly?" he asked in a voice that seemed to come from the very depths of the earth itself. "Or am I mistaken?" Mrs Daly stood back, surprised by such a fantastic figure and by his question.

"You are not mistaken, sir," she answered him. "This is indeed Gráinne's home and I am her mother. But who are you?" For a moment the figure didn't answer.

"My name is Thady Walsh," he said at last, "and I own some land over in Killycard in the County Monaghan. It is from there that I've come in order to see your daughter. May I come in?" Despite his fearsome voice, he spoke civilly enough and Mrs Daly opened the door a little wider, allowing him to enter.

"Come in," she said, "and right welcome. Now tell me, sir, how you know my daughter and what your business with her might be."

Thady Walsh stepped into the low cottage, gathering his cloak around him. His clothes were dark but everything about him oozed wealth, from the ugly gold clasp around his throat to the embroidery on the very edges of his cloak. As he stepped across the threshold, Mrs Daly waited for him to remove his hat, but he never did so. Even in the lamplight, his face remained in shadow, maybe even deeper than it had done outside. Both of them noticed that when he entered, there was a faint, sour odour in the air which grew heavier as he came forward to the fire. Mrs Daly thought that it might be the smell of damp or mouldy clothes – for all his old-fashioned grandeur, Thady Walsh's attire might not be very well looked after. Still, she said nothing and motioned him to a seat.

"I saw your daughter once at a funeral in Crossmore," he said, "and I was struck by her common simplicity. As for my business with her – it is of a personal nature." He sat down as Mrs Daly had invited him to do and crossed his legs, moving with a certain stiffness that suggested old age. "You will realise," he went on, "that I am an old man who has made his money and is now well settled. I was once married but, alas, my wife is" – and here he paused – "no longer with me. I have decided to marry again and am looking for a suitable wife. I had occasion to be in the graveyard at Crossmore when I saw your daughter attending a funeral there and was greatly struck by her quiet and modest demeanour." Mrs Daly took a sharp intake of breath and Gráinne, who was sitting in the shadows by the hearth, started back.

"You are correct, sir," said Mrs Daly. "Gráinne was indeed at her uncle's funeral in Crossmore several months ago but I do not recollect seeing you there. Were you amongst the mourners?" Thady Walsh hesitated for a moment but his eyes still glittered below the wide brim of his hat.

"Ah no – I was there on . . . another matter. But I was greatly impressed by the way in which your daughter conducted herself and wondered if I might pay her my compliments and perhaps call on her from time to time. I realise, of course, that I am an old man, far older than she, but I am not without money and my intentions are extremely honourable. As a token of my earnestness, I give you this. . . ." Reaching inside his cloak, he produced an old gold coin which he held out to Mrs Daly. It was more money than the good woman had seen in a year. She stretched out her hand to take it and then thought better of it.

"You are very kind, sir, but Gráinne is my only daughter . . ." she began.

Thady Walsh reached inside his cloak again. "It is not enough? As I told you, I am not without means and I only wish to show my appreciation of your daughter." He opened his metal-clad hand and there were three gold coins in the palm. "It is merely my intention to call with her and enjoy her company. I live in a lonely place and have little opportunity to enjoy the company of a modest woman. And it is also my wish that you, Mrs Daly, be in attendance at all times." He held forward the money. "Take it as a token of the arrangement between us." Mrs Daly made to reach for the money but then hesitated once more.

"The decision must be Gráinne's," she answered him. "I cannot answer on her behalf." Thady Walsh turned his shadowy head in the direction of her daughter.

"Your consideration for your child does you credit," he said in that awful voice. "What does the girl herself say?" Gráinne looked towards her mother's face, tired and drawn in the lamplight. She then looked at the gold coins in Thady Walsh's hand – more than the two of them could ever hope to earn.

"Take the money, mother," she said. "For Mr Walsh may call upon me if he so chooses." Thady Walsh made a noise that was somewhere between a sigh and a feral growl of anticipation and his eyes glinted.

"Excellent!" he breathed, allowing the coins to fall into Mrs Daly's hand. He rose very stiffly from his seat. "We are in agreement! I shall detain you no longer for I have other work to be about. But I shall call with you by and by. Depend upon it. I look forward to our next meeting." And he walked back to the door, his movements rather stiff and jerky. Mrs Daly let him out and she and Gráinne listened as the sound of the horse's hooves died away down the road towards Castleblayney, eventually disappearing into silence.

"Mother," said Gráinne, "You must never leave me alone with that awful creature – not even for a second. He may be very wealthy but I think he is a horrid man. Did you see how he never showed us his face but kept it hidden under that strange hat? Maybe he is a monster or deformed in some way. I . . . I'm a bit frightened of him." But her mother was looking at the three old gold coins. There was enough there to feed and clothe them for a long time.

"And what if he is monstrous?" she asked. "He is certainly generous, Gráinne, and we should not look our good fortune in the mouth. He can sit here well enough and I will stay with you and make sure that nothing befalls you. We can put up with ill looks if he is as free with his money as this." And so it was settled.

In the weeks and months that followed, Thady Walsh called at the Dalys' cottage three or four times and he always called late in the evening. Gráinne and her mother would be sitting by the fire as it was starting to get dark, when they would suddenly hear the sound of the horse, clip-clopping slowly as if from a distance, taking its time and drawing nearer to their house. Then there would be a hammering on the door and when it was opened, Thady Walsh would be there. He would come in and sit and stay for part of the evening before leaving again around midnight. And every time he came to visit, he left several of the old coins behind him as a gift.

He was always dressed the same way, they noticed – the same queer old unfashionable knee britches; the same dark, heavy travelling cloak and always the same strange wide-brimmed hat that threw his face completely into shadow. His hands were always covered with metal gloves and his cloak was fastened at the throat by the ugly gold clasp which he never loosened. Nor did he make any move to remove these when he came in, not even the hat, which stayed firmly pulled down across his brow, so that they could never properly see his face. Once however, they did catch a glimpse of his cheek as he moved and the lamplight caught it. As she saw it, Mrs Daly raised her hand to her mouth, for the skin was brown and dead, partly blue and mottled so that it was the colour of old metal, running up to a glittering eye which seemed to be sunken deep in the head. Then Thady Walsh moved stiffly in his chair and the vision was gone. Both Gráinne and her mother also noticed that the rank, dense smell of old clothes seemed to grow stronger on each visit and gradually the two of them came to the conclusion that Thady Walsh seldom washed either his body or his clothes. Nor did he eat or drink anything, although Mrs Daly frequently offered to make him a meal. He always declined politely, saying that he'd already eaten or that he was not hungry.

His talk was very general – he seemed to know the countryside round about quite well but he mentioned people who were long dead and some landmarks that were long gone, as if it had been many years since he had last been in the area. Of more recent things, he appeared to know very little or nothing at all and Gráinne and Mrs Daly found this extremely puzzling. Nor would he answer questions about his own family, other than to say that he had once been married but had no children, and would gently deflect any enquiry concerning it.

"My family is an old one," he would say, "with its own ways and traditions and it generally kept itself to itself. I'm afraid that my forebears did not mix much with the people around them and that I have inherited some of their character. I prefer solitude and my own company to those of my neighbours. As for family history, the ancestors kept few records about themselves – this was their manner – and consequently I know very little about them. My mother died young and my father acquired land and that is all that I can tell you." Then he would steer the conversation onto another course. Nor would he even speak about his former marriage – "It is still a matter of great pain to me" – and there the matter had to lie.

When he had gone, Mrs Daly would gather up the money that he had left behind. All of it was in old gold coin, long out of common circulation and therefore quite valuable. In fact, so valuable were these coins that she was sometimes able to get a little more than their face value and consequently she and Gráinne were able to build up a little nest egg for themselves. It seemed a small price to pay for putting up with the awful Thady Walsh for a few hours on occasion. This arrangement, however, was not destined to continue.

One evening when Thady Walsh called, he seemed stiffer than usual and he had difficulty even in sitting down in a chair.

"Though my visits here have been most pleasant," he said, "I am afraid that they can no longer continue. I have grown too old and too frail to travel the long distance between here and Killycard and must remain at home from now on." Gráinne and Mrs Daly exchanged looks of relief for, quite frankly, his sombre presence and stale smell was starting to annoy them. But they were not prepared for his next comment. "When I first came here, I mentioned to you that it was my intention to take a wife and that I had always looked upon Gráinne very favourably. It is now my intention to ask her to become my wife and to come and live with me in my abode over in the County Monaghan. As you will have gathered, I am a man of some means and can well provide for her and for yourself, Mrs Daly, if she will do me the honour." The two women looked at each other in fearful astonishment. "Let me assure you that you will both be well provided for. I realise that this has come as some surprise to you both and that Gráinne may wish to consider it for a time. I can give her a week and I must then have her answer, for my time grows short and my body grows frail and my next visit here will certainly be my last. This is a good offer and one which is heartfelt. I am old and set in my ways but I beg you not to dismiss such an offer lightly." He spoke more passionately than either of the women had heard him do before. "I shall leave you to consider my proposal," said he, getting up with some difficulty, his glittering eyes fixed squarely on Gráinne. "I am a man who is used to getting his own way," he added ominously.

As the sound of the horse's hooves faded into the dark, the two women looked at each other. Gráinne made a face.

"I'll never marry that dreadful creature!" she declared. "I would sooner die!"

But her mother was looking at the gold coin that Thady Walsh had left for them on the mantelpiece.

"Let's not be too hasty," she answered. "Certainly he may be old and ugly, but he is wealthy. Didn't he say that he owned acres of land round about and that he had plenty of money put by? And he is old and frail – he says so himself – and he may not be in this world all that much longer. And when he was gone, you would inherit all as his wife. It might be a good return for a year or so of living with him for he can't last all that much longer, certainly not by the look of him." But Gráinne was still unconvinced. However, she was wise enough to realise that she stood no chance of getting a better offer amongst the farmers, young or old, of the local countryside.

"I'll think about it," she promised. "But see what you can find out about who this terrible creature is and if he indeed does come from money and property. Ask the local priest – the clergy know everything."

In fact, now that events had taken such a serious turn, Mrs Daly had already resolved to do this. So she went to the local priest, a Father Cashman, and asked him if he knew anything about the Walshes of Killycard over in the County Monaghan. The elderly priest shook his head.

"I've never heard of any such family," he admitted. "But I can certainly make enquiries for you among some of the other priests. It may take a little time, though." Mrs Daly said that she would wait and returned home.

The more they thought about it, the more Thady Walsh's offer seemed like one that they couldn't really refuse. Mrs Daly too was old and was not in good health – if she died, how would Gráinne fend for herself? Thady Walsh had given them enough money to last them for a while but it mightn't last forever – certainly not long after she was dead. Perhaps it was better for the girl to marry the old man and go to live with him. After all, she had no other suitors.

And so when the slow-moving horse came down the road from the Castleblayney direction at the edge of evening a week later, Gráinne's mind was made up. She told Thady Walsh that she would marry him. If he was overjoyed at the news, he gave little sign.

"It's done," said he, getting up jerkily. "I'll go and arrange the wedding and make arrangements to convey you to my country where we can be wed." Mrs Daly looked at him curiously.

"Surely Gráinne will be married in her own church and amongst her own people," she protested. "I've already spoken to Father Cashman on the matter and he's more than willing to marry you both . . ." But Thady Walsh held up a gauntletted hand.

"Ah no," he said, gently but firmly. "I've told you that my family is an old one and a trifle . . . peculiar in its ways. We have always been married in our own country. And there is no need to . . . ah . . . trouble your Father Cashman. I have a brother who is a priest himself and will perform the ceremony. This is the way that it's been done in our family for generations."

"But it's a long way for me to travel!" exclaimed Mrs Daly. "I have no way of getting to Killycard unless you come and fetch me." Thady Walsh laughed, deeply and unpleasantly.

"Ah, the marriage will not be taking place in Killycard," he said, "but in Muckno where my family is involved in the local church. This is where my brother will conduct the service for members of my family only. As I told you, we have always kept ourselves to ourselves and this is our way – we do not welcome outsiders at our ceremonies."

"But I am Gráinne's mother!" exclaimed Mrs Daly. "I want to see my daughter married . . ." But Thady Walsh waved her protests away.

"Alas, I can make no exception. This is the way it has been done with us. You will receive payment for your daughter by and by but you may not attend the wedding. Now, we will be married in two days from today for I am anxious that the wedding will take place as quickly as possible, and I shall send some of my serving men to fetch Gráinne. They will come before nightfall to bring her to the church where I'll be waiting for her. I shall send you some money by way of a marriage dowry presently." And he waved away all objections, rising stiffly from the chair. "Make sure that she is ready when my men call for her. And there is no need for any grand show or wedding dresses. My family is a simple one and plain in their ways – the best dress that she has will suffice. Good night, Mrs Daly. I shall await your daughter in the church at Muckno." And with that he went out into the night.

Next day, both Gráinne and her mother were beside themselves with worry. Mrs Daly went down to the Parochial House to see Father Cashman but he was away in County Monaghan and would not be back for two days. The day of Gráinne's wedding drew closer and their anxiety increased. On the evening of the second day, Gráinne had no other option but to put on her best dress and await Thady Walsh's servants. Father Cashman still had not returned, though his housekeeper expected him back sometime that evening.

Just before ten o'clock, there was a hammering on the Dalys' door and, opening it, Mrs Daly found four small men standing there. They were all dressed in black, their faces unutterably pale, with black Van Dyke beards and hard glittering eyes like Thady Walsh himself. They spoke no word but motioned Gráinne to come with them, beckoning her to a queer old-fashioned litter which was surrounded by dark and heavy curtains. She went with them and climbed into it, pulling the curtains behind her, and that was the last that her mother saw of her. The little men lifted the litter and carried it off down the road towards Castleblayney whilst her mother stood at the door watching.

They were gone not more than an hour when Father Cashman arrived at the door, his horse sweating. He had ridden all the way from County Monaghan at full gallop.

"I have asked everywhere around Killycard and there is no Walsh family in the area. However, I spoke with Father McKenna who is an old man now and he remembers a story of a family of that name who had land in the area, but they allegedly came from Muckno. They were a dark and evil family – one of them was an unfrocked priest who had been expelled from the Church because of some hideous sin. Thankfully, Father McKenna said that their line had long died out in the countryside and all of them were dead." Mrs Daly gazed at him in horror.

"Muckno?" she cried. "That is where this . . . Thady Walsh said that his family attended church. That is where he has taken Gráinne to be married! And he said that he had a brother who was a priest and he would perform the ceremony there." Father Cashman frowned.

"There is no church in Muckno," he said, "only an old roofless ruin above the lough that hasn't been used for over a century. How can it be that Gráinne is to be married there, for there is only a graveyard there . . .?" Mrs Daly threw her hands to her face in sheer terror.

"The dead!" she almost screamed. "Oh Father, can it be? This . . . this Thady Walsh is no more than a corpse! And he has taken my Gráinne with him . . . oh, what have I done? Is my dear child to be married to a stinking cadaver?" Father Cashman stepped back, touched by the horror that she was feeling.

"I . . . I've heard of such things in the remote mountain parishes," he whispered "where men and women sometimes marry dead creatures, but I never thought . . ." He composed himself. "I'll ride to Muckno now and finds out what's going on. If it is as we suspect, then it's not God's will that the living and the dead be joined together in matrimony."

But Mrs Daly had collapsed into a quivering heap, her mind gone with the horror of it all, a condition from which she never recovered.

Father Cashman galloped through the night, down the Castleblayney road with only a bright moon to guide him. Sensing his anxiety, the horse went as fast as it could and soon they were approaching Lough Muckno, lying placidly under the stars. On the rise above the tranquil waters lay the ruined church, its roof open to the sky. And yet as Father Cashman approached, he was aware of strange lights that came and went amongst the tumbled walls. Reining in his horse, he leapt to the ground and although his heart was in his throat, he ran forward into the ruin.

The roofless church lay quiet, but at the far end, where the southern gable poked up, Father Cashman saw what seemed to be an open door, although he knew that there was no door there. An eerie and putrid light tumbled out to illuminate the briars and bushes which had grown up in the main body of the derelict church. And in this light, the priest thought that he could see figures moving. He ran forward through the long grasses and as he approached, the light blazed forward, lighting up the tumbled stones and moss-covered walls of the fallen building.

The priest found himself looking into a great hall which had been hung with tattered pendants and banners. Here a table made of polished wood had been placed and on it were the ruins of a grand feast amongst which now rats and crows came and went. Nevertheless, around this table sat several indistinct shapes, blurred by the horrid light, but visible all the same. But it was the far end of the hall that drew Father Cashman's attention, for there was a great four-poster bed with old and heavy drapes around it and at its foot stood what he guessed must be Thady Walsh. The creature had removed its travelling cloak and now stood in a

81

surcoat of faded velvet, which matched his faded knee britches. He had also taken off the wide-brimmed hat to reveal his face in the graveyard light. The skin was livid and was stretched taunt across the skull but was streaked by veins of blue and mottled with mould; part of a cheek had begun to fall in on itself and the lips were starting to draw back, revealing rotting teeth below. The hair had all but gone – only a few strands hung down across that ghastly face – and the bridge of the nose was now starting to decay and fall away. Only the great eyes, well sunken in the head, burned with bright and terrible fire as they fixed on the priest standing in the open air at the other end of the hall.

"Leave this place, priest!" the terrifying voice rang out. "Leave me to enjoy my wedding night. This is not for the likes of you!" Terrified by the monstrous tableau in front of him, Father Cashman tried to make the sign of the Cross but his hands were shaking too much and his arms were in the grip of a fearful paralysis.

"In the Name of God, be still in your graves," he shouted. "Let the girl go!" The thing that called itself Thady Walsh threw its decaying head back in a frightful laugh.

"God?" he replied. "God? Your God has no place here. Your God is dead and hanging upon a tree – now leave this place or it will be the worse for you."

The priest looked beyond that awful, shrieking creature towards the bed. There, peering round the heavy curtains, he saw another face that he knew – that of Gráinne Daly – and in her eyes there was a look of abject terror that chilled him to the bone. The sheer dreadfulness of the situation overwhelmed him, his senses reeled and he collapsed unconscious on the ground.

It was morning when he came to amongst the briars and grasses within the ruined church and with the dew on his coat. He lay in the centre of what had once been the aisle which had led up to the altar, facing the now blank wall where that dreadful door had been. Of course, it was no longer there – just the heavy stonework of an ancient church. Rising from the ground, Father Cashman made his way over to it, to see if he could find any trace of the now-vanished entrance. There was no sign of the doorway but where it had been there was now an ornate memorial tablet set into the stonework, its lettering badly worn away, marking the grave of a notable family. And with a thrill of horror the priest realised that the family name that it commemorated was Walsh. With a trembling finger he traced along the lists of those who had been buried – most of the names were too faded to be legible, but there was one down near the bottom which revived the horror within him. He stared and stared but could scarcely believe what he saw:

"Thaddeus Walsh of Killycard"

The date of his death was completely faded, but there seemed to have been a more recent inscription below the name which was slightly clearer and which echoed like the laughter of demons in the priest's mind:

"and also his wife Gráinne".

* * *

Note: At one time this story – or a number like it – were well known across Ireland and the tale was said to be the basis for Sheridan Le Fanu's nightmarish tale "Shalken the Painter", which he set in

Holland rather than in Ireland. Just to add fresh terror to the tale, my grandfather used to tell me that near to where he himself was born there was an old burying ground situated well back from the road and surrounded by a low wall. It was very old and badly overgrown, the worn and often illegible gravestones poking out from among the long grasses, just inside its boundary. Nobody could remember its name and, if there had once been a church there, no trace of it remained. Sometimes at twilight, just as the sun was declining and long shadows were creeping across the fields, the figure of a woman would come to the wall from inside the graveyard and stand, looking wistfully towards Armagh. Nobody knew who she was, but she was always dressed in black and her face seemed very pale. She was only there for a moment and when those who had seen her looked again, she was gone. Nobody could explain it. Some said that she was a ghost, others that she was no more than a trick of the light. My grandfather wasn't sure. "You never know," he would add with a wink. "It might've been Gráinne Daly herself."

7

"COME HOME"

County Laois

It was sometimes believed in certain country places that powerful actions or intense emotions might leave a mark on the landscape. Such a belief was probably rooted in the old Celtic ideal that humans were in some mystical way connected to the land on which they lived and that one would affect the other. Thus, violent acts and murders often left an impression on the countryside, like a sound on a recording, and might be "played" again by somebody who had the abilities to sense them. This was often offered as an explanation for ghosts and phantoms – that they were actually the "recordings" of dramatic past events held in the land, to be detected by certain individuals. Similarly, periods of great emotion or distress, either from a community or from an individual – grief, anger, loneliness – might also be imprinted on the world around to be "reactivated" at some future date. Powerful events such as the Irish Potato Famine, it is said, can sometimes stir up echoes which can reverberate down the generations even to the present day and there are some who have claimed to have seen "ghosts" relating to that period in time.

Not everybody, of course, had the ability to either see or hear such "recordings", it was believed, only those who were sensitive enough or who had "special abilities". In country areas such people were often referred to as "spae folk" (in the North of Ireland) or "ghost seers" and were treated with respect and awe by the community around them, as they were believed to have some sort of mystical connection into the Otherworld – the world of fairies and spirits. Indeed, their abilities were considered to be something akin to the "second sight", a tradition held by some seers in the Western Isles and in the Highlands of Scotland. Such visions, however, sometimes appeared to the viewer as actual events or sometimes with an almost dream-like quality – it depended upon the temperament of the person concerned.

Occasionally, however, ordinary people also briefly caught a glimpse of past events, often in moments of personal stress or in individual reflection. Like for the ghost-seers, such visions could occur at any time of the day or night and were often put down as ghosts or daylight wraiths. It was thought that they were induced by the circumstances in which individuals found themselves – for example, those who were sick or grieving were more likely to see such things than those who were not. Those who were intoxicated might also be prone to see such things – although, of course, their testimony was always open to question.

It was also said that certain places throughout the countryside were more susceptible to holding such "memories" than others and that those who visited them were more likely to experience visions of former years. Lonely roads, isolated houses, remote hollows, many sites well away from the hurry and bustle of the workaday world might be – and were often considered as – such places. It was well to avoid them, as who knew what ancient and terrible recollections and emotions lay there, locked into the land?

The following story, centred round one such location, is said to be true and I have no reason to doubt the honesty of the teller. He is not a country person steeped in country ways or beliefs but rather a man more comfortable in towns and cities. Nor is he young or gullible. He is exceptionally well-educated and with an artistic temperament which is nonetheless extremely well balanced. Today, he primarily earns his living as a writer, although he worked in a number of other jobs at various points in his life. He told me the story several years ago and I have since obtained his permission to repeat it here on the condition that I do not disclose his actual name and that I give only a general indication as to the location where it all happened. I was pleased to give this undertaking in order to be able to recount his story, which is both eerie and mystifying. About two years ago I also travelled with him to the location that he mentioned. The house, which had a considerable local "reputation" as a "ghost place", is still there and, though it was a high, bright day in the middle of summer, the evening was drawing on and I felt a distinct chill in the air which, I imagined, might not be altogether from this world. At that moment, the memories hidden in the land seemed very close.

When I was in my mid-twenties, I suffered what some would call a kind of breakdown, probably brought on by overwork. The doctors diagnosed it as nervous exhaustion and recommended that I take a complete break away from all the things that were weighing me down at the time. I had been working in a clerical job but had also been trying to make it as a writer – working late into the night and getting up very early in the morning in order to tackle my manuscripts, which I fondly believed were works of great fiction. On top of this, I'd got into a bit of debt – not a great deal but enough to add to the pressure on me. I didn't really see how I could take the doctors' advice.

Thankfully, I had a number of friends who were perhaps more concerned about my welfare than I was about myself. One in particular took me in hand and forced me to rest.

"You've got to get away from the town," he told me, "from phones ringing, from post that has to be answered and from people calling. You need to get away somewhere very secluded, where nobody knows where you are, and get your head together again. And just to help you, I've found you the ideal spot – a house in County Laois, tucked away in a corner of the Bog of Allen. A friend put me in touch with the old lady who owns it now and I rang her and offered her a little bit of money for two or three weeks – no, don't offer me anything, I'm glad to have done it. I told her that it was for a friend who was coming out of a bad time and she was very understanding. The house is yours for two or three weeks and it's already paid up. I think that she was glad to get some money for it – she's owned it for a while, she was saying, and she's had a bit of trouble letting it for it has a bit of a history to it."

"What d'you mean by that?" I asked him.

He shrugged. "She didn't really say. I don't think she was very sure herself. There's some talk in the locality about it being a 'ghost-place' or some sort of nonsense. She's not from the area so she didn't know anything about it. I think that she's tried to lease it out to some local families but they wouldn't touch it. Apparently they're quite superstitious around there. If anything it'll help you for you'll not be bothered with people coming round and disturbing you."

"It all sounds very intriguing," I answered. "Are you saying that this place you've got for me is haunted?"

"I don't think so. It's just some old country superstition. I honestly don't think you'll see a ghost and the main point is that you'll be well away from all the pressures that you've been under recently. Use the place to get a bit of a rest. It's very isolated and should give you plenty of solitude."

He was right, for at first I couldn't find the place. It was isolated all right, for it was not on any main road. After asking around for almost an hour, I was directed to a simple farm trail which led across a bog and into a clump of trees. The house itself stood on the very edge of the bog and was well hidden from anyone passing by on the road about a quarter of a mile away. The lane that led to it was so narrow that I knew I'd never get my car up to it, so I drove about a mile down the road where I'd been told I'd find the house of a very accommodating farmer. He agreed to let me keep my car in his barn "if I didn't stay too long" and though he was very amiable I had the distinct impression he had reservations about me staying at the house, even if he said nothing. Leaving my car behind, I made my way back to the lane.

There was nothing special about the house – it was simply a plain two-storey dwelling built out of dark stone with a small outhouse tagged onto its side almost as an afterthought. It was a square building with a low roof which hung down over the upper windows and made the place look slightly sinister. The front door, which had once been a garish shade of red, was now peeling, as were the window frames, both upstairs and down. In front was a narrow garden which stretched down to the very edge of the bog, where it met with the lane from the main road. An attempt had been made to cut the grass and to keep it tidy but down towards the swamp and the lane, the gardener seemed to have given up, for long grasses and bulrushes flourished in profusion. I pushed the door open and stepped inside – the place smelt of must and damp, the reek of a house which has stood empty for too long.

The inside was dingy and wooden – a vast open hearth clogged with clinker from the chimney in one corner of a narrow kitchen, which doubled as a living room; a small pantry which led to a back door out into the bog; and a narrow hallway into which a staircase descended. And that was basically all that was downstairs. The upstairs consisted of a narrow landing with a rather dangerous-looking banister and two small rooms which served as bedrooms, together with a small, cold narrow room containing a washstand with taps that didn't work. Water, I discovered, had to be brought in from a small well by the back door. There was no toilet either – other than a dry toilet out the back in a little hut half hidden by bushes. There was also no electricity; the only lighting in the house was from oil lamps which the owner had left for me. So the house was very basic, but it would do for me. There was a table and a small range on which I could cook in the living room, together with a low sofa, which was slightly damp, and a couple of chairs. An old worm-eaten bookcase with a pile of mouldy books made up the furniture downstairs; two single beds (one in each room) together with a dressing table and a chair in both bedrooms were all the furniture upstairs. There were several cupboards in the pantry in which I could store dry foods and not much else. As I said, a very basic place, but then I wasn't after grandeur.

My first days in the house passed pleasantly enough. I did a little walking and caught up on some reading. I lit a fire in the fireplace and was surprised when it burned at all. In all that time I saw nobody – nor did I want to see anybody – although I did glimpse a figure standing looking at the house from out in the bog. Doubtless, it was somebody who'd seen the smoke from the chimney and wondered if the house was inhabited. However, when I looked again, the figure had gone.

I'd brought my own food with me and my tastes were simple, so I wasn't too bothered about meals. I ate when I was hungry and slept when I was tired. I wrote a little, but not much. And at night I lay on the narrow bed, almost overwhelmed by the utter silence of the bog around me. Sometimes, I'd hear a dog bark, far away, or a bird cry out in the dark but mostly there was just silence. I slept as I've never slept before or since.

It was on the second night there that something odd happened. I'd been out for a walk in the bog that day and the Laois air had made me tired – I was still getting acclimatised – so I was in a particularly sound sleep. But something wakened me. At first I wasn't sure what it was. But then, as I came to, I had the unmistakable impression (don't ask me how) that somebody was standing under my window in the patch of green that served as a garden below. I thought that somebody had just walked round the front of the house and was standing facing the lane which led out through the bog to the main road. Whoever it was didn't move but just seemed to be standing there. At least that was the very strong impression that I had as I lay on the bed. Dismissing it as a fragment of some dream, I turned over on the bed and began to drift back to sleep. Then from below, the sound of a man's voice, deep and sorrowful, called out – just two words, "Come home!" For some reason, in my drowsy state, I thought that it sounded very far away. I was awake again and I thought at first that it was somebody who knew me who had come down and was calling to me, trying to gain admission to the house. Still half asleep I climbed out of bed and went over to the window to see who it was. Although I couldn't raise the window itself (damp and mould prevented that), I looked out, half-expecting to see one of my friends standing below. There was nothing, just the moonlight shining on the bogland. The garden below was empty. And yet I was sure that I'd heard somebody call – or was I? Maybe it had all been part of the dream. I looked around from my window, resisting the impulse to go down to the door and see if there was anyone there. I went back to bed and fell asleep again. I was disturbed no further during the night.

The next morning I went out into the garden, checking to see if I'd had a visitor, but found no trace of anyone near the house. I busied myself during the day with some writing and as evening drew on, I cooked myself a main meal and settled in for the evening to do some reading. Gradually, the tiredness of the day got the better of me and in the end I climbed the wooden staircase to the bedrooms above and was soon snoring.

When I opened my eyes again, it was still dark – it must have been just after midnight or very early in the morning.

I had the distinct impression that I'd been woken by somebody speaking close by or making a noise under my bedroom window. I lay for a moment but there was no other sound or movement and, thinking I'd been dreaming again, I rolled over to go back to sleep.

"Come home!" This time I heard the voice quite distinctly. It was a man's voice, heavy and laden with grief. Indeed, all the woes of the world seemed to be contained in those two words. It seemed to come drifting up from under my bedroom window where the front door opened onto what passed for my garden. The effect was like plunging me into a bath of cold water. Suddenly I was fully awake and sitting up in bed. I sat for a moment, waiting for the voice to speak again but there was only silence. Cautiously, I rose and walked over to the window. As on the night before, there was nobody near the house, only the moon shining down onto the front of the house. The bog all around seemed very peaceful. Perhaps what I thought I'd heard was just an echo of the breakdown that I'd just been through – at least that was my reasoning. I went back to bed and lay down but I didn't sleep.

"Oh, come home!" In all my life, I have never heard a plea so mournful or so heartfelt. It was a man's voice, filled with catches and sobs, laden with grief and anxiety. And there was no mistake; it came from outside, just below my window and somewhere near the front door. I sensed somebody moving, along the front wall of the house and into the garden. Once more I got up and ran to the window and again I saw nothing, just the emptiness of the bog stretching away to distant dark hills. But I had absolutely no doubt that I'd heard a man call out, for the poignancy and loneliness in that cry had almost been too much to bear. Again I got up and, lighting the lamp, went downstairs. The place was in darkness with nobody about. I looked in the pantry and checked the back door – it was locked. I went to the front door, opened it and peered out into the night. The garden was drenched in moonlight but there was nothing moving – or was there? At the far end, where the lane started across the bog, was a huge, dark rhododendron bush, surrounded by shadows that spilled out into the grass and as I watched, I thought I saw one of them move.

"Hello?" I called. "Is there anybody there?" The only thing that answered me was a bird crying somewhere out in the boglands. I walked down to the bush, holding my lamp in front of me as if for protection, but there was nothing there. As the light advanced on the bush, the shadows fell away, revealing only a stretch of empty grass. I went back to the house, puzzled by what I'd heard. Was somebody trying to play a rather cruel trick on me, I wondered? But then who would know that I was here? It was all very puzzling. You may be sure that I got very little sleep for the rest of the night, but in that time nothing happened, nor did I hear the cry again.

In contrast to the first few days at the house, the next day seemed to drag slowly. I tried to read but I couldn't get the memory of that lonely call out of my mind. Truthfully, I've heard few things sadder – it had been the lost cry of a broken heart and it somehow reverberated in my mind. I went twice to the well at the back door and once to a turf stack down beside the dry toilet to get fuel for the fire. Whilst I was there, I chanced to look across the bog and saw the figure that I had seen previously standing a good way off, amongst some clumps of bushes which rose out of the morass, looking towards the house. It was a man, dressed in a dark coat and trousers and with a cap pulled down on his face. He looked like some kind of labourer or local farmer and even from a distance I thought he seemed a bit shabby. He must have glimpsed me for he turned on his heel and was gone, striding swiftly through the bog as if to get well away from me and the house. I went back indoors.

The day passed and I made myself a simple evening meal. As I said, my appetite had not fully returned after my illness and my wants were not great. Then I read until late and it was time to go to bed. I will tell you that I climbed the wooden stairs with some apprehension, as I had really no wish to go up there and when I did fall into bed I lay awake for a long time. Eventually, I must have dozed off.

"Come home!" The voice, although still as grief-ridden, seemed somehow stronger and more distinct. "Oh, please come home!" It stirred me from a light doze. Suddenly I was awake again. Crossing to the window, I looked out. The land below was in darkness. Clouds masked the moon and I could barely make out even the rhododendron bush down by the lane. But even as I looked I knew there was nothing there. If somebody had been playing a joke on me, they were probably gone by now. I turned back to bed.

"Come home!" I was just pulling back the covers to the bed in order to get in when the voice called again. This time, I was sure that I heard a footfall on the step at the front door. I rushed back to the window to see if I could catch who it was. At the very far end of the garden, a little way from the house and by the big rhododendron bush there was a light of some sort burning. It was not from a torch or anything like that – rather it seemed to be a lantern held aloft by an unseen hand. Somebody, I imagined, was standing at the mouth of the lane and was carrying a lamp, either for signalling or for some other purpose.

"At last!" I said to myself in triumph. "I'll see who you are now!" And, not even bothering to pull on a dressing gown, I hurried down the stairs, across the short hall and flung open the front door. The garden was in darkness – there was no light at all at its end by the rhododendron bush. I walked down to the mouth of the lane but there was nothing or nobody there, the garden was very still. I even walked a little way along the lane and into the bog. There was a movement to my right but it was only a waterfowl that I'd disturbed, which went flapping away across the marsh. A dog barked somewhere far away. I looked around, hoping to see the lamplight bobbing away to disappear across the bog, signifying that somebody human was carrying it, but I saw nothing. Was it my imagination? Had some vestige of the breakdown returned? I made my way back to the house but couldn't sleep. I sat for the rest of the night, reading by the oil lamp and hoping somebody would come again. But there was nothing.

If I wasn't going crazy, then somebody had to be playing some sort of game with me. The next day, round about midday, I went to the mouth of the lane and looked out across the bog. This was roughly about the time I'd seen the man standing out there and there he was, walking a little way away in the direction of the road.

"Hello!" I called to him but he didn't seem to hear and just kept walking away from the house until a clump of low trees hid him from my sight. But I resolved that if I saw him again, I'd corner him – for I was convinced that he might have something to do with the mysterious nightly goings-on. I had also decided not to go to bed but to sit up – not lighting the lamp – and wait and see if anybody came about. That way I might be able to test whether I was sane or not.

I cooked myself a meal on the little range and then sat down to read. As darkness stole across the Laois countryside, the bog fell silent. I snuffed out the lamp and sat down on the sofa to wait in the gloom. The phosphorescent hands of my watch crept around with almost intolerable slowness but nothing happened. I waited and waited but all was silence itself outside. Weariness must have overcome me and gradually I drifted off.

It must have been the sensation of somebody passing in front of the lower window that wakened me. Whether it was a footfall or somebody actually brushing against the glass, I don't know, but whatever it was it stirred me. From somewhere close by came the now-familiar anguished voice with its repetitive call: "Come home! Oh, come home!" I ran to the window which looked out towards the lane. Down beside the rhododendron bush, the light was burning again – yellow, smoky, almost orange, like the light from a lantern or an oil lamp. Without hesitating, I ran through the hall, opened the front door and was out into the nightbound garden. The light was still there, burning brightly beside the blackness of the rhododendron bush and slowly I advanced on it. Now, at last, I'd see who had been tormenting me!

The garden was gloomy and full of shadows but as I drew nearer to the rhododendron bush I imagined that I saw a figure standing close to it. However, it was so indistinct I

97

couldn't determine whether it was a man or a woman – although by its partly glimpsed bearing I assumed it to be the former. I was aware of no more than a clot of darkness, a dark bulk off to the side of the bush, suggestive of a figure of some sort. It seemed to be holding up a light – something that looked like an old fashioned lantern or a hurricane lamp that threw out a sort of jaundiced light on the edges of the great, dark bush. Instinctively, I knew that this was the being which cried out so pitifully each night. Indeed I sensed the words without the figure having spoken.

"Who's there?" I asked, my own voice shaking slightly. "Who are you?" The shape didn't reply. In fact I sensed that it seemed totally unaware of my presence there but was concentrating on something in the dark towards the end of the lane or out in the bog.

"Come home!" the voice drifted to me across the intervening space. It seemed echoey and far away now and a hundred other voices seemed to be mixed in with it, whispering along its edges. "Oh please come home!" Although frightened, I made to step closer, to make out what the shape in front of me might be. At the same instant, there was a movement off to my right – something stirred in the undergrowth. It might have been a bird or a rabbit or some such animal but, instinctively, I turned my head in its direction. In that instant, the shape was gone, the light winked out and I was alone in the garden and in the dark once again. Somewhere out in the bog a fox barked sharply.

"Who is it?" I called again, for I still hoped that some human agency lay behind the appearance. However, I was now beginning to think one of two things: either it might be a part of my illness which had lingered on, or – and this terrified me – it might be something supernatural. I could feel a cold sweat break on my forehead. Far away in the night, I thought I heard the cry again, just as plaintive as before but fading away: "Come home!" The night suddenly seemed very cold and I turned back to the relative warmth of the house. I now thought that it *might* be some sort of supernatural manifestation.

You can be sure that I did not sleep at all that night. I sat on the sofa listening for the voice calling from somewhere nearby and occasionally I would cross to the window and look out, expecting to see that queer, jaundiced light at the foot of the garden once more. But there was nothing. As daybreak rose over the bog, I fell into a light doze, sleeping fitfully until the early afternoon. I ate only sparingly, fearful that my sanity was going and as night came on I sat, almost unmoving in the lamplight in the sitting room, waiting for the plaintive cry to come and burying my head beneath the cushions of the sofa when it did.

The next day, I more or less moped about the house, trying vainly to write something, convinced that I was on the edge of another breakdown, whether induced by ghosts or by my own morbid imaginings. A sort of blackness, loneliness, almost bordering on despair, had descended on me and I couldn't shake it. An explanation of sorts would, however, come in a sudden and unexpected way.

I had been out at the dry toilet, which as may be remembered, lay at the back of the house, away from the well. As I returned to the house through the bushes I suddenly became aware of somebody standing by the back door and trying to peer in the back window into the pantry.

For a second, I froze and stood my ground. I had not lit a fire that morning and perhaps the person might have been checking that I was still in residence. He was the man whom I'd seen out on the bog, a local, labourer-like individual, dressed in a dark torn coat and trousers and heavy workingman's boots. He was moving along the back wall of the house rather furtively, creeping up to the edge of the window and peering round it in a highly suspicious manner. Carefully, I crossed the intervening space and laid my hand on his shoulder, making him jump. He turned and for the first time I saw his face, framed by a shock of dirty-white hair. It was a local face, broad and tanned by the weather, set below heavy, dark eyebrows. There was no guile or malice in it, only a look of genuine surprise and fear.

"I meant no harm," he said immediately in a thick, heavy country accent. "I was only checking to see if there was still somebody in the place or if you'd gone."

"I've seen you watching this place two or three times before," I snapped back. The terror and lack of sleep had made me irritable. "Why should you be so interested in me or in this house?" He seemed to cower back.

"I meant ye no harm," he repeated. "I sometimes use the well an' I wanted to check if there was anybody about. I was surprised that there would be anybody livin' in this place at all an' I thought that ye mighta gone."

"Why would you think that?" I answered him hotly. "You've been watching me well enough for the last few days." I could sense that he wanted to be away but here might be a chance to get to the bottom of the mystery about the house. He shuffled to one side and I was frightened that he might make a run for it.

"The place has a bad name about it," he said. "There should never have been a house built in this spot an' that's the truth".

"What do you know about somebody shouting in the night?" I demanded. It might well have been him, I imagined. "Somebody who calls out and keeps me awake at night? Is that you?" His eyes widened and he seemed to relax a little.

"Ye've heard it? The man that cries?" he said. "An' ye thought that it might be me?"

"You or somebody else. Somebody trying to frighten me or make a joke of me!" I replied hotly. He gave a small laugh and his fearful manner relaxed a little bit.

"An' you think that it's me? Well, it's not me. But I know about it. Nobody knows *what* it is. Some people say that it's an echo or a memory." He looked around towards the back of the house. "Nobody remembers who built this house, for it was built just outside living memory. But they said that it should never have been built in this place. Maybe somewhere nearer the road, but not here."

"Why not?" I asked. "What do you mean?"

He paused, unwilling at first to say more, but then he went on: "There are some around here who believe that this is a fairy place – a special place. They say that there used to be an old ringfort here which went away back beyond the time of the Church and into pagan times. They said that it was a very magical place and that it could *remember*. There are some that will tell you that the land has memories too and that very special people might be able to see those memories from time to time. People who have *the gift!*" He said this as if it should mean something to me and looked at me pointedly as he spoke.

101

"Then this . . . this *thing* that I heard is some sort of prehistoric pagan ghost?" I asked him, but he shook his head. He was still looking to my right and I still thought that he might make a run for it.

"No, not from the very oul' times," he answered. "I never mind this house being built but I do mind one or two who lived in it – not for long, though. I think some o' them heard what you must have an' this place always had a kind of *feelin'* about it. But there useta be an oul' fella in this country whose father is said to have heard about a man who lived in it. He lived there with his daughter – his wife bein' long dead – an' he seems to have been a decent enough fella. But the daughter was very headstrong an' liked her own way, an' he was very proud an' wouldn't give in to her. The pair of them clashed every day an' in the end he told her to get out an' so she did an' she went to Dublin. I suppose he thought she would only go for a few days an' then she'd be back with her tail between her legs, but he never saw her again. She was murdered, y'see, somewhere in Dublin. Her throat was cut from ear to ear." And he made a motion with his right forefinger across his own scrawny throat. "There was a sailor took up for it." There was another pause. "Nobody knew for a long time what had happened but all the time that she was away, the father was distraught. Even though he was very stern an' strict, he still loved her. It got to him in the end – went for his mind – and he used to stand at the end of the lane calling on her to come back an' telling her that he forgave her. He got stranger and stranger in his ways, for he was a man that never mixed much with people."

"And did he ever find out what had happened to her?" I asked slowly, almost afraid of the answer.

"Oh, aye. And when he did find out they say that he did himself in. He used to come out at all hours of the night, callin' for her – sometimes with a lamp, an' sometimes not. The guilt had got to him, y'see, an' he blamed himself for driving her away from the house – away to Dublin! In the end it all got far too much for him. Some people that know the story say that he wandered into the bog out there an' was drowned; some say that he hanged himself from the stair-banisters of his house." I thought of the narrow and dangerous banisters at the top of the stairs and shuddered a little. "There's some'll tell you that he just died of a broken heart, but nobody knows. The oul' fella that told it to me didn't know. But they say that *somethin'* still hangs about the house – still callin' for her to come home. There's people that'll tell ye that they've seen a light in the bog an' that's the oul' fella lookin' for his daughter an' never findin' her. People'll say it's a ghost but it's more likely to be a remembrance held in the land round about. There's places that are like that. Oul' people knew about them but the young ones don't." He looked at me oddly. "Ye say that ye've heard it yourself?"

"I've heard a sound," I answered, "like a call. But I can't truthfully say what it is. You say that other people might have heard it? Have you heard it?" He gave me a sort of odd smile, still edging around me towards the bog as if anxious to be away.

"Some people say that they hear it on still nights – callin' out across the bog – but I never have," he replied. "I've seen somethin' that looks like a light, though, along the edges of the bog but the priest said that it was just marsh gas! An' he says that the call is no more than the shout of a fox or some other such thing. But I don't know." I stood there for a moment, unsure of what to say or of what question to ask him next, but he continued: "Maybe it's nothing more that a *memory* that the land holds. This was supposed to be a *fairy* place – a house should never have been built here. I wouldn't lodge in it for a fortune. It has a really bad feelin' to it, I think." And with that he darted past me and through a gap which separated the house from the bog. "But I have to go now. I've urgent business somewhere else. I can't tell you any more." The last sentence was slightly garbled. It was an odd way to leave. I made to run after him and then thought the better of it. What would I ask him and what more would he tell me? I knew all that I needed to know, I suppose. I watched him run across the boggy ground, his boots splashing up water as he went and then I turned and went back into the house again

Knowing the history of the place did me no good. Nor did it grant me any comfort. If anything, it worsened my situation there, for an almost tangible atmosphere of gloom had settled over the house, an atmosphere which I could now trace back to the lonely, grieving man who had once lived there. The house itself now seemed to hold a heavy air of oppression about it and, as I went from pantry to living room to narrow hall and between the bedrooms upstairs, I couldn't help but think of the sad, anxious man who had once done the same. I slowly began to realise that, although the house had been rented for two more weeks, I couldn't possibly stay. For the good of my health and for my sanity, I reasoned, I had to leave it as soon as possible. And yet, I wasn't altogether sure. Maybe the feeling was no more than a notion that had been stirred in me by the strange old man's tale. Maybe it was just foolishness. Maybe there was no basis at all in the tale and he'd just told it to me in order to frighten me.

My car was still stored away in the neighbouring farmer's shed and I now walked up the road to check that it was all right. Whilst I was there I spoke to the farmer who was working in the yard. He was a burly, pleasant fellow who looked a "no-nonsense" type of person. I didn't talk about the house or its alleged history directly but I did mention that I had seen an old man skulking about in the bog. He simply laughed.

"Ah, that'd be Thady Rafferty," he replied. "He's always about there. Have you spoken to him?" Not wishing to disclose what had happened, I told him that we had exchanged a few words but no more. He laughed a little again.

"He's a strange one all right. Comes from a strange family; brothers and sisters were all the same – queer dreamy people, always seein' things or hearin' sounds that nobody else could see or hear. They say that he has notions about the bog, says that it's full of fairies and such like. Full of old tales about druids and ghosts, he is. He's really not all there." He looked at me knowingly. "I wouldn't listen to anything he tells you, for he has strange notions. Sometimes I think that he should be put away somewhere, for he's always trying to frighten people who don't know him. But there's no truth in what he tells people." However, when I casually mentioned the house to him he looked at me oddly and wouldn't be drawn on it.

"He told me that some man had hanged himself there," I probed, "after his daughter was murdered in Dublin."

105

He turned away and refused to meet my gaze. "If there was, I never heerd of it," he replied in a tone that suggested that I should let the matter rest.

"Would you stay in the house of a night then?" I chided him in a sort of half-joke. He didn't answer me for a minute, but busied himself arranging meal bags.

"No, I wouldn't," he replied finally. "It's a damp old place – too close to the bog – and I have a problem with my chest. It wouldn't suit me at all. It might suit a younger person like yourself though," he added more cheerily as if to lighten the mood. However, he would say no more about the house and that was really an end to our conversation.

When I returned to the building, the overwhelming sense of melancholy struck me again as soon as I walked in through the door. Loneliness seemed to envelop me like a dark cloak as I stepped into the tiny hallway and as I looked upwards, I thought for one brief second that there was a suggestion of a shadow, hanging against the upper banisters above. In an instant, the impression was gone but it lingered with me for the rest of the day. That night, the voice in the garden seemed to call slightly more loudly for the daughter of the house to come home and the light down by the rhododendron bush seemed to burn just a little bit brighter. If these were the memories trapped in the land, they were seemingly getting stronger. In fact, they were now starting to overwhelm me. I had to get away from the house and from the bog.

As morning approached, I packed my things and the remainder of the food that I had brought with me. After ten, I walked up the road, past the farmhouse where I had stored my car, to return the keys to the woman who owned the house. I simply told her that the climate of the place didn't suit me, that it hadn't proved as restful as I'd thought and that I was going back to Dublin. I told her that she could keep whatever money had already been paid for her inconvenience. She looked at me oddly but said nothing. I expect she guessed what had happened. I then walked back to the farmer, collected my car and left the Laois countryside behind me as I headed back to the city.

The house, as far as I know, is still standing on the very edge of the Bog of Allen. I went back to it once but I doubt if I'll go back again. I think about it occasionally – more than I'd like to – and wonder if the voice still calls there at night and if the light is still burning in the darkness by the rhododendron bush. I know that I only saw shapes and shadows in the moonlight but the voice, the feeling of loneliness and despair, have haunted me down the years more forcefully than any ghostly vision. Maybe for all his strangeness, the old man, Thady Rafferty, was right and what I heard and felt were no more than the memories of the land. If that is the case, do those memories still linger there? Would *you* go back and find out?

* * *

Note: The idea of ancient memories being held in mounds, forts and earthworks is a common one in several parts of Ireland. Indeed, there is an old saying that "any house built in a fairy fort (an earthworks) is bound to be haunted" and there are fragmentary stories from all over the country of the sounds and sights of former years being heard or seen within the earthen walls of ringforts and such like. So, is the idea of ghosts and the walking dead no more than the actual memory of the land upon which we live, somehow trapped forever like an insect caught in aspic? A fascinating idea and one perhaps for the scientist as well as the folklorist to tease out.

8 THE BLIND ROOM

County Roscommon

Perhaps like everywhere else, the ghosts of children – particularly those of very young children – hold a special place in Irish folklore. Perhaps it is their innocence and vulnerability that make such phantoms especially appealing to storytellers and arouse some deep compassion within ourselves. The idea of a life cut short at a young age also stimulates our concern and pity. Sometimes, however, such phantoms can also be the most persistent and dangerous form of spectre. Children, deprived of their rightful and anticipated place in the world, can become extremely petulant and spiteful towards the living. The spirits of stillborn children were particularly dangerous – never having lived outside the womb at all, they felt cheated of life and were either continually seeking a way into the world or else looking to harm the living who were enjoying the existence that they themselves had been denied.

There were a number of places in various parts of Ireland – perhaps tucked away in some isolated corner of the country – that were given over to the burial of stillborn children and those who

109

had died immediately after birth (and therefore had not been baptised by the Church). Many of them were no more than fields or small hills donated by local farmers and were called "caldreagh". They are also sometimes referred to as "killeens"/"cillins", although the true definition of this word is sometimes disputed. Some of them were used for the burial of suicides whose act of self-destruction traditionally had placed them outside the prayers of the Church; but mostly they were children. A rather famous one was said to lie near the village of Mortyclogh near Cormcomroe Abbey, County Clare, but this was a rather disputed site and it is not clear if it was actually referred to as a caldreach. Whatever such places were called, people were ill-advised to cross them, especially after nightfall. The souls of undead children swarmed there like flies, anxious to take over the body of the traveller and so gain some form of material existence in the living world. Such sites were widely considered to be badly haunted. Dangerous though these places were, anywhere that an unbaptised child had been laid was equally so, if the circumstances were right.

What sorts of children were buried in such isolated and unconsecrated graveyards? Stillborn children might be, but also children who had been born in secret. In Catholic Ireland, sex before marriage or sex outside of marriage was considered to be a serious sin. Children were sometimes the evidence of this. Consequently, some births were kept secret, even from the Church, and the babies were quietly disposed of, being laid to rest in some unmarked grave. Such places might be considered especially dangerous as the child, deprived of both its life and its parentage, might become even more vicious and malignant.

The following story was told to me by the descendant of a housekeeper in one of the large houses in County Roscommon. My informant was unsure as to exactly which great house it was, as the person who relayed the story to her was slightly wandering in her mind and the location appears to have changed during the course of the tale, which is said to have occurred nearly a hundred years ago. The main name given for it was Castlemartin House, which changed in the course of the story to Castleshea, but no such names or locations exist. She also named the family who owned the property as the Martins, but no such family held lands in County Roscommon and it is possible that the old lady – the housekeeper – confused them with someone else. There is no exact indication as to the location of the house itself, although there was a Castlemartin House in Kilkenny. However, it may have been Strokestown Park House but it might just as easily have been Castlecoote House in the west of the county or the King House near Boyle. This confusion does not, however, detract from the chill which is generated by the tale and is no obstacle to it being included in this collection. I have taken it upon myself to adapt its form slightly to suit a reading audience but the details of the story remain the same as when I heard them.

Come here till I tell ye! This happened years ago when I was only a slip of a girl and first taken in service in County Roscommon. In fact, it happened so long ago that I can hardly remember anything exactly as it was. But I'll try to mind it as best I can.

I was only about thirteen when I left my father's house in Mayo and travelled to Roscommon to work for my aunt, who was senior housekeeper in a big place they called Castlemartin. The house was very big and very old and was the home of some grand English family who were never there. But the place had to be maintained and looked after, so there were still servants living there and my aunt was in charge of a good number of them.

I can remember the cart that had collected me from home sweeping up the great drive. It was not quite dark but the evening was coming down and it seemed to me, child that I was, that the house was lit up like a town. There were lights all along its length and in the poor light of the afternoon, they showed me just how big and long the place was. It was spread out in front of me, lights twinkling in its windows, like some sort of fairy land to which the cart was taking me. It was just like another world.

The drive to the house was very long but we got there eventually. We went round, past the grand front door and under a low arch and into a yard which had stables off it. There the carter stopped and pulled up his horses.

"This is far as you go, Miss," he said in his heavy accent. In all the trip, he had barely spoken to me once; maybe he was too shy to do so. He was an oldish man and he had a very polite way about him. "Get down and I'll get somebody from the kitchens to come and get you." He got down himself and went across the yard towards one of the yellow-lit windows. "Wait there and somebody'll get you by and by," he called back to me. And then he was gone into the dark at the corner of the yard.

I waited, oh, I don't know how long, in that shadowy coachyard, looking up at the lights that were coming on in the windows far above me and feeling very alone. At that moment I wished that I'd never left my father's house in Mayo to go into service in such a place. It was my aunt who had persuaded my father after my mother had died and he was barely fit to look after us all. My aunt was a widow – I'd heard it said that her husband died very young – and had been in service for a long time and I barely knew her. But she had got me this post, which was more than I could have hoped for at home, and so I waited.

In the end, a girl not much older than myself came to bring me in. She was dressed in a dark blouse and skirt with a white apron, stained and smeared, knotted about her waist. Her hair was tied up in a bun under a whiteish cap.

"Are you Mrs Casey's niece?" she asked in a very sharp voice. I said that I was. "Well, come in then. Your aunt's waitin' for you." And she turned on her heel and walked towards the darkened house with me following.

And so I came to Castlemartin House. My aunt, who I had seldom seen before that day, welcomed me with a cold kiss on the cheek in a huge kitchen where a great black range threw out heat and made the place – big though it was – feel like a furnace. My aunt was a tall and very severe-looking woman. My father had always said that she had a good heart but a sharp way with her. There was not much family friendliness from her, anyway.

"You'll be a maid of all work," she told me. "And you'll work hard and ask no favours from me, for I've had to pull a few strings to even get you here." She looked at me closely, with her thin face very pinched. "Here the fact that you're family counts for nothing. I've done my bit for you; now it's up to you to work hard for me and give me no bother." I said that I would. "Good. And now, Nuala" – she pointed to the girl who had brought me in – "will show you where you have to sleep. Get unpacked and we'll sort you out some sort of dress from the blind room." She spoke as if I should know what she meant, but in truth I hadn't a clue.

The maid that she had called Nuala lifted a lamp and walked over to the door, ready to take me further into the darkening house. My aunt walked over to the roaring fire to warm her backside at it. "When you have sorted yourself out," her tone softened a little, "come back down and I'll get one of the others to fix you something to eat, for I'm sure you're hungry after your journey. You can tell me a bit about your father and how he's keeping." The hard light flickered in her eyes once more. "Oh – and you must always refer to me as Mrs Casey and *never* Aunt Margaret. Here I'm as good as your employer and you must always remember that." I said that I would and followed Nuala out of the kitchen, up a flight of wooden stairs and into the rest of that great house.

The family who owned the place were not at home, Nuala told me. They spent most of their time at other houses that they owned in England and only came to Roscommon once in a while. There were rooms in this big rambling house that lay empty for most of the year but which, according to her, had to be tended and cleaned just the same. My aunt was in charge of this and, according to Nuala, she was a hard but fair mistress.

"All the same," she went on, "I don't like being in one of those big, cold, empty rooms on my own. You can be away in one of the wings and you might as well be in another country for all you see and hear of the rest of the house." And I thought that she shivered a little in the lamplight. She said no more.

She led me up several narrow wooden staircases that were quite clearly used by the servants and were not for the owners of the place. I followed her along narrow passageways, which she claimed the owners didn't even know about, let alone use. This was so the servants could go about their business without bothering the great family. At one point, however, she led me out onto a fairly grand landing from which a number of other passages led. In order to get my bearings, I looked down one of them. It was long and dark and gloomy, but I could just see a lamp burning in a bracket at the far end where it connected with another passage and a figure standing there and watching us pass. I thought that it might be another maid or a washerwoman; she seemed to have a bundle of clothes in her arms as she stood there. As far as I could see, she was dressed in a long grey gown with a long white apron which came up over her chest and looked to be fastened about the neck as well as at the waist. On her head was a cap, similar to the one Nuala wore, but it was pulled down so that I couldn't see her face. However, she was staring at us so hard and taking such an interest in the pair of us that it made me feel uncomfortable. Nuala pushed open the door into another corridor and I turned for a moment to look in her direction, about to ask her about the peculiar maid, but when I looked again the figure was gone and there was only the lamp burning in the bracket. If Nuala had seen her too, she gave no sign but led me down the corridor to my own room. Nor did I ask about it, although the strange maid's stare had unsettled me a bit.

I was to sleep in a small room at the back of the house. It was little bigger than a box room, with a single bed in it. The walls were very dreary and a single window looked down on a narrow yard, with a pump directly below. There was a small grate in one corner of the room which Nuala told me could be lit only if the weather was very cold. She also told me that I might get another maid in with me from time to time, though where she could have slept, I hadn't a notion. There's little else to say about my room except that it was very drab and dreary; however, it was somewhere to lay my head and I was grateful for that.

I went back to the great kitchen where my aunt had some soup and bread ready for me. There was also a maid's dress that I could put on. From her chair by the fire, my aunt conducted the conversation between us, asking about my father and my brother and sisters – all of which I answered as truthfully as I could. I asked my aunt about the great house and the family who lived there but her answers were a little vague. She was a woman, she told me, who lived "below stairs" and knew little about the goings-on of the family who lived above. They simply came and went. She told me that I should make a friend of Nuala, whom she said was about my age and a good worker, but that I was to ignore Paddy Sweeny, who worked with the horses out in the stables and whom I hadn't met yet but soon would. He was an old man from the area and was always trying to frighten the young maids with fanciful tales.

"He'll tell you old stories about ghosts and fairies," my aunt told me. "He'll tell you too that this old house is badly haunted. But don't listen to him for the stories are all in his head and there's not a word of truth in any of them. It's only giddy girls that would believe such nonsense, and you're not one of those!" She spoke with such confidence that I wholly believed her.

I sat and drank my soup while she went through the members of staff whom I should get to know – and those I shouldn't – who worked all over the big house. For some reason I thought of the peculiar maid in the old fashioned dress who had watched me so intently from the end of the passageway and reasoned that she might be one of those I would meet eventually.

"You should try your dress on," instructed my aunt. "I think it should fit you but if it doesn't we can get Kitty Reardon up in the blind room to sort it out for you. You can go up and see her and introduce yourself to her, for I'm sure you'll be seeing her time and again as you're growing." Kitty Reardon, she told me, was the seamstress who looked after the clothes and uniforms of the yardsmen and maids. She was, according to my aunt, a hearty and pleasant woman who never seemed to let anything overly worry her. "It would take somebody like that to work up in *that* end of the house," she added significantly.

"Why so?" I asked, munching on some bread that she'd given me. I was feeling a bit more at my ease now.

"It's a lonely old place up there," my aunt explained, "and very cold. And the room that she works in always has a bad feel to it, I think. It never seems to bother Kitty Reardon but it would bother me if I had to work up there, even for a little while, away from the most of the house with only the occasional maid nipping in and out. I'm very seldom up to see Kitty but when I am I always think there's a bad air about it."

"Why do they call it the blind room?" I asked, taking a spoonful of soup. I thought that it was a curious name. My aunt stretched her hands out to the blaze of the hearth, although the great kitchen was very warm.

"It's because there's no windows to it. Never were. I think in the days before I came that it was a sort of maid's parlour, although it was never used much. There used to be a hearth and a fireplace and all in it but it's all boarded up now. It hasn't been used as a parlour since I've been here. It was always a place that we stored linen and now it's a place for the seamstress to sit. Kitty Reardon has to work with the door open so that the air can circulate – no windows, you see – and I don't think that she's ever in there for too long. Paddy Sweeny'll tell you there's a ghost or some such nonsense in the room but I don't think that Kitty Reardon has seen anything in all the years that she's been working up there." And there the matter was left, as my aunt seemed not to want to discuss it any further. She switched the talk to something else and I finished my meal.

The dress of the uniform that I'd been given didn't fit. I was a slight young thing and it was a little bit too big. However, a bit of tucking in would soon sort it out, my aunt said.

"Go up and see Kitty Reardon, up in the blind room, and she'll sort it out for you," she advised. "I'd think that it'll only take a minute or two – a couple of tucks here and there – and after you've heard about her, now you can go and see what she looks like."

The seamstress's room lay in the west wing of the house, which was not used all that much. It was full of rooms that were all closed up for most of the time, even when the family was home. It was the older part of the house and was full of dark back staircases and little rooms that had once been used for servants. The blind room was on the corner, at the top of a flight of narrow stairs that led up from a lower pantry. They were very steep and you had to be careful climbing them and take them quite slowly. I climbed up, holding my uniform dress over one arm and gripping an old handrail that ran along the side. That's how steep they were!

As I climbed a movement at the head of the stairs caught my eye. Looking up, I saw one of the maids standing for a minute right above me and looking down as I came up. She was a tall, thin-looking woman dressed in old-fashioned clothes – a dark dress and a white apron that looked badly stained – with a maid's cap on her head and tied about the chin in a way that was long out of use. I couldn't really make out her face but it seemed to be very thin and drawn, with hard and glittering eyes and a tight severe mouth. She carried a bundle of blankets in her arms, pressed tight against her chest. For a minute, I thought that this might be Kitty Reardon and I had my mouth open to speak to her but she suddenly turned and went round the corner at the stair top and passed out of my sight. I came up the stairs and turned the corner after her, finding myself in a short corridor that ended in a blank wall but with a door off it into a small room. Assuming this was where the maid had gone, I followed her into the room, which was very bare but was piled high with bed linen and odd clothes and so forth, stacked on shelves and in boxes all around. In the middle of it at a little sewing table sat a small, plump woman of about fifty with a round and pleasant face and her grey hair tied back into a bun. She was working on an old pair of britches by the light of a tiny oil lamp. This turned out to be Kitty Reardon but she was completely alone in that little room.

There was no sign of the maid I'd seen at the head of the stairs and there seemed to be nowhere in the room or in the short corridor outside that she might have gone.

"Come forward, child," said Kitty Reardon cheerily enough. "You're Mrs Casey's niece, aren't you? You got something for me – a dress to be taken in by the looks of it." I looked around the room, searching for another door through which the maid might have gone. "What's the matter, dear? Don't be scared. I won't bite you!"

"I was looking for the other maid who came in here," I explained. "She came in right in front of me but she seems to be gone."

Kitty Reardon frowned, her jolly face creasing for a minute. "What other maid?" she asked. "There's been nobody up here for over an hour. The last person was Paddy Sweeny who came up and sat with me for a spell but he's been gone some time. No, there's been no maid come in here – you must be mistaken." But she spoke with a little more seriousness and her frown grew a little more worried-looking as if she *might* know what I was talking about but didn't like to say. "Now, what can I do for you. Is it a dress you want adjusting?" I said that it was and she made me take my own dress off so that she could measure it properly.

There was no more talk about the strange maid, but there was another curiosity in the blind room. On an open bit of the wall between two piles of clothes was an odd shadow. At first I thought that it might be that of a small bird or a huge insect with its wings spread wide, for it moved and fluttered and seemed to change shape from time to time. As it did so, it seemed to make a low, faint buzzing sound, like an angry bee trapped under a glass jar. I looked around me again but I could see nothing that might be casting such an odd shadow. All the same, Kitty Reardon seemed to pay no attention to it or even to notice that it was even there.

"What's that, Kitty?" I asked, pointing to it. She turned and followed my pointing finger with her gaze.

"What's what?" she replied, then she seemed to notice the shadow as if for the first time. "Oh, that. That's just some old thing – it's been here for years, for as long as I've been up in this room. It's just some odd shadow or trick of the light, but it never bothers me. And I never bother it either." And she laughed a shrill, hearty laugh and sat back in her seat. I gathered that Kitty Reardon let very little annoy her.

"Doesn't the drone of it annoy you?" I pressed. "I know it would me."

But she simply laughed again. "Lord God, child, it never bothers me at all," she said. "It drones away behind me but it doesn't trouble me. It's just some old noise in the house." I thought her voice sounded a wee bit troubled, but I never said. She finished measuring me, with plenty of general chat and nothing more was said either about the strange maid or about the queer, buzzing shadow, but I guessed that they might be lurking somewhere in the corners of both our minds.

Kitty Reardon was the first of the servants whom I met in that great house and over the next few days I met some of the other maids, Mary Cassidy the cook – a dour, complaining woman – a couple of menservants and the yardmen. One of those I met was Paddy Sweeny, who was thought to be something of a "character" among the others.

121

He was an oldish man who worked in the stables outside – although he seemed to do as little work as possible, for he was always sitting in the kitchen, smoking his pipe and exchanging gossip with everybody around him. He watched me very thoughtfully from under his heavy eyebrows as I carried water in a heavy bucket across the kitchen.

"Has the wee girl seen the ghost?" he asked my aunt suddenly. She had been taking tins down from a cupboard in the corner of the kitchen but she turned on him with a withering look that seemed to have no effect on him.

"What ghost?" I asked him warily.

He drew on his pipe. "The Grey Widow," he answered mischievously. "One of the grand old ladies that used to live here. It's said that she walks the upper passages in the West Wing, all clad in her finery, going from room to room and terrifying young maids. She can walk through doors and walls, so they say, and you can wake up in the middle of the night and find her standing at the foot of your bed looking lost and mournful. They say that she's looking for something in this house but can't find it. It's enough t'give a young girl like yourself the creepies."

"Paddy Sweeny!" my aunt snapped sharply from the door of the cupboard. "Stop all that old talk at once and stop trying to frighten the maids. There's no such thing as ghosts, as well you know, and I've never heard of such a thing as a Grey Widow ever since I've been here. This is something that you've made up yourself in order to frighten young girls. It would suit you better to get back to whatever work you might be at. Go on now!" He rose from his seat with a kind of a half-smile, the pipe in the corner of his mouth.

"There *is* a ghost about here," he half-whispered as he went past me. "Keep your eyes open for it." But my aunt silenced him with another of her looks.

The strange maid I'd seen at the top of the stairs and at the end of the long corridor bothered me a bit. I asked Nuala who she might be, trying to describe her as well as I could – the odd dress, the bundle in her arms, her strange old-fashioned cap. I told her that she might be a washwoman as she always seemed to be carrying a bundle of clothes. Nuala made a face.

"It might be Maggie Daley," she said after some thought. "She sometimes does washing round here but she only comes on certain days. She's a right bitch, that one, all right. Nothing ever pleases her or goes right for her. And she's got a sharp tongue. She has a queer way about her too – never mixes too well with the other servants. Keeps herself to herself. I think she has a want in her head." She paused. "Or it could be Ellen Walker who sometimes works in the laundry. She's from the North and a bit strange." She lowered her voice slightly. "She's a *Protestant*, you see." She spoke as if she were referring to a disease and that this explained everything. I simply nodded, though I was unsure exactly what she meant.

There the matter lay, although when I met both these women shortly afterwards, they looked nothing like the maid whom I'd seen at the top of the stairs. However, there were so many other servants coming and going about the place that I thought I had probably missed her and would run into her eventually.

I was a maid of all work and my aunt sent me first of all

to work in the laundry and later to help Nuala with some of her cleaning in the smaller, more out-of-the-way rooms. During my time in the laundry I was up and down the stairs to Kitty Reardon in the blind room so often that I think my own feet would have known the way without me to guide them. I fetched her up armfuls of bedsheets, curtains, tablecloths and yardsman's drawers, all needing mending, and stood at her side beside the sewing table in that narrow room whilst her needle flashed and winked in the lamplight.

"I declare child," said Kitty Reardon in her cheery way one day. "I think that shadow on the wall has got deeper and the noise has got louder. Now what would that noise be?"

She was right, for the low droning buzz kept up a kind of irritating racket in the background whenever we were talking or whenever anybody came into the room. Kitty, tolerant soul that she was, didn't appear to mind it too much but if I'd had to work there for most of the day it would have driven me mad.

"What *is* that sound?" I asked. It sounded like an insect, trapped behind the woodwork and trying to get out.

Kitty Reardon shook her head. "I don't rightly know," she admitted. "Just an old sound about the house. All very old houses have strange sounds about them. This one's been here in this room ever since I came here and it doesn't really trouble me all that much. There's supposed to be some stories about it, but I never half-listen and I couldn't tell you a word of them." I think that she may have lied about that. "I used to think it was the wind or some sort of machinery down below on the lower part but now I'm not sure. And it has certainly got worse of late. I might get Paddy Sweeny to take a look for me." But of course, she never did – that was always Kitty's way.

When I wasn't in the laundry, I was cleaning rooms in the distant western wing of that great house. The rooms there were often big and empty and few of the family went there when they were in residence. Nuala was always frightened or at least hesitant about going there, for the rooms were always cold and full of shadows.

"There's a *creep* about it," she would say. "Paddy Sweeny says it's *ha'nted*. There's things in them rooms that crawl in from the countryside round about and lodge there. That's what I think anyway. I'm never settled there." I didn't find it so, although it was a bit lonely away from the bustle in the rest of the house. But I went there anyway, to clean the dust from the desks in the writing rooms and empty drawing rooms, without any fear. That was until old Mrs O'Farrell came to visit my aunt.

I came into the kitchen one afternoon to find a strange woman sitting in the big chair by the grate. She was a big woman, very tall, but old and a bit bent, with a broad countrywoman's face that was lined and covered in wrinkles. Her walking stick hung on the arm of the chair as she leaned forward. She seemed cold even though it was a reasonably warm day. She spoke to me very kindly but in a low, husky voice, which sounded more like a man's. She had a broad country-sounding accent. I thought that she seemed very much at ease in our place.

My aunt looked up. "This is Mrs O'Farrell," she said. "Mrs O'Farrell used to be the housekeeper here before I came. This is my niece, Mary, who's working as a maid here." The old lady was very pleasant and later on when my work about the kitchen was done she invited me to sit down and have a cup of tea with them. From time to time I noticed her looking curiously at me. She had a very peculiar old-woman's stare and as she looked at me, I thought that she might be thinking of something else. She had a curious look on her face.

"Are you the youngest of the maids here, child?" she asked.

"She is indeed," replied my aunt, answering for me as was often her way. "She's barely beyond thirteen." The old woman seemed satisfied and nodded.

The talk around the table was very general – about what was going on among the staff, about Paddy Sweeny (whom she knew) and about the family upstairs coming and going. As we were talking, one of the other maids came in and asked my aunt something. She rose and went with her out of the kitchen. This gave old Mrs O'Farrell a chance to lean forward towards me in a very familiar manner. There was eagerness in her tone as she spoke.

"Tell me, child," she said in a low voice so that my aunt wouldn't hear. "Have you ever seen anything . . . strange about this place?" I shook my head. "People that . . . shouldn't be here?" Again I shook my head, unsure of what she meant. She seemed a very strange old woman. Her talk over the table had been rambling and without any real purpose, the sort of conversation the very old might carry on. But now she seemed very focused and her voice took on a strange intensity. "Tell me, have you ever heard a child crying late at night?" Again I shook my head, as I never had heard such a thing. She seemed a wee bit disappointed. "I would've thought that one so young . . . but no matter. You've seen nobody about the place that you couldn't account for?"

For some reason, the strange maid sprang into my mind – I had never really tracked her down – and I told Mrs O'Farrell about her. "She wears an old fashioned dress and a strange cap so that you can't really see her face."

Instantly, there was a glimmer of light in the old eyes. "And where did you see this maid, child?" she enquired.

"I've only seen her a couple of times," I said truthfully. "At the end of the corridor and going up to the blind room where Kitty Reardon works. But I'm sure that I'll run across her as soon as I get to know the place."

The old woman looked at me with a long stare. "Maybe," she replied. "But I'll tell you something, Mary. That maid mightn't belong to the world of living people at all." She was beginning to sound like Paddy Sweeny when he was making a joke of me with stories about the Grey Widow. Mrs O'Farrell, however, seemed deadly serious. "They said that there was a maid killed herself here a good while ago. Long before even I came here. I heard about it from an old man who had worked here as an ostler and who still lived in the area. He was a very old man and he just about remembered the story, which had happened just before he was born but when his father had been working here. He said that this maid had given birth to a child away in one of the rooms of this house. The father had deserted her, and them upstairs had threatened to sack her, for there was no way that they could keep a maid and her baby about the place. There was nowhere for her to go and no way for her to support herself or the child. So she hanged herself in one of the rooms. What became of the baby nobody knew. There were some that say she murdered it and hid the body somewhere. But it was a terrible tragedy all right."

Mrs O'Farrell leaned slightly closer across the table, putting her old face close to mine. "They say that the spirits of a suicide or of a murdered child'll never rest quietly – that's what the Church says anyway – but they also say that it's only the very young that see them. I came to work here when I was about your age, or maybe a wee bit younger, and at night, I used to be wakened out of my sleep on two or three nights by a child crying somewhere in the house. Even though I looked for it, I could never find it and there were no children in the house at the time. And I thought sometimes that I saw a woman coming and going when there was really nobody there. It was because I was young, you see. Now that I'm old, I see nothing, only shadows. I'm nearly blind anyway."

"And you think that the woman that you saw was the maid?" I asked in wonder. "The one that hanged herself?"

She sat back in her chair a little bit. "I don't know, but I know that I did hear a child crying and I couldn't find it," she answered. "It might have been a young owl crying, as some people told me it was, but I've never been sure. As I grew older, I stopped hearing it and my nights were never disturbed again. I think that it was because I was so young. I would've –" But at that moment my aunt came back into the kitchen and Mrs O'Farrell changed the subject.

I never had a chance to ask her any more, for she left shortly after and several months later I heard in general conversation that she had taken a fever and died. But she left plenty of thoughts buzzing about in my head. I would have liked to ask her where the maid hanged herself and who she was and if they had any clue as to what happened to the baby, but I never get the chance. I had to get on with my own life.

As I said, I had to clean some of the rooms of the west wing, well away from the rest of that great house. This was the part of the house that Nuala didn't like to work in, for the rooms were cold and empty, but I didn't mind it. It was easy work, for there was little dust and there were really no fires to set or anything. But it was a wee bit eerie. You seemed to be cut off from everything, in your own world of empty corridors and even emptier rooms.

Since Mrs O'Farrell had told me the story of the hanged maid, I had found the west wing more spooky, as I was convinced that this was where the suicide had happened. The coldness of the place seemed more bitter and I was convinced that I was being watched, even when I was alone. There were a couple of times when I turned suddenly, expecting to see somebody there but seeing nobody. At times I wished that Nuala would come with me but she had duties somewhere else. I dreaded being sent over there late in the day when the sun was going down and the passages were full of shadows. A couple of times I was going along some of the corridors and I thought that I saw something turning a corner away in front of me at the far end of the passage. It looked like a maid carrying something but I could never be sure. All the same, I expected to see the strange maid again, rather more closely. And I wasn't disappointed.

Late one evening I was finishing off in one of the rooms at the far end of the west wing. It was quite a small room and was always called "the writing room" because it was supposed to be where the ladies of the family came to write their letters. It was set about with old, heavy mahogany furniture which was hard to clean and took a little time. I was just finishing off, cleaning around the edge of a desk in the far corner, when I happened to look up. I had left the door of the room open into the corridor outside and where I stood I could just make out a figure standing on the other side, watching me through the crack in the doorframe. There was something very sly about the way she had done this but, I thought, something very desperate about it too. I froze where I stood and the figure seemed to draw back into the corridor.

For a long moment I stood there, rooted to the ground. The figure on the other side of the door had not been very clear but I was sure that it was the dead maid. I would have called out but I knew that I was alone in that part of the house and so I stayed where I was for a long time. Eventually I found the courage to step out of the room and into the corridor. There was nobody there but away at the end of the passage I thought I saw a shadow moving among all the others – a shadow that seemed to be holding a bundle of some sort. Almost at once, all the fear left me and I was overcome by a great feeling of misery and loss. This must, I believed, have been exactly what the strange maid had felt as she went to her death. I could feel tears welling in my eyes.

"Oh, you poor thing," I said aloud, hearing the emotion in my voice, even though I was not sure who I might be speaking to. "How you must have suffered." A small tear ran down my cheek. There seemed to be a faint sound – somewhere between a sigh and a sob – from away down the passage. It had a strange echoey edge to it and seemed to come from a long way away. Then all was silent again. I ran back to the main house but told nobody about it – not even Nuala, who was the nearest thing to a friend that I had there.

In fact it was a long time before I mentioned the hanged maid and then it was to Paddy Sweeny, who was warming himself in front of the fire on a cold day, long after Mrs O'Farrell had died. There were just the two of us in the kitchen and I can't remember how the talk about her came round – maybe it was about things that had happened in the house long ago. When I asked him about her, Paddy sucked long and hard on his pipe before he answered.

"Ye've been talking to oul' Mrs O'Farrell afore she died. That was always a thing she talked about – she even said that she'd seen the maid's ghost two or three times when she worked here as a maid herself. The priest says that them that has taken their own lives'll never get into Heaven but has to wander about. But do you know what I think? I think that she murdered her own child, a wee infant, and it's the spirit of that child that keeps her here about this house."

"But nobody knew what happened to the baby," I reminded him. He took another draw on his pipe.

"It's near certain that she murdered it afore she killed herself," he said. "But they never found the body. They found her all right, hanging in one o' the rooms."

"Which one?" I asked; but he shook his head.

"Nobody's sure," he replied. "At least, that's what Mrs O'Farrell told me. I only know what I know from her. Some say that she did it from a beam in the dinin' room, other people say that it was far more private and that it was in the servants' quarters, but nobody knows. Them that were here at the time's all dead now. So it's hard to say." He seemed to want to avoid the subject, as if he didn't really like talking about it.

"Could she have hanged herself up in the sewing room where Kitty Reardon works?" I kept on at him. "My aunt says that it used to be a place for the servants."

Paddy Sweeny nodded slowly, looking deep into the fire. "It used to be what they called a footman's pantry in the days when this was a much grander place. There was a fire in there and the butlers an' such could go there for a bit of peace and quiet when they weren't on duty. Some of the maids and yardsmen used it too. I never mind it being anything more than a sewing room, though. But that's where the deed could've been done all right."

"Did you ever hear the maid's name?" But he shook his head.

"I never did. There were names put about but I don't think any of them were true." At that moment, another maid came in and the conversation switched – much, I think, to Paddy Sweeny's relief.

However, I still remember his words, which I thought were important at the time: "Maybe it's the spirit of the murdered child that holds her here." In the local area I knew that the souls of dead children were considered to be very powerful, so maybe Paddy was right and it had something to do with the spirit of the child. But it was all very puzzling.

There is only one more thing I have to tell. After what happened in the west wing, I hadn't seen the ghostly maid for a long time but I could sometimes feel her presence about the place as I went about on my tasks. From time to time I passed by a mirror and looked up, half-expecting to see her standing watching me from some concealed corner, her bundle in her arms.

The story drew to an end one dark day coming into winter, which was the last time that I ever saw her. I had an old apron that needed sewing and in a moment that I had to myself I went up to the blind room to give it to Kitty Reardon. I climbed the stairs and turned the corner, but found the room empty and Kitty not there. The shadow on the wall buzzed more loudly than I'd ever heard and seemed to keep changing shape right in front of my eyes – sometimes filling out and at other times falling in on itself. It seemed to be a living thing and it frightened me greatly. The feeling that I was being watched in that room was so strong that I could bear it no longer. I ran out, leaving the buzzing shadow as it moved along the wall.

Then I stopped, for on the landing outside stood the awful maid. She was dressed as I remembered her, in an old-fashioned servant's uniform with a stained white cap tied about her head. And she carried the familiar bundle in her arms from which, as I looked at it, the chubby arm of a child reached up towards her face. I looked at that face, for this was the closest that I'd ever seen her, and I saw how grim and drawn she looked – the jaw set firm, the eyes red from crying, the hair caught in curls around the cheeks. She must have been very pretty once but sadness and the awfulness of her life had taken their toll. I didn't know what to do, I just stood there. She didn't seem to see me but moved straight past me where I stood – I won't say that she walked, it was more like she glided – and right through the open door into the blind room. Walking past Kitty Reardon's sewing table, she walked straight into the wall, where the shadow fizzed and bubbled, and was gone. The shadow hissed and seemed to grow, but the ghost didn't reappear.

That was the last time that I saw her. In a moment, Kitty Reardon returned – she had been across in another part of the house fetching some tablecloths that needed mending – and found me in distress.

They fetched Paddy Sweeny and my aunt and I told them what had happened. After some whispered conversation between them, Paddy went and got some tools. He forced the wooden boards around where the shadow buzzed, so that they came away. Behind it were the remains of an old fireplace and grate with an old blocked-off chimney.

But there was more. Paddy Sweeny put his hand up the chimney. On a little ledge just above the grate, he found something else, which I wasn't permitted to see. However, I did catch a glimpse of what lay in Paddy's arms. It looked like a bundle of filthy rags, covered in dust and soot. This was taken away and the fireplace blocked up again. Kitty Reardon wouldn't go back there and the sewing room was moved to another part of the house. The blind room was boarded up and the sealed door was painted over, and that's the way it stays even today.

And that was the end of it. At least for me. A few weeks after it all happened was my birthday and I turned fourteen. I never saw the ghostly maid again. Was she finally laid to rest by what we found in the sealed-up chimney? Somehow I don't think so. I think that the ghost still walks the corridors and passages of this great house, still tied here by the spirit of her murdered child. In later years, some of the younger maids used to ask me from time to time about a strange maid that they sometimes saw away at the end of a corridor or going into a room in the west wing. I never say anything but I've no reason to doubt that it's *her*. Now it's older maids who come here to work – not the slips of girls that there were in my day – and probably they don't see anything at all. And the shadow never went away, even after Paddy Sweeny took the bundle from the chimney. It was still there, buzzing and bubbling and hissing, though not as fiercely. Maybe the spirit of the child had somehow established itself in the very woodwork of the blind room, like a bad stain, and couldn't be shifted. If it's still there, behind that sealed door, I wouldn't know.

I'm an old woman now and all the others who might remember these things – Paddy Sweeny, Kitty Reardon, my aunt – are all dead. Even Nuala, who was my best friend in those early days has, I think, gone to her grave. I married one of the yardmen and, when he died in a fall, I took over as housekeeper here when my aunt passed away. We never had any children and this huge house had become my home.

I'm almost as old now as Mrs O'Farrell was on the day that she came to see my aunt, and just as stiff. I have to walk with a stick now, the same as she did. Sometimes, though, when the house is quiet and there are no maids about, I take a walk as best I can along the long, echoing corridors of this house and wonder if the dead maid is still there, haunting the shadows like some memory of long ago. And does she still carry her bundle, the child that was hers and that she killed? I don't know and I doubt if I'll see her now. Maybe around us all, the ghosts of those who have gone long before crowd invisibly, unsuspected by us all.

* * *

Note: The idea that only young people could see ghosts is a very interesting one. In many parts of Ireland, it was believed that only children and animals could truly see the phantoms of the dead. Animals continued to see spirits throughout their lives but once the child attained a certain age, the ability to "ghost see" was removed – at least that was the belief. Some people, however, managed to retain that ability into old age and were known as "ghost seers" within a community. In other parts of the countryside – such as the place where I was brought up – it was believed that only one person in certain families could see ghosts. On a personal note and within my own family, I unfortunately do not possess that power but my brother, an accountant, claims to have seen a ghost many years ago. Perhaps there might be something in that belief after all!

9 THE DEAD CART

County Tyrone

Unfortunately, I cannot give the name of the person who recounted this story, except to say that it was a blind woman who lived somewhere in the Sperrin Mountains of County Tyrone. I heard the tale at an impromptu story-telling session near Sheep's Bridge on the edge of the mountain country. A number of us had gathered for what was entitled "a cultural evening" of music and story-telling organised by one of the local councils as part of a cultural programme which it was running. My job was to get the local people – many of whom came from rather scattered communities – thinking about their heritage and culture. Because it was near Hallowe'en, the talk drifted to stories of ghosts and fairies. An old man had been telling a story about a young child who had allegedly been carried off by a dark spirit in the glen up in the Sperrins. At this point, the blind woman came in. She was guided by another woman and took a seat near the back of the hall. From the look of her, I assumed that she was a country woman – a great bag of a black skirt, a grey but torn jumper, stained with all sorts of things, and heavy black workmen's boots. She also seemed very old and worn. For a while she listened as others told tales of haunted houses and fairies on the mountain roads, and then she told her own story. I have recorded it here for a couple of reasons – firstly, because it is clearly an authentic tale from her area; and secondly, because it mentions a phenomenon, once current in Celtic lore, but which has now been almost forgotten: the dead cart.

In certain rural communities it was assumed that those who died did not go straight to their eternal reward immediately upon their demise. Rather, they sometimes hung around as vague insubstantial shadows, until a certain time of the year when they were gathered together for transportation to the Afterlife. This might be done by the fairies – the concept of the "fairy funeral" – or, in certain areas where the Celtic ideal was deep, by the dead cart. Each year at the darkest time, the cart would travel around the countryside carrying the souls of the recent dead into eternity. It was usually drawn by six black horses and it was unclear as to who actually drove it – some said that it was the Spectre of Death; others that it was the Devil himself. In Ireland, according to the writer W.B. Yeats, it was known as the Cóiste bodhar *or Coach-a-bower, meaning the "deaf coach" because its passing usually made no sound. In Brittany, however, it was the Cart of the Ankou (the Ankou being an ancient Breton god of death) and the turning of its wheels made a creak which could be heard for many miles around. This sound was the harbinger of approaching death. There are still a few areas in Ireland where a belief in the death cart is still firmly held and the Sperrin Mountains seems to be one of them.*

The following is the story that the blind woman told and it seemed to resonate with her listeners as they drew together in that lonely mountain hall with the wind faintly whistling across the slopes outside.

"Ye speak about ghosts and things," said the blind woman almost dismissively, "but they're all just imaginings – shadows seen in the half-light of an evenin' and mistaken for something else. And a lot of it is just oul' hearsay, that only the foolish would believe. But I can tell ye a story that actually happened, for I knew the woman that it happened to and she was a good and decent woman." She turned her sightless face in the direction of the old man who had been speaking when she first came in. "Aye, an' you knew her too, Daniel – Mrs James O'Hagan that lived up in Conniglen, away up in the mountains."

The old man murmured his assent. "True enough. A very decent woman. An' her husband was always a very decent man."

The blind woman nodded. "That's a fact, Daniel. An' they were always very close. They had never any family that I knew of an' that maybe drew them together. When James died, his wife was left up in Conniglen, which is a lonely place at any time o' the year." Again Daniel agreed with her.

"Oh, a wild lonely place," he said. "Ye might see nobody up among them mountains for days. Never a being."

"The only thing that ye'd see up there," the blind woman went on, "is the birds sailin' in the air an' the shadows of the clouds on the mountains. That's all ye'd see and it might be like that for weeks. Is it any wonder that Mrs O'Hagan was very lonely after her husband died? And her without many neighbours near her?" She leaned forward in her chair, warming to her story.

As I said [continued the blind woman], Mrs O'Hagan was a decent woman and her neighbours began to get worried about her. Mrs O'Neill, who lived away down the glen, used to walk up to see her from time to time but she had a big family an' couldn't often get away. Every time she came up, however, she thought that Mrs O'Hagan looked a wee bit more failed. It was the lack of company an' pinin' for the husband, y'see. She needed somethin' t'lift her mind and she wouldn't find it away up in a place like Conniglen.

"There's a bit of a fair down in Pomeroy, Mrs O'Hagan," said Mrs O'Neill. "Ye should go down to it for it would surely lift yer mind. There's people about an' there's music an' dancin'. It would put the spring in your step surely."

But Mrs O'Hagan shook her head. "Pomeroy's a long way away," she said, "an' how would I get down there an' home again? I'd have to walk an' I'm too old for walkin' such a distance at my age." She wasn't a young girl runnin' to a dance, y'see.

But Mrs O'Neill wouldn't hear of it. "Frank Sweeny that lives on up the Glen a bit has a married sister that lives in Pomeroy," she told her, "an' he would go down an' see her on the Fair Day. He has a horse and cart and will give you a lift down there an' a lift back home again, I'm sure. I'll ask him to call by and talk to you. One way or another, we'll get ye to the fair." Mrs O'Hagan protested that she didn't want to give anybody any trouble – that was the sort o' her – but Mrs O'Neill's mind was set.

"I'll have Frank Sweeny call with you tomorrow," she promised.

And true to her word Frank Sweeny did call and offered Mrs O'Hagan a lift to and from Pomeroy on his cart. "I'll be glad of the company," he told her. "It's a long, lonely road down to Pomeroy from up here in the mountains without anybody to talk to." And so it was settled.

On the day of the Fair, Frank Sweeny called by Mrs O'Hagan's house an' the two of them set out for Pomeroy on his cart. They chatted all the way down, for Frank was a very decent man when he hadn't the drink on him – he was a sort of harmless bein'. And although she was a fairly quiet woman, Mrs O'Hagan chatted away to him quite pleasantly.

Anyway, they soon reached the outskirts of Pomeroy. Frank drew the horse and cart up in front of a big gate with a stone pillar on the very edge of the town.

"There ye are, Mrs O'Hagan," says he. "I'm goin' to my sister's place but I'll be back this way at about six this evenin' an' I'll give ye a lift back up to Conniglen. So be here waitin' for me if you would," Mrs O'Hagan thanked him and climbed down. Frank Sweeny turned the horse and was gone in the direction that he said was down to his sister's place, but Mrs O'Hagan thought that he might be going to the pub for a drink. That was the way of Frank; he was a decent creature but it didn't take much to lead him astray.

The Fair was a grand place altogether. There were stalls and booths all around and Mrs O'Hagan spent the day looking at what was on offer. She met a couple of old friends and they stood and chatted and she went for a cup of tea in a café with one of them. All the same, despite the loneliness of the place, she soon found herself thinking about Conniglen and wishing that she was back up there. Her life in the glen had fallen into a kind of routine that she was beginning to miss. So, as the evenin' wore on she began to count down the hours until she could get a ride back home with Frank Sweeny.

Soon it was six and nearly time to go. The Fair was nearly over and all the stalls and booths were packing up. Saying goodbye to the last of the people that she'd met, Mrs O'Hagan started out to the edge of the town and the big stone gatepost where Frank Sweeny had dropped her off. There it was. She gathered together the things that she's bought in the Fair and hunkered down in its shadow to wait for Frank. Everywhere people were goin' home. Some o' them called out an' some o' them waved but there was still no word of Frank Sweeny. And still Mrs O'Hagan waited. A couple of times people stopped with her and asked her did she want a lift but they were goin' in the direction of Omagh or Strabane and she always said no. She would wait for Frank.

She waited and she waited and still Frank Sweeny didn't come. Mrs O'Hagan shook her head for she thought that he still might be in a pub somewhere. She thought about goin' to try and find him; but what if he arrived when she was gone and she missed him? And anyway, pubs were a man's place an' she was a respectable widow woman. So she stayed where she was in the shadow of the gate.

The day started to darken and there was a skiff of rain on the breeze. Round about, the first lamps were being lit in the windows of the houses; but still Frank Sweeny didn't come. It was then that Mrs O'Hagan decided to walk towards home. Maybe Frank was lying drunk somewhere, but would come to himself and would overtake her on the road. She'd have a few sharp words to say to him all right but she was sure that would be the case. So she left the gate and turned along the road in the direction of Conniglen.

If she had to walk the whole way home, it would take her most of the night, but so sure was she that Frank Sweeny would be coming after her that she strode out confidently up the mountain road and out of Pomeroy. The drizzle that had blown in over the town started to get a little bit heavier, but still Mrs O'Hagan walked on. The houses started to fall away behind her. At one point, a dog came running out of a yard, barking, and stood in front of her until its owner called it in from the lamplit doorway.

The road was getting very steep now and she'd been walking for the best part of an hour. As she walked, she kept listening for the "clip-clop" of Frank Sweeny's horse or the sound of his cart wheels on the road behind her, but although several carts passed her, none of them belonged to her neighbour and none of them stopped. Once, a tinker man, driving a flat cart, loaded down with old bits of metal, shouted down to her but she ignored him and kept walking. A woman, throwing out the day's water from her doorstep, wished her a "goodnight" as she passed.

It was still not completely dark but the scattered houses that she walked by all had yellow lights in their windows. As she walked by a cottage on the roadside, she heard the sound of a radio coming from somewhere inside and once she almost tripped over a cat that was lying in the gloom beside a gate. By now all the traffic from the Fair had fallen away and the road stretched out, before and behind her, long and empty. Still Mrs O'Hagan kept walking. And still there was no sign or sound of Frank Sweeny.

About five or six miles beyond Pomeroy and well up along the mountain road, there's an old crossroads which has a bit of a bad name to it. They say that there were people hanged there in the oul' times but I'm not sure. Anyway, a little beyond it on the road up into Conniglen there used to be an oul' church standing. But it has long fallen down and today not a trace of it remains although the graveyard around it is still there and is still used, I'm told, for burials from time to time. There is a gate with two big stone pillars leading into it by the side of the road.

By the time Mrs O'Hagan got as far as the crossroads, the rain which had been edging the wind had come on a little heavier. Not really heavy but enough to wet her – it was the last gasp of a passing shower. She thought that she'd better stand in for a moment until it passed and she cursed Frank Sweeny for his lateness. Stepping off the road, she crouched in the shelter of the gatepost of the old cemetery, waiting for the rain to pass.

The shower lasted no longer than five minutes and then it was gone. A huge, fat moon drifted out from behind the clouds and lit up the countryside for miles around. With the rain gone, it was going to be a beautiful night. Mrs O'Hagan stepped from the shelter of the gatepost onto the road and made to turn up towards Conniglen. Then she heard something away down the road towards Pomeroy. It was the slow and steady "clip-clop" of a horse an' the distant creaking of an oul' cart, drawing closer.

"There's maybe Frank Sweeny comin' now," she said to herself, "An' not afore time. If it is I'll give him a bit o' my mind when I talk to him." And so she stepped back a little nearer the gatepost an' waited for Frank to arrive.

The cart came out of the growing darkness very slowly. It was pulled by an old sway-backed horse that moved along slowly and the cart itself seemed old and very dilapidated.

"That's not the cart that I came down on," thought Mrs O'Hagan. "Maybe something's happened to the other one and Frank's had to borrow somebody elses'. That's why he's so late." She looked at the driver. He was sitting in the very front of the cart, the reins between his hands, very hunched over, so that she couldn't see him properly. But she did see that he wore a big, broad-brimmed old fashioned hat, which put his face into deep shadow. For a moment, she wasn't even sure if it was Frank Sweeny who was driving the cart.

"He didn't have that old hat when he came down to the Fair," she said to herself. But then she reasoned. "Maybe his sister gave it to him to keep the rain off him." As the cart drew nearer, the driver gave no sign that he even knew she was there. "Typical of Frank," thought Mrs O'Hagan, "he's still the worse for wear from the pub. He's probably half-asleep and doesn't see me." So she moved out of the cemetery gates and onto the road. As the cart drew nearer, she saw that there were two or three other people sitting in it behind the driver. Maybe Frank was giving some of these others a lift home too, for despite the drink, he was a very kind man and wouldn't see a person stuck.

Although she was standing by the roadside, the cart showed no sign of stopping but it was moving so slowly that it was possible to climb onto it. For a moment Mrs O'Hagan was about to call out but then thought better of it and, as the vehicle rolled past her, she made to run round the back of it and climb on. Frank might be asleep and the old horse seemed to know where it was going. The tailboard on the cart was down and she was able to hoist herself up and onto the bare boards. If he'd seen her, Frank Sweeny gave no sign. In fact, he didn't even turn round but continued to

145

hunch down at the very front as if guiding the horse. The cart rattled slowly over the road and on the wooden boards, Mrs O'Hagan could feel every bump and pothole that it went over. She looked at her companions in the cart but in the poor light, she couldn't see who they were, nor did they look in her direction as she climbed on. One was an old man, one was a woman with a heavy shawl about her head and shoulders and there were two small children at the farthest end of the cart, just behind the driver. They either seemed deep in their own thoughts or else they were all asleep. Mrs O'Hagan said nothing; she was just grateful for the ride.

About a mile beyond the crossroads, the road forks in two. The right fork goes on up into the mountains an' up to Conniglen, while the road to the left cuts across the mountains and down to Sheep's Bridge. When the cart reached this fork, to Mrs O'Hagan's astonishment, it cut off to the left as if it was goin' to Sheep's Bridge.

"Where's Frank goin'?" she asked herself. "Is he maybe so drunk that he doesn't know where he lives?"

She called out: "Frank? Where are you takin' us, Frank?" But the figure in the front of the cart didn't pay any heed and the vehicle kept on down the road towards Sheep's Bridge. "Maybe he wants to drop one of these other people off first," said Mrs O'Hagan, for she knew Frank was kindly like that. Directly in front of her was the woman with the shawl, sitting with her back towards her, and Mrs O'Hagan reached out her hand to grab her by the shoulder and to ask her if someone was being dropped off.

"Can I ask ye, Missus –" she began and then stopped, for as she touched the woman's shawl, she found that it was cold and very damp. And as she looked closer, she saw that there were traces of mould along its edges. In response to the touch, the woman turned and Mrs O'Hagan found herself lookin' into the livid face of a corpse. The skin was very pale and streaked with grave-earth, the hair hung out from under the shawl in dirty strands and the eyes were wide an' starin' like garnets. They were completely dead and as Mrs O'Hagan watched, a graveyard spider scuttled across the cheek an' down into the woman's mouth, which was wide in a scream and edged with blood. And the worst of it was that Mrs O'Hagan *knew* the woman she was lookin' at. She had been a neighbour woman up in the Sperrins but had moved down to Pomeroy and, according to what Mrs O'Hagan had heard, had died nearly a year before.

"Oh my God!" she looked away and caught a glimpse of the children, who were squatted down in the front of the cart. Half the face of the little boy had been eaten away but one dead eye watched her constantly from the shadows in the corner; a rat poked a head out from under the little girl's dress. This, realised Mrs O'Hagan, was a cart of the dead. In her younger days, she had sometimes heard about the Dead Cart that travelled the roads collecting the souls of the departed from roadside cemeteries, but she never thought that she would actually be on it! She looked towards the driver, inching up the cart towards him.

"You're not Frank Sweeny!" she screamed. "In the Name of God, who are you?" At this the driver turned his head, the old-fashioned hat that he wore sliding back a little, and in the moonlight Mrs O'Hagan saw that his "face" was nothing more than a grinning skull.

"Merciful Mother of God!" shrieked Mrs O'Hagan. And as the skull looked directly at her, she heard a voice, low and

147

rumbling like distant thunder but with a sort of echoey tone to it. She could barely make out the words that were said but she sensed them rather than heard them anyway.

"Let her go!" it said. *"She is close to her time but it has not arrived yet!"* As if in reply the driver pulled on the reins and the cart slowed down until it had almost stopped. In sheer fright, Mrs O'Hagan fell from the back of the cart and ran back to the fork in the road. There she hid herself under a bush and was still crouching there when morning came and Frank Sweeny came along the road in his own cart, looking for her.

It had been as Mrs O'Hagan had suspected. On leaving her he had gone to the pub where he'd had more than was good for him and afterwards he'd gone down to his sister's, where he'd fallen asleep on her sofa. She, either forgetting or not knowing about Mrs O'Hagan, had let him sleep. It had been almost midnight when he'd woken in a panic over Mrs O'Hagan and had set out to look for her on the road.

He brought her home and put her to bed. She was cold and terrified and would hardly speak much, except to answer the most simple questions. Would you blame her after the horrors that she'd seen? He fed her some whiskey and sent for her neighbours. Mrs O'Neill came up to stay with her and look after her for a while. For a long time after, she wouldn't stay in the house on her own and when she did, she always had to have a light burning when it grew dark. She wouldn't even go to sleep unless there was a lamp burning. And she was never the same, for when she heard the sound of cart wheels or of somebody with a horse on the road near her house, she would become very afraid. She had been a quiet wee person before but now she drew into herself and would sometimes jump and cry, even at the slightest noise about the house. The memory of that night just wouldn't leave her, y'see. Just over a year afterwards, she died. I wonder if the Dead Coach came all the way up into Conniglen when she did?

The blind woman finished her story and sat back while a bit of a murmur went round the hall like a ripple.

"I've told you all my story," she said "and it's a true one. Some of ye's know that it is. And now I'll bid you all a goodnight." Nudging the woman beside her, who had brought her to the hall, she stood up. Her friend guided her out into the night. Another lady closed the hall door behind them. For a few minutes there was silence – people not really knowing what to say – but eventually the conversations resumed.

Later I asked the old man whom she had called Daniel who the blind woman was. He said that he had known her years ago but he couldn't remember her name. She'd moved away to live with some relative – maybe even a son – who farmed away up in the mountains and he hadn't seen her for years. But, he added with a bit of a laugh, she obviously remembered *him*. He knew the woman that she was with for she was a neighbour of his own, and would ask who she was and get back to me. I never heard from him again. But he did say that the story was true for he had heard it himself from other people and he knew the woman from the story, and her husband.

Down the years, the blind woman's story has stayed with me and on dark evenings I often wonder if, away from the modern world, the Death Cart, actually does travel the lonely roads, lifting those who have died and carrying them into the Afterlife?

149

* * *

Note: The idea of a cart – or in some instances a coach or carriage – which collects the dead, has persisted down into the twenty-first century. As recently as last year, I spoke to a man – not all that advanced in years – in Sligo, who claimed to have both heard and seen a death coach. It was much more elaborate than the cart described by the blind woman: an ornate black coach pulled by six black horses, but it had the same ominous significance. It acted almost like a banshee foretelling a death within the community. The idea of the death carriage has even found its way into English ghost-story literature with the publication of the writer Amelia B. Edwards's "The Phantom Coach", which has similar overtones to the tale recounted by the blind woman. Perhaps there is something within this old story after all. . . .

Sheehogues and other Horrors

10

SOMEONE ELSE

County Clare

In Ireland, as elsewhere in the world, religious festivals were considered special, both for the individual and for the community in general. In the pagan world, observances at certain times of the year were considered essential for the continued wellbeing of a community but, as the Christian ethos spread across the country, this notion became a much more personalised one. Rather than being a communal rite, the onus was placed on the individual and his or her prosperity and good fortune depended upon the personal observance of such special and holy days.

In the Christian calendar, these designated religious days included the Sabbath – once a week – and also times which marked certain events in the Christian story and within Church history. Major events included such dates as Christmas, Easter and the Feast Days of important saints and martyrs. These were invariably to be spent in prayer, fasting and holy contemplation, and believers neglected such duties at their peril, for to do so was a mortal sin and would ultimately reflect upon their immortal souls.

153

Such neglect would allow the forces of darkness to take possession of them and drag them down to a Lost Eternity. At least, this is what the Church taught in order to ensure compliance.

One of the most important dates in the Christian year was, of course, Easter, the time when, according to Biblical teaching, Christ had risen from the tomb. Although originally a Celtic/Saxon pagan festival – when the fertility goddess Eostre was worshipped – the date came at the end of a time of fasting and contemplation (Lent) which had lasted for forty days and which represented Jesus' privations in the wilderness. This gave the festival an added significance in the Christian mind. During both Lent and the Easter festival, people were expected to abstain from various foods, from alcohol and from milk products, since these were considered to be symbols of earthly pleasures. Indeed Lent and Easter times were often known as the Black Fast because even the tea was black, due to lack of milk in it.

Although some work was carried on during that time, the Church insisted that it be kept to a minimum so as not to deflect from prayer. This was not always strictly adhered to by their congregations (indeed the Easter period was said to be the best time to take on hired labour as, being on their Lenten fast, they did not require much feeding!) and so the clergy began to warn of dire consequences for those who broke the prohibition. Excessive work at such a holy time was a sin, they asserted, and would leave the sinners prey to the dark forces which often ranged about the countryside. They would fall victim to fairy magic, or worse.

The following cautionary story reflects this ideal as it demonstrates how the breaking of a religious festival can attract supernatural retribution of the most frightening kind. Although originally from Clare, it was told by Cahal O'Brien from Mayo, where he had heard it and some of the names may have been changed.

At last the Lenten Fast was over and we were all heartily glad. A few of us gathered in Bartley Dolan's pub to have our first drink after Easter and to share each other's company and chat.

"By God, that's the best pint of stout I've tasted in a while," said a big farmer named Lynch, raising the glass to his lips and drawing the cream from the top of it. "I've been lookin' forward to it all over Lent." He leant his arm against the bar where he was sitting and took another long mouthful, relishing every drop.

"Ah, sure you could've had a wee glass over Lent," replied Jimmy Moran with a bit of a smile. "As long as you never told the priest, the Church would be none the wiser." He was a small man with a thin moustache, dressed in a kind of tweedy suit and perched at the other end of the bar. They said that he worked as some sort of accountant in Ballina, but I couldn't be altogether sure. He had a great reputation for stirring things when he had a mind to and I don't think he was over-fond of the Church.

Lynch looked at him, his tongue catching the last few bits of cream from his lips. "I'd hate to break the Fast," he admitted. "You never know what might happen to you if you did. The priest says that these Holy Festivals are very solemn and not to be taken as a joke."

"That's only the Church talking," said Jimmy Moran. "They tell you these things to keep you in fear of them."

"I wish that more people would take a drink over Lent," said Bartley Dolan, who had been cleaning glasses behind the bar. "I hardly make more than a few pence before Easter. Not even the Protestants come in here over that time. By the time Easter's over, I'm nearly in the Poor House." Bartley was a stoutish man, going bald, who blinked at his customers from behind thick glasses. The pub actually belonged to his mother, who was bedridden, but Bartley, who had never married and who looked after her, was owner in all but name. He was always pleading poverty although we all knew that he wasn't short of a penny or two.

"There you are!" answered Jimmy Moran triumphantly. "The Church is depriving honest publicans of their wages. And all so's they can boss you about an' keep you under their thumb. If they'd only make Lent for a day or so, it would be far better. Bartley here would only lose one day's takings."

"All the same, it's ill luck to break the Lent," said Ryan from his seat by the fire. Bartley always kept a good fire roaring in the grate. "I heard of boys who done it an' no good ever came to them."

Jimmy Moran snorted loudly. "Sure an' what harm could befall us?" he asked, looking directly at Lynch. "You do your work over Lent – there's still cows to be milked and bastes to be tended to. An' nothin' ever happens to you, even though the Church says you shouldn't be working at all." And he sat back on his chair as though there was no arguing with him.

"But that's different," protested the big farmer.

"How is it?" asked Moran with an air of authority.

"You're breaking the Lenten time and nothing happens to you. And there's more than you works all through Easter, aye, an' Christmas too, an' nothing befalls them. No ill whatsoever. As I said, it's only the Church talking. Drink an' work away an' nothing'll happen to you. A lot of old superstition, that's all it is!" And he sank back into the chair with a kind of smug, self-satisfied look about him.

"I'd not talk about such things so lightly," said a voice from the window. All the heads turned. "It's a mortal sin to neglect your religious duty and to ignore a Holy Day. I know that to my own cost!"

It was an old fellow called Delaney who spoke. He was not one of the regulars who came in of a night for a bit of neighbourly gossip, but only visited Bartley Dolan's from time to time when there was a thirst on him. Some people said that he came from County Clare and, in truth, he had a bit of a Clare accent to him, but he usually kept himself to himself, drank his drink and mixed with nobody. He had seated himself on a low stone bench by the window, where he cradled his pint on his knee and looked out at the late evening fog that was rolling around the pub. He watched the assembled company from under the peak of his cap with sad, weary eyes that some of them found a bit troubling. Jimmy Moran gave a laugh that had no humour in it. Maybe the old man frightened him a little.

"You're sounding like a priest yourself, Mick," he said. "Is the Church paying you for such talk?" And he put his glass back on the counter and made to change the subject.

"Let him talk," I said. "What is it that you know about breaking the Holy Day?" I had always thought that there was *something* about old Mick Delaney, some secret that he

157

wanted to keep hidden; and anyway, none of us was going anywhere in the fog outside and I was in the mood for a good story. Delaney looked back at me with the look of someone that has said too much and would have turned back to his pint without any further comment had it not been for Ryan.

"Cahal's right," says he from the chair. "You can't let Jimmy Moran away with a comment like that. Tell us what you mean an' put him in his place." He had no great liking for Moran, I thought.

"You're among your neighbours too," I added.

Delaney took another swallow of porter and sat back in the stone window seat. "All right then," he said. "But it was yourselves that asked about it. And every word I tell you is true and is my own, not the Church's – for I was there when it all happened."

He took another swallow and his eyes assumed a strange haunted look. Outside something in the fog rattled at the window behind him and he moved forward as if to avoid it. The fire in Bartley Dolan's grate crackled and spat and even Bartley himself had stopped polishing the glasses behind the bar. We all listened.

I was born *[began Delaney]* in a small fishing village on the coast of County Clare. The name of it needn't concern you; in fact, I don't think that there's more than a handful of people live there now. But when I was growing up, it was a lively enough place.

We weren't a big family. I had three sisters, all of them married fishermen, and one older brother, Pierce. My father had been a fisherman too but he'd drowned when Pierce

and I were very young and I never really knew him. Our mother was the centre of our family when we were all growing up – a good solid religious woman who did the best that she could for us all. We were no different from any other family in our village.

My brother and I followed our father to the sea – that was the way of it in our village. Pierce bought himself a boat and I was part of his crew. In those days, the fishermen would set out along the Clare coast with a crew of about six men, to chase the fish up beyond Scattery Island and sometimes bring back big catches. My brother Pierce was counted one of the best fishermen in the whole village, for he'd made a few very spectacular catches and he fairly revelled in that reputation. Indeed so did I, for I was proud to be part of his crew.

But there was another man in the area who could give him a run for his money. That was Philip Mohan, who lived at the farthest end of the village, just beyond the chapel. Philip was just a bit younger than Pierce, and was very good-looking – a big burly fellow, well tanned by years of sun. He and his brothers Connor and Liam crewed a boat that fished the waters round Scattery at all times of the year. And they came back with some fine catches – catches that would sometimes rival anything that my brother and I had made. Pierce and Philip were the best of friends – that was the way of it among the fisherfolk – but I knew that, deep down, although it was never stated, there was a great rivalry between them. When Pierce made a great catch, Philip Mohan would be the first forward to shake his hand but I could see the glint in his eyes that told me of the jealousy behind the smile. And it was the same for my brother as well.

Well, sirs, one year during Lent, but well before Holy Thursday, Philip and his brothers took a boat out as far as Scattery and came back with a grand haul of fish. Some said that it was the greatest catch ever caught in our village in long years and it had all been caught in a day or so. I'll tell you that Philip Mohan was the talk of our village for days afterwards. As usual, Pierce was one of the first down by the quayside to see his catch and congratulate him. But, like I said, there was a jealousy behind all the smiles. The more that the people of the village praised Philip Mohan and the more the local girls ran after him and played up to him, the more that jealousy grew, day after day. At night, Pierce would toss and turn on his bed – I slept in the same room as my bother – and I knew full well what dreams were tormenting him and what was eating away at his very soul.

A couple of days before Holy Thursday and the beginning of Easter, Pierce took me to one side.

"Mick, I'm going to take a crew out to Scattery tomorrow," he told me. "If there's fish to be had out there, I want my share. You'll come with me?"

I looked at him in both surprise and fright, for the fishing was slowing down before Easter. Boats were coming in and tying up until after the Holy Time was over. No boats were going out; indeed, some might have considered it a great sin to do so.

"Are ye wise, man?" I asked him. "It's Easter – nobody fishes then. Wait'll after the holiday's past and I'll go with you then, surely. But not over Easter. Ma would never allow it, anyway." Our mother was a very religious woman and took her holy obligations very seriously.

Pierce waved my doubts away. "I was talkin' to Philip

Mohan," he answered. "He says that there's big shoals of fish up by Scattery. He says that he could've filled his boat twice over – aye, and more. But they'll be movin' north and we'll miss them if we wait any longer. We can be up to Scattery and back in a day if we put our backs into it – back for Holy Thursday and Good Friday and the Easter service. Take my word for it." He spoke with such certainty that I truly believed him.

"But can you put a crew together?" I persisted. "There aren't many who will crew with you for fear of missing the holy day."

Pierce shrugged. "I'll have my crew," he replied. "The thought of a share of the money'll outweigh the fear of missin' a holy time. And anyway, we'll be back long before Easter starts, that I'll promise you."

"And what about Ma?"

"You leave Ma to me." He gave me a smile and a wink, for he knew that he was her favourite son and that ever since our father had died, she had looked on him as the man of the house. He could usually wrap her round his little finger when he had a mind to. "Be ready to sail for Scattery soon." And I knew by his tone that he'd get his way.

And so it was. Pierce managed to put a crew together to sail with him as far as Scattery. He had myself; two brothers named Tom and Donal O'Brien; a big man called Paddy John Faree, who had crewed on many boats and was regarded as something of an atheist by most people; and an old fellow, Peadar McMahon, from up the coast who was a fearful old drunk and would go anywhere for a bottle of spirits. Not the best of a crew but one that would certainly take us as far as Scattery. And, of course, there was Pierce himself, who was considered to be one of the best boatmen in our village. He had also managed to get my mother's approval for our going as long as we were back in time for the Easter Vigil. Like I said, he could twist her round his little finger.

The night before we were to sail, however, my mother called me to her.

"You're going with Pierce," she said in a voice that was weary with resignation. She knew that there was nothing she could say that would turn him, for he was very single-minded. I nodded and she went on: "I've pleaded with him not to go at a holy time but his mind is set. But I want you to take something with you." She handed me a medallion on a long chain to wear about my neck. Looking at it, I saw that it was inscribed with Latin words.

"Take this with you and wear it always," she instructed. "It was blessed by a bishop in Rome and is a very holy thing. It'll protect you out on that sea, for there's no telling what dangers might be out there waiting for you if you break the holy festival. Promise me that you'll do this."

I gave her my word that I would.

"Pierce is my son and I love him dearly," she told me, "but he's very headstrong and won't be told anything. Make sure that you have him back for the Easter Vigil." I told her that I would and she grasped my hand. "Make sure you do," she whispered.

The next day we set sail. The sky was overcast but there was a stiff wind blowing from the west which was good for fishing. The crew was eager and Pierce was sure we would have a big catch – even bigger than Philip Mohan's, a week earlier. We rowed hard and soon we were off Scattery Island, where we put down our nets. The first catch was good enough – not great, but not bad either. However, Pierce said that there was more to be had and I could see in his eye that he wanted desperately to beat Mohan's haul. We dropped the nets again. The second catch was poor; not many fish to be had in that cold sea.

"We've probably missed the best of them," said Paddy John Faree as we pulled the nets in. "If we'd been here about a couple of days or so ago, we'd have had more fish than we knew what to do with. But they've probably gone north up the coast to Mutton Island." And he was probably right.

"Then that's where we'll go," declared Pierce. "If there's fish up around Mutton, we'll catch them." The men gasped and muttered amongst themselves, for a trip all the way up to Mutton Island would mean that we would not be back in our own village in time for the Easter Vigil. They were understandably nervous, for this was a mortal sin.

"If we can catch no fish off Scattery," I said, "I doubt if we'll catch too much off Mutton. Let's go home and we can fish after Easter when we've more time."

Pierce, however, was determined to go right away. He was used to getting his own way and wouldn't be denied. "If we delay any further, we'll miss the fish altogether," he snapped back. "If we put our backs into it, we can make Mutton and still be back for Easter." There was no arguing.

And so we pulled up the Clare coast for Mutton Island, getting farther and farther away from our village as Holy Thursday approached. From time to time, we would stop and put our nets down, but we caught very little. The crew grew more and more irritable the farther north we went. Old McMahon, who had brought a bottle of spirits with him, began to whine and complain when it ran out and there was no more to be had; the two O'Brien brothers bickered and argued over the smallest thing; and I wasn't happy about the way things were going. I continually thought about the promise I'd made to mother, and was cold and distant towards Pierce.

"If we go any farther north, he'll have us fishin' off the Donegal coast," said Paddy John dryly, as we pulled in the nets with little in them. And I had to agree with him.

We unconsciously marked the hours as they passed and as Holy Thursday and the Easter Vigil drew closer we seemed to become even more unsettled. Tom O'Brien fought with old McMahon and Pierce had to separate them. And there were practically no fish to be had.

"They've moved farther north," Paddy John remarked. "Any big shoal is probably off Ulster by now." But Pierce swung on him angrily and told him that there was a huge catch waiting for us off Mutton Island if we held our nerve and went after it. But the omens didn't look good.

We were not far from Mutton when the fog came in. At first, I'd seen it on the horizon, a long, low bank heaving and moving across the water away at the distance. It extended in every way, as far as the eye could see, and it was thick and white, so thick that none of us could see even a glimmer beyond it. At first it just seemed to lie out along the horizon, but then it seemed to travel towards us with a slow, leisurely movement.

"Pull for the shore," shouted Pierce. "Before that damn thing overtakes us." The men put their backs in and began to row desperately for the coast, which we knew lay not too far behind us. But although we rowed, not a trace of the shoreline could we see. The fog seemed to quicken as if it knew that we were trying to escape it. It writhed and rolled after us as if it were a living thing. Our muscles straining, we pulled and pulled, trying to make that shore, but it refused to show itself.

I think that all of us pulled as we have never pulled before, for there was something horrible about that approaching fog – something that frightened us all to our very core – and we were all anxious to beat it. I was sitting beside Paddy John at the oars and when I looked at him out of the corner of my eye, I could see the sweat standing on his forehead in beads. He was a big man but he was badly frightened.

"We should be seeing the shore now," said Pierce, half to us, half to himself. "Where the Hell is it?" There was no trace of the coast on the way that we were heading – none at all. And behind us the fog seemed to quicken even more, swirling towards us over the waves like a hungry thing. We strained some more. And then it was on us!

Delaney paused and took a sip of his drink. Close by, the window rattled, as though someone was trying it in order to get in. The suddenness of the sound made some of us jump. The door opened and one of our neighbours came in, blowing on his hands and complaining about the evening mist gathering in the hollows outside. The fire crackled and spat in the hearth. We all were listening intently. Setting down his drink, Delaney went on.

I had been in fog banks before *[he continued]* but never one as terrifying as that. In an instant, the outside world was cut off to us and we were encased in a realm of pure white and total silence. The fog was so thick that I could hardly see my hand in front of my face, let alone those around me in the boat. They were only vague shapes which I couldn't really make out unless they came very close. It was cold; I've never felt cold like it – a real penetrating cold that got right into your bones. But the most frightening thing was the quiet. It was as if we were completely cut off from the entire world outside and not a sound from beyond penetrated the thick blanket of mist. It was as if we were the last six men left alive in all the world. The only sound that we heard was the gentle lapping of water against the side of the boat and the rattle of the oars in their rowlocks when we moved.

"We'll wait this out," said Pierce, his voice echoing strangely in the murk. "It'll soon lift." But I knew that he spoke more in hope than in certainty.

And so we drifted in the fog. We knew (or thought we knew) that Mutton Island lay to the north and the Clare coast to the east but beyond that we knew nothing. We just moved slowly through that damned, continual fog, not sure where we were going.

At first we tried to talk amongst ourselves, to make light of our situation. The young O'Brien brothers told a few humorous stories and old McMahon ridiculed a couple of his drinking companions for our delight, but soon we grew weary and the talk dried up. It seemed to have grown colder and we drew closer together for warmth.

The hours seemed to pass with an agonising slowness and the fog showed no sign of lifting. There was no breeze and the white tendrils wreathed around the boat as if they were trying to catch us and drag us into the sea. Still we were only vague figures to each other, little more than shadows, so thick was the mist. We sat on, waiting, each man lost in his own thoughts.

"It'll lift soon," said Pierce, a forlorn hope edging his voice, but if anything the fog became thicker. "A wind'll rise and lift it."

But no wind came and the men shifted and moved. They were getting very uneasy about being back in time for the Easter Vigil.

I had been sitting half asleep when Donal O'Brien put his hand on my shoulder.

"Mick," he whispered into my ear, "how many of us are in this boat?"

It was an odd question. I was sitting in the back of the boat and I looked around me at the dark figures swathed in fog.

"There should be six of us," I answered him softly. "At least there were six of us when we crewed out."

"That's what I thought," he replied, "but I thought for a minute there that I counted *seven* of us."

I shook my head. "You maybe miscounted," I said. "There should only be six of us here."

I counted the figures. There were only six shapes in the fog ahead of me.

I turned to Donal. "I was right, there are only six."

But he had been counting too and he still made seven. I counted once more and this time I made seven myself, but it might have been because old McMahon had moved slightly and I'd counted him twice. I counted again, but once again I made seven. It seemed that there was somebody else in the boat with us. I thought that whoever it was might be sitting in the very front, but I couldn't be sure. I inched forward to where Pierce was sitting.

"Count how many of us there are," I whispered to him. "Donal thinks that there might be seven of us here."

He snorted derisively. "The fog's makin' Donal stupid. There are only six of us," he said. "Look, I'll count for you. . . ."

He counted.

"What the Hell? I'm counting seven!"

He counted again but this time he only made six.

"Somebody's movin' about. Either that or it's the fog playin' tricks. Everybody sit still until I count."

He counted the shadowy shapes again and this time made seven.

"Sit perfectly still." There was fright in his voice now.

He counted again and this time made six. Then Paddy John counted and he made seven. We couldn't actually see who was who, but the shapes in the mist were very confusing. And all the while we were locked in a world of absolute silence, drifting steadily through that damnable fog.

"It's the mist," Pierce insisted. "It's playin' tricks with us." Old McMahon had begun to whine about it being a punishment for missing the Easter Vigil and I knew that the others were getting very unsettled as well.

"I know what we'll do," said my brother. "I'll call out your name and you answer an' raise your hand so's I know where you are." It was a sensible plan and we all agreed.

"Right," he said. "Mick?"

I raised my hand. "Here."

"McMahon?"

The old man raised his arm too. "Here."

"Tom?"

"Here."

"Donal?"

"Here."

I was surrounded now by shadowy figures with their arms raised through the mist.

"Paddy John?"

"Here."

Pierce sat forward in the boat surveying the raised arms. "And me too. That's the six of us."

Then, at the very front of the boat, we all saw it through the mist – a shadowy figure with its arm not raised. It looked like something wrapped in a dark sheet, sitting slightly forward, hunched over and gathered in on itself. We saw it like a shadow through the fog but only for a minute, for the mist came in like a bank and swirled about it and suddenly it was gone.

"The Devil!" the oath was out of Pierce before he knew it.

"*Here!*" Nobody could tell where the voice came from but it was an old man's voice, heavy with age and with evil. It came from the front of the boat and yet it seemed to come from the fog all around us as well.

"Oh Holy Virgin!" cried McMahon. He fell back in the boat and began to sob. Pierce started forward to where he thought that the figure had been but there was nothing there except wreaths of mist. He made to grab at something but all he caught was empty air.

"We're all done for!" wept McMahon. "We're all in Hell an' we're done for!" The two O'Brien boys began to chatter nervously and I have to confess that I was terrified myself.

"Who the Hell is it?" shouted Pierce. "Who answered me? What is it that you want with us?" He shouted defiantly but I could hear the absolute terror in his tone. "Answer me now!" And from somewhere close by – from the sea or from within the boat itself – there came a sound like a low chuckle. It may have been a seabird on the water and hidden by the fog – some of them have cries that sound very human – or it might have been something else, but it was a nasty sound, heavy with menace. But nobody replied to Pierce's question.

The window in the alcove rattled again, just as if somebody had quickly walked past it. Ryan started in his chair by the fire and even Jimmy Moran gave a quick oath from the bar. Bartley Dolan got up again cursing something about "a faulty catch". Lynch took another swallow of his drink and the room waited, hanging on the old man's every word.

I was terrified *[said Delaney]*, for I knew, like everybody else around me, that something unholy was in the boat with us – something that had joined us because we had broken a holy feast. And then I remembered what my mother had said when she had handed me the holy medal before we'd sailed.

"It was blessed by a bishop in Rome and it'll protect you when you're on the sea." I could almost hear her voice through the mist. "No bad thing can touch you if you wear it about your neck." I reached inside my shirt and felt the medal against my skin. I ran my thumb along its surface, feeling the indentation of the Latin words and as I did so I murmured a silent prayer.

For a moment, nothing happened, but then through the fog we heard a sound – the first natural sound since the mist had come down. It was the clear thin sound of a bell, calling to us from out of the mist. And, as if in response, the fog itself slowly began to thin.

"By God," cried Pierce, "I can see the coast!" As so we could, vaguely at first through the wreaths of mist, but there all the same. And as I looked around me, I saw that there were only six of us in the boat, all looking shoreward.

We were below the cliffs at Killard – God Himself may know how we got there – but from the hills above, the bell of a small chapel was calling the faithful to their Easter Vigil. And every man standing in that boat silently crossed himself.

Mick Delaney drained his glass and finished his tale. We all watched him in silence, none of us knowing what to say to him.

"We went home, sorely chastened, to the Easter Mass and for almost a month, not one of us put to sea again. Indeed, in the end I gave up the fishing and worked on a farm for my living. And I am the last of that crew left alive. Six months after, Pierce was drowned in a sudden storm off Scattery. He was a great loss to our village. Tom and Donal O'Brien crewed on a boat out of Doonbeg that never came back; old Peadar McMahon drank himself to death and they found him dead in his bed with the whiskey bottle beside him. Paddy John Faree was killed in a fall from the roof of a house that he had been thatching near Kilrush. And I'm the one that's left, the one with the holy medal that my mother gave me." He paused for a moment. "And sometimes I get the feeling that I wasn't so lucky after all and that my own end was only postponed for a while. I'd been willing to break the holy festival too and had gone with my brother to catch fish when I should've been on my knees in the chapel. That is why I've never neglected a holy time since. You never know what sheehoguey things might be lurking about, wanting to take advantage of your sin."

He rose from his seat a little unsteadily. Bartley Dolan caught him by the arm to guide him to the door. "Take it easy, Mick," he said with a smile. "It looks like you've made up for your Lenten Vigil." And he winked at Lynch over by the bar. He opened the door and let old Delaney out. A few wisps of fog rolled in and, despite the fire, the temperature of the bar dropped.

Delaney turned in the doorway. "I bid you all a goodnight," he said, his words slurring a little even though he'd not had all that much to drink. He was an old man, however, and drink can affect the old greatly. "And I would recommend that you keep your high days and holy days and that you never neglect your religious obligations. The Church knows what it is talking about – believe me." And with that he turned and allowed Bartley to ease him through the door and out into the night.

"A grand story," said Lynch from his seat by the bar. "It'd fairly make you think. Maybe there *is* something behind the Church teaching after all."

Jimmy Moran snorted. "That's all it is," he said cynically. "A story. Told by an oul' man with too much t'drink in him.

It was a good story, I'll grant you, and one which'd fair put the wind up you – but that's all it is. An oul' boy's imaginin'." Bartley Dolan came back in rubbing his hands on the bar cloth.

"It's a cold night for Easter," he said, "an' there's a heavy fog gathering out there in the corners of the fields."

"Did you see oul' Mick off?" asked Ryan from his chair.

Bartley went round the counter and lifted some empty glasses. "Aye, he's on his way home," he replied. "But I'm not sure if he went alone. I took him to the door and set him out on the road, but I got the impression that there was somebody waitin' for him in among the bits o' fog. I had the notion that I saw somebody standin' under the big tree a little ways up on the other side o' the road. I thought that it was somebody watching Mick and that he was startin' to move off as soon as the oul' fella drew level with him, fallin' into step behind him. But when I looked again, there was nobody there and Mick was on his own, headin' up the road home. It was all a bit strange but I must've been mistaken." And we all laughed, but without much humour.

"Oul' Mick's story has got to you as well, Bartley," said Jimmy Moran, winking at the company. "You're gettin' as jittery as some oul' granny sittin' by her fire on a winter's evenin'." Again we all laughed, still very nervously, and even Bartley himself joined in.

"I suppose so," he said ruefully. "But it was a damn good story. Now, who's for another drink? Same again, Jimmy?"

And there it would all have ended but for one small and curious thing. At the turn of the road and at the head of the laneway to Mick Delaney's cottage there was a steep bank

173

falling away into a little glen and a narrow stream that flowed through it. On his way home that night old Delaney had somehow missed his footing on the edge of the road and had fallen down the slope and into the glen. That would have been bad enough but he had fallen awkwardly and had broken his neck. He was dead before he was found the next morning.

"It was all very strange," said Bartley Dolan afterwards as he stood behind the bar polishing glasses. "Oul' Mick walked that road for years, drunk and sober, at all hours of the day and night, and never a thing happened to him. He knew it like the back of his hand. So why should he fall at that particular time? An' I was sure that when I let him out that night, I saw somebody under the trees, walkin' behind him, but I couldn't be sure who it was or if it was a person at all. Very strange . . ."

"Aye," said Lynch lifting his pint, "an' nobody could hold his liquor like oul' Mick. It's very curious indeed." Ryan, sitting in his usual chair by the fire, said nothing. Nor did I. Outside the pub, the evening mist gathered, while somewhere across the fields nearby, a chapel bell sounded, calling everyone to evening prayers.

* * *

Note: The above tale, which is a fine example of a "story within a story" is reputedly true, although a number of variants of it – not all to do with fishing – occur all over Ireland. At one time these tales were actively encouraged by the Church for obvious reasons and a number of them can actually be attributed to priests and clerics. A story, reputedly widely told by a Father Maguire from

County Monaghan, reveals the dire fate which befell Frank McKenna who went hare-coursing in the Sperrin Mountains of Tyrone on a Sunday, thus neglecting Mass, and whose ghost was supposed to haunt the area where he died, is another such example. Although some such stories are undoubtedly spurious, there may indeed be an element of truth in others.

11

THE DEVIL'S FOOTFALL

County Cavan

As evening drew on in remote country areas, it was as well for folk to close the door and lock the windows for, as the light declined, who knew what manner of supernatural being might be passing by unseen on the road outside. And an open door was always an invitation to such beings. Once into the house, it was usually extremely difficult to get them out again and they could torment the inhabitants for weeks, months and even years afterwards.

Those who lived near fairy forts and mounds were especially at risk – for not only fairies inhabited such places. Other dark and problematic creatures did so as well and they went back and forth at twilight, passing by the doors and windows of houses, usually unseen by those within. Such beings might well, if they took the notion, venture into the building through an unlocked door or unfastened window or through some crack or gap that they found.

The hygiene or tidiness of the house often dictated whether such entities took an interest in it or not. If a house was filthy or even in a state of disrepair, it would attract questionable supernatural creatures to it and would allow them access to those within. For example, if the dirty feet water – i.e. the water used for washing the feet at the end of the day – was not thrown out it would draw ghosts and sheehogues about the house. Similarly, bread or cheese, left uncovered or going mouldy, would have the same effect. For instance, Jeremiah Curtin records a story from the parish of Drimoleague in County Cork which concerns a dead man who was able to enter a house because the family involved had not thrown out the dirty "feet water" and there was soured milk in the pantry. This malevolent corpse was then able to murder the three sons who lay asleep in the building and to drink their blood. But had it not been for the general untidiness of the place and the neglect of its inhabitants, the being would never have been able to enter. Undoubtedly, there is a warning about cleanliness and good housekeeping contained in this tale.

Another way in which such a being could gain admittance to a property was to be invited in by someone within the house – usually unwittingly. The entity could perhaps pose as a traveller who was seeking rest and under the ancient Irish laws of hospitality could not be refused. Or they might take the guise of someone in distress, seeking aid. However, once inside a house they would reveal their true identity and torment those who were kind enough to bring them in. Even opening the door to one of these beings was considered to be an invitation. One story from County Longford tells of a beggar woman who was brought into the house to be warmed at the fire by a kindly householder who took pity on her supposed frailty. When her host's back was turned the old woman vanished and seemed to become a sort of poltergeist which terrorised the household by smashing crockery and by its persistent rapping long into the night.

The following tale from the border country of County Cavan contains similar elements to the Longford story and serves as a

warning to people to be wary as to who passes by their house –
especially in the late evening. It was told during an interview in
1993 by the blind travelling musician Phil Bernard MacDonnell,
who came from the area in question.

Where the road runs up from the village of Blacklion to the crossroads at Gowlan, there is still an old fort standing, dating back into dark and pagan times. The locals call it Moneygashel Rock and it has a very bad name to it. From the back door of the house where I was born and brought up we could look down over the fields to it and I recall on many a night standing at the corner of the house and watching the place lit up like a town with a strange glow and not a one near it. Nobody would go near it after a certain time at night for fear of being "taken" by whatever lived there – at least that's what they said through the countryside. And there may have been some truth in it, for odd shadows used to come and go across the fields to and from the Rock and they said that they came from unseen things that sometimes ventured out and about when the light was changing.

There was a family living among the fields many years ago – I remember my father talking about them – called McMahon. They lived in a small limewashed cottage that stood by the side of a pad-road (a turf or mud road) that ran through the fields and beyond Moneygashel Rock. It suited them well enough, for they weren't a big family – a couple of boys and a girl, and the father and mother. Not big for those times. The father was a labouring man but he had notions above himself and fancied himself as a bit of scholar. He was always reading and although he was a decent enough man, he had a tendency to look down his nose at his neighbours – not cruelly, you understand, but it was just the way of him.

Now the daughter's name was Mary and she was about seventeen or so around the time I'm telling you about and she was sweet on a young boy – one of the Maguires who lived over by Belcoo on the other side of the Border but who worked for Colonel Nixon up above Blacklion. By all accounts, he was sweet on her as well. Her father, however, didn't approve of the match for there was a big family of the Maguires and they said that some of them had been in trouble with the police on the Northern side of the Border. It's said that he didn't think the boy was good enough for his daughter and forbade Mary to see him, saying in no uncertain terms that he wasn't to come about the house. But as has been rightly said, the more you try to turn the course of romance, the more you'll fail. Mary was a headstrong girl and was determined to keep seeing the boy. And, as has also rightly been said, love will usually find a way.

As I was telling you, young Maguire worked for Colonel Nixon and his road home took him past the end of the pad road that led up to Mary McMahon's house. There were times that she was alone in the cottage – the family were sometimes away cutting turf in the moss – and on these occasions she would go down and spread out her apron on a big stone just at the turn. When young Maguire saw it, he knew that Mary was waiting for him up in the house and he would call with her on his way home. This was the sign, you see.

One evening, the family were away cutting turf in the moss and Mary was left to look after the house. As soon as the family were gone, she went down to the end of the pad-road and spread her apron on the big stone to let young Maguire know she was waiting for him. Then she went back to the house and to her work.

Just as it was starting to get dark, she saw that the turf creel by the side of the fire was empty and went out round the side of the house to fill it from the stack. The corner of the house lay between herself and the pad road, so she couldn't see who was coming or going but she had left the door of the cottage open. And as she filled the creel, she heard a footstep coming up the road from the direction of Moneygashel Rock. It was a slow and leisurely step, like a man taking his ease in the late evening sun, not hurrying himself to get home. Thinking that it was young Maguire on his way home from Colonel Nixon's, she called out to him.

"I'm at the turf stack. Go on into the house and I'll be in in a moment. The door's open." The footstep paused for a moment and then turned into the house. Mary continued to fill the creel before going back into the kitchen. Although she had expected to find Maguire standing waiting for her, the room seemed completely empty. Thinking that he was hiding and ready to jump out and surprise her, she put the creel down and began to look around. But there was nothing.

"Where are you?" she called, but there was no answer. "Stop fooling about and show yourself." There was a sound from behind her and she turned quickly, but it was only a bird easing its throat on the end of a briar just beyond the open door. "Come on now!" she was starting to get uneasy.

Again there was no answer, although she was sure that she had heard the footfall going into the house. She moved from room to room but the cottage was empty. However, set in a niche above the fire was a little piece of glass that the family used as a mirror and as she passed it, Mary thought that she glimpsed the reflection of something out of the corner of her eye. In the farthest corner of the room, she thought that something watched her very intently, although she couldn't make out exactly what it was. It looked human but it was completely hairless and naked, with very pink skin. It wasn't moving but remained where it was, seemingly following her every movement around the room. However, the image was gone in an instant and when she turned to look in the glass, there was nothing there at all but her own reflection. By now the girl was becoming frightened and she ran from room to room, trying to find a source for the strange image, but there was nothing there. Then she heard the voices of her family as they made their way back from the moss, coming home to have their supper.

Mary said nothing to them as they came in and they appeared to notice nothing strange about the cottage. There was one thing, however – none of the dogs which had been with them would come into the house but stood, bristling and growling in the doorway, as if sensing something that they didn't like. No amount of coaxing would bring them in. Finally, Mary's father cursed them and shut them outside for the night. But this was the only thing – at least for a while.

Later on when the supper was finished and as she was doing the washing up, Mary felt something tug playfully at the ties of her apron, pulling them loose. Thinking that it was a family member she turned to scold them but there was nobody there, for they were all seated around the fire and well away from her. She turned back and went on with the washing but someone or *something* poked and nipped her. It was a faint sensation but again when she turned there was no-one behind her. It was all very peculiar.

Late that night, the family went to bed. Mary slept in a small room at the back of the cottage which was sparsely furnished and had a large, uncurtained window that looked out over the adjoining fields. It was a bright moonlit night and the light streaming in through the window played across the stone flags of the floor. Although she could see that she was alone in the bedroom, Mary had the strangest sensation that there was someone in with her, standing watching her from a corner of the room. Nevertheless, she undressed and got ready for bed and slid in between the sheets. As she did so, she had the impression that someone got into bed beside her. She had blown out the lamp and as she lay there in the dark she was conscious of a faint movement under the bedclothes to her right. She put out her right hand and touched something beside her that felt like naked skin and which was deathly cold. There was no mistake! With a loud scream, she jumped out of bed and as she did so, the clothes on the other side of the bed were thrown back as well. As she stood there in the middle of the floor, a shadow began to form in the moonlight that came in through the window. It was a tall figure, like that of a man, but the arms were impossibly long and the head was twisted to one side as if the neck were thrawn (twisted). It stood in the shaft of moonlight, unmoving.

Mary's screams had brought her father and brother in to see what was going on and they saw the eerie shadow as well. As the light from their lamp fell onto it, it seemed to move and writhe as if it had a life of its own; its arms waving and forcing them back beyond the doorway. And then it was gone as if it had never existed. All that was left was the stone flagged floor.

You may guess that there was not much sleep in the house that night. The experience had been terrifying for everyone but especially for Mary, who refused to go back into the bedroom. And no wonder. She spent the night in her parents' room and it was all that they could do to get her calmed down. However, she didn't tell them what had happened and her father was at a loss to explain what the weird shadow had been about. Maybe she hoped that would be the end of it, but it certainly wasn't.

The next morning as she stood by the basin, washing the breakfast dishes, something put its arms round her and tried to kiss her on the base of the neck. She turned but there was nothing there and as she did so, something unseen pulled the strings of her apron loose and grabbed at her skirt. She jumped back and as she did so, a couple of burning peats fell from the hearth and danced across the floor. Plates rattled on the dresser and a cup lifted itself from the table and fell to the flags, breaking into a hundred pieces. A pail of water that had been standing by the door lifted itself up and spilled all over the floor whilst something chuckled softly somewhere close by.

The family never had a bit of peace for the rest of the day. Plates and cups danced along the dresser, members of the family were pelted with potatoes, mysteriously brought in from outside, and hot peats flew about the room as if they had a life of their own. A sheet which had been hung in front of the fire to dry suddenly rose up and formed the shape of a man with his hands menacingly outstretched. It was all so terrifying that at last Mary broke down and told her father what she'd done and about the strange footfall on the pad-road that she'd invited into the house. She had thought it to be young Maguire, but he'd been sent on a message to Enniskillen by Colonel Nixon himself, hadn't come back until late and had gone straight home. She didn't know what had come into the house.

"It was some sheehoguey thing from Moneygashel Rock that was going past in the twilight," her father replied. "Such things are always going back and forth before nightfall." And as he spoke, the Thing (whatever it was) laughed at him out of a bucket by the fireplace. Although very afraid, her father knew what to do about it.

A little way below on the road into Blacklion, there was a retired priest living. He was an old man but very wise and he knew all about ghosts and fairies. It was said that he had performed one or two exorcisms in his time and it was to him that Mary's father went. Father Judge, for he was so called, listened gravely to the story.

"By bringing the being into the house, your daughter has done a very dangerous thing," he said very seriously. "These things are not to be trifled with. They are like weeds that take root in a garden and I can tell you that it's as well you came to me now for if you had waited much longer it would have taken nine priests and nine bishops to cast it out. But let's see if we can dislodge it ourselves." And he lifted his coat and Bible and followed Mary's father home.

At the cottage, things had got worse. Crockery had been smashed on the floor and smouldering peats lay everywhere. Blankets from the bedroom had been pulled out and now danced about around the kitchen, taking odd and bizarre shapes which looked like people or animals, whilst voices laughed in the buckets and pots. The place was bedlam. Telling the family to stay outside, Father Judge stepped into the middle of this terrible racket. He was a tall man, silver-haired and with a beard like a Bible Patriarch and he looked very imposing. Standing in the middle of the kitchen, he raised his hand.

"In the Name of God, be still!" he shouted. Burning sods jumped at him out of the fire and a plate was fired at his head. The old man never flinched. "I command this in the Holy Name," he repeated. Things quietened for a moment although one of the windows rattled in its frame.

"Away, priest!" shouted a voice from the bucket by the fire. "Away, you black crow! What business have you among decent people?" And the Thing laughed like a mad person. A lesser man might have turned in the doorway but Father Judge didn't let on he'd heard it. He opened his Bible to intone the words of exorcism but it was knocked from his hand by something that he could not see. Cups rose by themselves and were banged down again on the dresser.

"Tell me in the Name of God who you are?" demanded the priest.

The voice from the bucket laughed back at him again and made several rude noises. "Fooney McHarkelton," it replied. Another titter of laughter rang around the cottage. "What ails ye, Fooney?" the Thing added in another voice, as if talking to itself. There followed a string of gibberish, some of which was quite obscene and concerned Father Judge himself. The priest paid such a rant no heed but continued with the rites of exorcism, praying earnestly as he did so. The being whooped and wailed all around him, telling him in a number of voices that it was the spirit of his mother who was now "a lost and tormented creature"; that it was the spirit of a serving man who had lived in the area and who had stolen something from his employer and several other persons. It bleated like a lamb and barked like a dog and caused more peats to jump from the fire. As Father Judge tried to intone the words of exorcism, it threw a potato at him, narrowly missing his left ear.

"There! Take that for your trouble, you old crow," the voice from the bucket told him. The priest tried to read the sacred words of exorcism but was drowned out by the din.

"I charge you to be gone from this place and to torment these people no longer, in the Name of God!" he shouted. Tins and plates rattled in the pantry.

"What ails ye, Fooney?" the Thing mocked him, aping his own voice.

For hour upon hour, Father Judge wrestled with the terrible Thing. He was nipped and punched and hit about the shoulders with lighted sods and pelted with potatoes. And the voice from the bucket continually hurled abuse at him, revealing some things about his past that he'd rather have kept hidden. The sweat fairly stood on his head but still the being mocked him. At length he left the cottage and went to where the family waited.

"It is stronger than I had imagined," he admitted to them, "but I do know something that will get rid of it." He turned to Mary. "The Being was invited into the house with both your words and your heart. That is what gives it it's strength. Tell it to go – *will* it to go as you have never willed anything before – and it will go. But you must want it to leave with your heart and soul."

"I do want this," Mary replied. She was terrified of the terrible Thing that she had brought into the house and desperately wanted some peace for herself and her family. So she accompanied the elderly priest back into the cottage and as soon as she stepped across the threshold the pandemonium started again. Potatoes and eggs flew around the room as though on strings; crockery rattled and bounced on the sideboard and animal sounds – the bleating of sheep and the barking of dogs – issued from the chimney. Her heart literally stopping within her, Mary walked to the very centre of the chaos and stood there.

"Wish it to go with all of your heart," Father Judge instructed her. "You're the one who brought it into this place and you're the only one who can cause it to go." And he opened his Bible and began to read again – telling the spirit to go. The Thing howled and gibbered and threw crockery at them both. And all the while, the sheets and blankets turned themselves into ever more frightening shapes and danced wildly in the air around them.

"Tell it to go," Father Judge told Mary, "and tell it to do so in the Name of God. Speak with the authority of the Lord of Hosts."

The girl swallowed hard, for the sweat was breaking on her. "Go from our house, in the Name of God!" she commanded. Peats danced across the floor as Father Judge read another exorcism.

"What ails ye, Fooney?" asked the voice from the bucket by the hearth, followed by an insane tittering. There was the sound of a woman crying from the chimney and more animal noises. Something like human excrement fell into the fireplace, but Mary stood her ground. "Go on," she shouted. "Go on now!"

Suddenly everything was quiet again. The plates and crockery stopped rattling on the sideboard and the sounds from the fireplace stopped. Potatoes that had been caught in mid-flight suddenly dropped to the ground and everything seemed peaceful. Then, from outside, came another sound. It was the slow, unhurried step of somebody walking away from the cottage, down the pad road towards Moneygashel Rock. It was an easy footfall, like a man taking his time in the late evening sun, and it grew farther and farther away.

Father Judge wiped his brow. "Whatever it was has gone," he said solemnly, "but it's left its mark here. This house will have to be ritually cleansed and a Mass said here before decent people can live in it once again for any length of time."

And that was the way of it. A special Mass was said in the cottage and the place was blessed. There was no further trouble from creatures from Moneygashel, although the McMahon family never really prospered after that. Mary, in particular, never enjoyed good health and always looked thin and wasted. In the end, she married young Maguire but they had no children and she didn't live many years after the wedding. Maguire remarried and had a big family – one of the biggest in the area – and his descendants still live about Gowlan yet. After a while, Mary's family left the cottage and went to live on the other side of Blacklion, but they never had any luck. Most of the good was gone from them, ye see, and they finished up without either land or much money. That's what comes from messing with sheehoguey creatures.

Moneygashal Rock is still there and it is just as ghostly a place as ever it was. Odd shadows still come and go across the fields around it at certain times of the evening and there is sometimes a dark coldness that hangs around it like a shroud – except at night, when it is lit up with lights and such. I wouldn't go there for a fortune after the sun goes down – by God, I wouldn't!

* * *

Note: Although locally styled as a "Rock", Moneygashal is actually an early form of cashel – an Iron Age fort – drystone walls circling a grassy interior. Its prehistoric (and probably its supernatural) significance is accentuated by a Neolithic tomb, a short distance to the north of the cashel. Moneygashel Hill has long been considered an important place of worship, some say for thousands of years. The undoubted antiquity of the place and the nearness of such a tomb has, it is assumed, led to ghost and fairy stories concerning it. Nevertheless, even today and in the strongest sunlight, Moneygashel Rock is still a sinister and eerie spot.

12

THE PRIEST'S LIGHT

County Fermanagh

Tragedy, particularly concerning very young children, often left an indelible mark on the folklore of an area. It was imagined that those who, say, died in infancy had somehow been cheated of life and their spirits could have an influence upon the physical world. The ghosts and souls of children who had been stillborn or who had died shortly after birth were considered to be the most dangerous.

I have already mentioned caldreachs elsewhere in this book (see "The Blind Room"), the places where unbaptised children and stillborn babies were laid to rest outside the jurisdiction of the Church. Indeed, there was one over the fields, a little way behind my grandmother's house, which all of us children scrupulously avoided for fear (as some of the local people put it) that "the dead babies would get us". Children who had died unbaptised or stillborn babies were always looking for a way back into the world and so such places were dangerous to cross, especially after dark.

Dead and unbaptised children presented other dangers too. They lay at the root of the similar idea of the "stray sod" which

191

sometimes led travellers astray. Anyone who unwittingly set foot on the patch of ground where an unbaptised child lay buried lost all sense of direction and was condemned to wander around aimlessly for hours (in some cases days) before retrieving his or her bearings and continuing with the journey. The only way in which this awful spell could be broken was to turn one's coat inside out and to wear it that way until the journey was completed. People could often finish up miles away from where they intended or walked in circles all night, until the sun came up and the spell usually dissipated. Of course, there was nothing to show where the grave of the dead and unshriven infant might be, for there were no markers or signs and so most instances of the "stray sod" happened accidentally.

There are only a few stories of this dreadful phenomenon – few people will readily admit to having got lost in familiar locations, perhaps even very close to their own homes. An interesting one, however, came from Belfast, where a workman was supposed to have wandered around a narrow timber yard all night, all sense of proportion lost. It was said that a dead tinker child had been buried in the corner and this gave rise to the spell. Tales of the sod are more common, however, in country areas where it may have been easier for, say, unmarried mothers to hide the dead corpses of their offspring in former times.

The following story comes from a townland about fifteen miles beyond Enniskillen in County Fermanagh, between the villages of Belcoo and Garrison. It was told by the person to whom it happened – the late John McFadden, who worked around the area.

I could tell you of many strange things that I've seen in my time. I worked in a house one time away beyond Letterbreen and there was a room in it that nobody would go into. Always shut up it was, with the door locked tight. This was in a big sturdy farmhouse and the people who lived there were big farmers and I was the hired man. All the time you could hear sounds and voices from the other side of the door but nobody would even look in for fear of what they might see. But I wasn't frightened at all by it. The only time that I was truly frightened – and I'll tell you about it now – was the time I stepped on the stray sod in Drumcully, over between Belcoo and Garrison. I was a young man then but I was surely frightened for I thought that I would wander forever and never get home. And I wasn't the only one, for Paddy Kelly, who's long dead, was with me and it happened to him too.

This is how it came about. Paddy and I had been at a céilí house over near Tullyrossmearn one night for a bit of craic. The place was well known and the woman of the house was known to keep a good drop of poteen for visitors. There were fiddlers from County Leitrim there and there were singers who had come all the way from County Donegal, and storytellers and dancers. There were glasses of poteen passed round – the best poteen that I've tasted in a long time – and Paddy and I had our sup. It was a great night altogether and it went on until the early morning.

About half one or two o'clock, Paddy and I thought we should be getting home. I was working over at a place up above Gowlan Cross, just beyond Blacklion in Cavan, and I had an early start and my mother would have my life if I was in at the clouds of the morning. So we thanked the lady of the house and started for home.

It was a good, clear moonlit night at the far end of summer and the place was as bright as if it had been day. The pair of us were living in Drumcully at the time and we both knew our way home; we could've walked it blindfold. But it's a twisty old road from Tullyrossmearn to Drumcully and there were plenty of shortcuts across the fields which we, being local boys, knew very well. Away across the countryside we could see the dim shapes of the sleeping farmhouses as we walked. Here and there a dog barked and I heard a fox shouting one time down among some trees off to my right.

"I'm very tired, John," said Paddy. "I could do with gettin' to my bed. Come on an' we'll cut across the fields an' that'll bring us home the quicker." It made sense, for there were a couple of paths across the fields that we could take.

"Right," I answered. "You walk on an' I'm behind ye."

Away on a low hill I could see a light still burning like a star over the sleeping houses round about. I knew that it came from the window of the Parochial House. At that time, the parish priest in Drumcully was a very severe and very devout man. He was always up until all hours of the night, reading his Bible and his Holy Commentaries, and he kept the light burning in his window. It shone out over the darkened countryside like a beacon, reminding us all of the authority of the Church. And as I walked along the road, it seemed to follow me like a distant eye, watching my every move. Not that we stayed on the road for long, for Paddy soon found a gate into a field and climbed over it.

"We'll take this way through the fields. It'll take about fifteen or twenty minutes off our time," he said. I followed him, climbed the gate and dropped into the field. We were now walking towards the distant light from the priest's window.

We crossed the field and came to an opening that led into another bigger field. Paddy went first through the gap. In the poor light, I could just make him out in front of me, moving like a shadow. I could see the moonlight on the shoulders of his coat as I followed him. And beyond him was the priest's light, shining like a star directly in front of us. Somewhere off to my right, a strange bird called, a high sound like a flute. I don't know what sort of bird it was for I'd heard nothing like it before. I wondered at it but I paid it no real heed.

Then, suddenly, Paddy was gone and there was only darkness in front of me. It was a darkness the like of which I've never seen before, almost total blackness. I looked around me to get my bearings, for I knew the field and had crossed it many a time, but I could see nothing that I knew. The priest's light was there but it was somehow off to my left and wasn't directly in front of me as it had been before. I took a couple of steps forward.

"Paddy!" I shouted. "Paddy! Are you there?" But there was no answer from the dark around me. I looked again but I couldn't make out the shapes of the farmhouses or the bits of the familiar countryside anywhere. I walked forward and as I did, the priest's light seemed to pass in front of me, like a shooting star, swinging over to my right.

As I said, I knew the field around me well enough. I knew that there were the tumbled walls of an old barn somewhere close by – maybe to my left – and I walked that way. I walked and walked and the field seemed to stretch out in front of me into that awful darkness. The only thing that I could fix on was the light from the priest's window and even this wouldn't stay steady. Sometimes it was to my right, at other times to my left.

And then the walls of the ruined barn came out of the blackness and I thought that I knew where I was. I knew that, to my left, the field fell away down a slope into a boggy bit of land. Beyond that was a wooden gate into another field. I wondered what had happened to Paddy – he couldn't be all that far away. Maybe he was lost too and couldn't find his way. In front of me was the light from the Parochial House, flickering away and I thought of the priest, seated close to the lamp, maybe dozing with his Bible open in front of him. Sometimes, he was known to stay up all night reading. I walked towards it, tripping over the uneven ground, expecting it to fall away in front of me down to the gate, but it didn't. I shouted again.

"Paddy! Paddy Kelly! Are you there, man?" For a minute there was no sound, then I heard Paddy's voice calling but it seemed to come from a long way away, maybe on the other side of the big field. The voice sounded echoey and seemed to shift a little.

"John! John McFadden! Where are ye, John?"

"I'm here!" I called back. "But where are you?"

"I'm in the middle of the field, John," he shouted back with a kind of a laugh in his voice that was more about fright than humour. "But I can't find my way out. An' I don't know where I am. I thought there was a gate here but there isn't."

"Hold still," I shouted back. "Stay where you are but keep talkin' an' I'll walk towards ye."

"I walked through the gap in the bank," he went on, "an' there I didn't know where I was. I started to walk across this field an' somehow I got lost. An' it's not that big a field, John – not that ye could get lost in." His voice now seemed to get fainter and was becoming lost among the echoes of the field. "Where are we, John?"

"I don't know," I shouted back, "but we'll get out of it."

And then, directly in front of me were the fallen stone walls of the old barn again. It was if I had just walked round in a circle and had come back to where I had started from. And away behind the walls, the priest's light was burning still, although I knew it couldn't and shouldn't be there.

"Paddy!" I shouted again, putting my hand against the broken gable of the old barn to make sure it was there. "Are ye still there?" This time there was no answer, only the bark of a fox from far away. "Paddy Kelly! Answer me, Paddy!" But the night was silent.

I turned left at the ruined barn and seemed to go down a hill. In a few minutes I was up to my ankles in water and thin, wiry bog grass. I reached the bottom of the hill and the gate into the next field should be in front of me. I squelched through the boggy ground, the water lapping at the mouth of my boots. In front of me was a big bank of broad-leafed plants – we used to call them cow's tongues – that I didn't remember. Big, broad things they were and there seemed to be a great stretch of them in front of me. I waded into them, anxious to get through them and find the gate, tramping down some foxgloves that rose up in my path. I looked up and directly in front of me was the priest's light, like some terrible eye watching me and mocking me. I tramped on through the plants but seemed to be getting nowhere.

"Paddy!" I shouted again, this time in desperation. "Paddy, where are you?" And then I was through and on solid ground, going up a small hill. And at the top were the ruins of the old barn again. I seemed to have come in a complete circle.

I looked around me. On all sides, the field seemed to stretch away into the dark and I hadn't a clue where I was. For a minute I thought that I might take shelter in the ruin – lie down behind the old gable and wait for morning – but the night had suddenly got very cold and I had only lighter clothes on me. I decided to have another try at finding my way out of the field. Maybe if I walked back the way that I'd come, I could go through the gap in the bank and find my way back to the road. I decided that I'd walk that way. In front of me was the priest's light, although I knew deep down that it couldn't be there. There was something very wrong here. But I kept walking across the field in the direction of the gap – or so I thought.

Again, I found my way barred by those big broad-leafed plants; they were all around me. I thought that I'd plough on and I started to tramp them down as I walked. They seemed to get thicker and thicker and there were briars and bushes in among them that tore at my clothes and so I was forced to turn back. I began walking across the field again and soon I was back at the ruin of the old barn again. I turned left and began to walk down the hill.

I knew that in the far corner of the field, tucked tight against the hedge, was an old standing stone, well worn by the weather. I knew this because I had worked round it many a time during the harvest. If I could find this, I reckoned, I could follow the line of the hedge down to the gate. I walked on and on but there was no sign of that landmark. By now I was starting to panic and panic badly, for I had visions of never finding my way out of the field. Although a part of my mind told me that this was nonsense, I imagined that I would wander in the darkness until my body gave out with hunger and thirst. All the same, I kept on walking.

The stone came out of the dark in front of me and I was right glad to see it. Now, I thought, I knew where I was. A little way on the other side of that stone was the hedge and I could follow the line of it until I got to the gate. Touching the stone to make sure that it was there and that I wasn't dreaming, I walked past it expecting to see the hedge right in front of me, but there was nothing there – just the empty field. I walked on, expecting to come to the hedge, but I seemed to be walking up a hill which I knew couldn't be and then in front of me I saw the old stone again.

"I'm walking in circles," I said to myself. Taking a fix from the twinkling light that now lay to my right, I started walking in that direction. This time I was walking down a hill and as I neared the bottom, I felt the ground turn wet and muddy under my feet and wiry bog grass stung my legs through my trousers. But still I walked on and the ground seemed to grow boggier and boggier until I was in a real danger of sinking well into it and not being able to get out again. I had to turn and walk back until I got to firmer ground. And then I heard Paddy's voice calling, some distance away.

"John? John McFadden? Are ye there, John?"

I made my way up a slight slope in the land. "Where are ye, Paddy?" I shouted back to him.

There was a pause. "I'm at the oul' fallen barn," he replied. "I'm still lost, John, an' I can't seem to get out o' this field." There was a kind of panic in his voice and I knew how he felt. "I tried to take my bearin's from yon light but it seems to keep movin' and if I follow it I'm lost. This is the second or third time that I've been at this barn. Where are you?"

"I'm over by the oul' standin' stone at the foot of the field," I answered. "I thought that I might find the hedge and follow it down to the gate but I can't seem to find the hedge. I've been tryin' to follow the light too but it's no use."

"Look, John, stay where you are an' I'll try t'walk towards ye. At least if we're together we can maybe find our way out. Stand yer ground and if ye can sing, I can follow the sound." And so standing on the edge of that boggy land I began to sing an old foolish song that we'd sung back in the céilí house. In truth, I felt a right fool. I waited and waited, but there was no sign of Paddy.

"Paddy?" I shouted. "Are ye still there? Are ye close by?" But this time there was no answer. I took a couple of steps towards the place that I thought his voice had come from but there was only the open field in front of me. And hanging low on the horizon – or where I imagined the horizon to be – was the priest's light, watching me. The anger got the better of me and I walked quickly forward, only to find my way blocked again by a great bunch of cow's tongues and briars that I couldn't get through. I was forced to turn again and after walking up a wee bit of a hill I came back to the old standing stone again. But by this time, the panic was on me and I turned left and kept walking, out across the field. It seemed to stretch on and on.

"Paddy!" I shouted. "Paddy Kelly!" I kept shouting for him as I walked. I came to the ruins of the old barn again and there wasn't a sign of Paddy. At that minute I felt lost and hopeless, as if there was nothing that I could do. I was beaten. I turned and began to walk back across the field, more slowly this time, and the priest's light in front of me seemed to blaze as if in great triumph. In front of me the land seemed to slope downwards but I just walked on.

Then there was a movement in front of me and coming out of the dark, there was Paddy Kelly, walking as slowly as me and trying to find his way across the uneven field. Forgetting everything, I ran towards him and he towards me and we threw our arms around each other like long-lost brothers.

"John," says he, "I called an' called on ye but ye never answered." I think there were tears of relief in his eyes but I couldn't see too well in the dark.

"I never heard ye," I replied. "But I called to ye as well when ye were up at the oul' barn but I never heard ye either."

He looked at me oddly. "John," he says, "what d'ye think that this is? Why can't we find our way out of a field that we've both known since we were boys? There's something very strange here."

I looked out in the direction of the twinkling light, the only thing that we'd continually seen since we'd entered the field.

"I think there's some sort o' witchcraft or somethin' at work here," I replied. "Somethin' that has confused our minds an' lost us our bearin's."

Paddy's voice dropped almost to a whisper. "D'ye think that we're bein' fairy-led?" he asked.

I looked at him, for the same sort of thought had crossed my mind as well. "Maybe" I said. "But how?"

He suddenly looked very serious. "John, did ye ever hear of the stray sod?" he asked.

I said that I had – it was an old spell, well known in the country areas of Fermanagh. If a person stepped on the unmarked grave of an unbaptised child or a suicide, they could wander for hours without any sort of direction, even though they knew the place that they were in very well. Maybe that's what was happening to Paddy and me.

"If that's the way of it," I said, "then we should take our coats off and put them back on inside out. My mother said that this was always the way to break the spell of the stray sod. What d'ye think?" He nodded gravely.

"It's worth a try," he said, "for I'm damned if I can find my way out of this field."

So, like two idiots, we stood in what I thought must be the centre of the field, taking our coats off and putting them back on again inside out. And as I did so, I thought that the priest's light, which had always been there in front of us, dimmed slightly and began to fade away like a star in the morning. Somewhere, away across the field, the strange bird called again, just once, and then it fell silent again.

There was a redness in the sky to our left and gradually the landscape seemed to come back into focus. We were at the head of a field all right, but it was not the field that we had been trying to cross. It fell away in front of us down to some cattle houses and beyond that was the house that we'd céilíed in the night before. Even as we stood there, the woman of the house came out to throw out the leavings of the tea pot into a bush at her door and we shouted down to her. She must have seen how badly the pair of us were shaken, for she brought us in and gave us some poteen that had been left over from the previous night in the heel of a cup. Paddy told her what had happened and that we thought it was the stray sod that had done it. I didn't say anything, for it was just an old country superstition and I didn't want the woman to think that I was very gullible. But she nodded her head. She had heard a story from her mother that a servant girl in one of the farmhouses in this area was supposed to have given birth many years before and that the baby disappeared. It was supposed to have been born dead and was buried in some of the fields nearby. Maybe we had accidentally walked across its grave and this is what had led us astray. The power of a dead infant can be very strong in some country places.

I walked home, keeping to the road this time, in the first light of the morning. The sun was coming up and everywhere, the farms were stirring and coming to life. A dog barked at me through a gate as I passed by. Away on the hill above Drumcully I could still see the light from the window of the Parochial House twinkling out over the countryside – the priest must have read and worked all through the night – but somehow it didn't seem as threatening as it had when I was wandering, lost in that strange field. Even so, I quickened my step in order to get home.

That was a long time ago when I was no more than a boy. Paddy Kelly's long dead and he never spoke to me about that night again. I think that he was still afraid about what had happened to us. So am I. I can still never walk across a field or hear the call of a bird in the bushes without thinking of that night. Nor can I look out across the countryside and see the light coming from the window of a far-away house without thinking of the priest's light and how it led us astray. But like I said, it was all a very long time ago.

* * *

Note: This is one of the most complete tales of the stray sod which exists in Ireland and few like it exist anywhere else. There are fragmentary tales, though, and not all of them in rural Ireland either. A good number of years ago, a teacher from the North of England, recorded how he had got lost on a green in the middle of a busy Newcastle housing estate whilst on his way to see his girlfriend. He had, he said, wandered around until morning trying to find his way out of the estate, even though he knew it extremely well. He put it down, half jokingly, to the influence of the stray sod. Maybe there is more to the legend than might first appear!

13

THE CROOKED BACK

County Kilkenny

It has long been believed in some parts of the countryside that there are certain areas throughout the landscape which are dangerous to humans and where they should not go. This is not because of any physical danger but rather because of supernatural retribution. These places were believed to be the haunt of genius loci *– literally, "spirit of place" – disembodied forces which protected the immediate area in which they were to be found. This might be a well, a lake, a ring fort or even a cluster of trees, and it was often considered that these forces may have been the remnants of old gods or spirits associated with the place in former times. Most of these, it would appear, were hostile to human encroachment upon their territory and would take swift action against those who trespassed in their domain.*

In folklore, the region which these forces inhabited was often known as "fairy ground" or "bad ground" and prohibitions were placed in rural minds against building there or conducting any form of human activity there for fear of antagonising these specific spirits. This of course, did not prevent people from going there and folktales are often littered with instances of disappearances, misfortune and even death for such flagrance. Indeed, in my own youth I can well remember a ring fort which stood close to our house in which no one would work after six in the evening. The story of one man who did so and who vanished there was well known in the district and served as a warning to others in the locality. (The man turned up about seven years later with no real memory of where he had been in the intervening years, although there was much general speculation that he had left his wife and had been living with another woman elsewhere! Nevertheless, the place was still regarded with some suspicion.) Similar tales come from many other parts of Ireland. A number of years ago, I interviewed a farm worker in County Sligo who told me a story about an old fort near Ben Bulbin, an area widely regarded as "fairy country".

"It was a place that I never felt comfortable even being near," he told me. "Even if I was working a few fields away, I could still feel it – a kind of a 'coldness' that seemed to come from it. And at twelve o'clock in the day, I'd see a woman walk across the fields and go into it and she never came out again. I saw her as clear as day, dressed in black and with a red scarf about her throat. Maybe she was a fairy, maybe a ghost or a spirit – for they said that there were suicides in that place – but I never ventured close enough to find out. But I know that I saw her at the distance. It was a bad place all right."

The following story concerns such a place in County Kilkenny. It has been slightly adapted, the location marginally changed to place it near the village of Bennetsbridge, between Kilkenny Town and Thomastown (the real location is not too far from there). It is based on a story that I heard from a doctor in the Kilkenny area and some of the names have been changed as certain people or their *descendants may still be alive. Like many other such tales, it portrays the eeriness of isolated places and hints at the forces that might still be lurking there....*

As the evening wore on, more and more people began to gather in the pub – farmers from round about, tradesmen finishing their day and travellers maybe on their way to and from Kilkenny town, stopping in for a drink on their way through. The place was full of smoke, clatter and chat. Most people congregated along the length of the bar, shouting orders, telling stories and generally having a laugh. It was the lively, friendly atmosphere of a country pub. For everybody, that is, except one: behind the bar, one of the three barmen watched the proceedings around him from under low and beetling brows and with a kind of gloomy scowl on his face. He looked as if he'd once been a strapping fellow but was now bowed over by some sort of curvature of the spine until he seemed to be almost hunchbacked. His face, partly covered by a heavy beard, looked as though it had been at one time pulled to the left by a stroke, leaving the left eye drooping slightly and deforming the man's countenance to some extent. From his position behind the counter, the barman surveyed the chattering company with a wary, almost hostile stare as though keeping an eye out for something amongst them that was hitherto unseen but which he knew might be there.

Seeing my interest in him, the doctor sat back at the table in the corner where we were seated and began to light his pipe.

"Something of a specimen!" he said, striking a match below the table's edge. "You wouldn't think that he was once one of the finest hurlers in all of Kilkenny."

My eyes widened and shifted to the crook-backed man on the other side of the bar. If he saw me looking at him, he gave no sign.

"Indeed you wouldn't," I agreed. "But who is he?"

"Charles Mangan," replied the doctor, drawing on the pipe. "Used to play for the Kilkenny county side and a patient of mine. One of the most eligible young men in the county too many years ago." My eyes widened slightly further.

"But what happened to him? A stroke maybe? It would've had to have been quite severe to leave him like that!"

The doctor's face narrowed and his previous good humour seemed to dissipate momentarily. "Ah," he replied, but said no more.

"Look," I said, "it was just a passing question. I didn't mean you to break your doctor–patient confidentiality. Forget that I ever asked – it's just that he is, as you say, such an odd specimen."

There was silence between us for a moment then the doctor spoke again. "If I tell you something," he said, leaning forward almost confidentially, "you must promise never to repeat it when Mangan is alive, although I'm not telling you anything that isn't already well known in this locality anyway. But if you give me your word, I'll tell you how he's supposed to have been twisted like that and my own take on it."

I nodded in assent. And I kept my word for many years, although now that Charlie Mangan is dead, I believe that I can tell the tale.

I was intrigued by the misshapen barman and my friend the doctor's manner only served to add to that sense of interest. I had the impression that I was about to hear some dreadful secret. If he knew that we were talking about him, Charles Mangan displayed no interest.

"Well," said the doctor at length. "Mangan is something of a character in this area. Like I said, he was a great hurler for Kilkenny but he was also well known all across the county for his . . . ah . . . raucous behaviour. He was a great drinker, you see, and because of his status as a hurler, a lot of women had set their caps at him, so to speak. You wouldn't think so to look at him now, but he was once an extremely handsome man. He lived with his mother, not far away from this pub – in fact he lives there yet – his father being dead for a while and he being the only son. There's a sister in America, I think, but he was certainly always about the house and his mother's favourite. I think that he was rather spoiled and used to getting his own way most of the time. He would stay out until the early hours drinking and chasing girls – and he broke manys a girl's heart in this countryside – and his mother wouldn't say a word to him. She's long dead now but I think that she let him away with far too much. There was a group of boys that he ran about with who were almost as wild as himself but Charlie Mangan took great delight in being the wildest of the bunch. There wasn't a dare or a trick that he wouldn't try, just for the devilment of it. You wouldn't think that to look at him now." He took a drink and cast a long look at the gloomy barman.

"A little way from here, there's a ruined church standing on a low hill a good bit back from the roadway. I once spoke to a historian who said that it dated from medieval times but he could tell me nothing about it. Some people round here will tell you that it's just an old ruin but others will tell you that it has a very bad name about it – it depends whom you talk to. Anyway, leading down to the very foot of the field where it stands is an old laneway which connects the fields with the road. The fields are accessed by an old stile which is set into a gap in the hedge under some trees at the very end of the lane. Now that *has* an extremely bad reputation and few local people will go anywhere near it, preferring to walk about half a mile farther on to access the fields around the old church by another gate. Why, I'm not sure – you'll hear plenty of stories about it. Old people say that it's the haunt of ghosts and fairies, that they gather under the trees and wait for travellers to come by so that they can terrify them; others will tell you that it's the entrance to another world and that you can vanish there, but nobody's really sure. All old local folktales and legends, you might say. But it's not the most pleasant of places anyway and I've never liked it myself. The branches of the trees have never been cut back and they hang over that old stile in a rather disturbing way, throwing it into shadow. And there's a coldness about it too – the stile itself is always wet and muddy even on the driest summer day and it's always dark with shadows coming and going, even when the sun is shining on the fields behind it. Even the lane down to it is eerie, with high hedges on either side, shutting out the sunlight." He shivered, even thinking about it.

"I spoke one time to a young boy in this area – one of the Latteys who live near the lane – and he told me that he'd seen a man and a woman dressed in strange old-fashioned clothes climbing over the stile and when he looked again they were gone, though there was nowhere for them to go. He was sure that they were fairies. However, he was a rather strange young man – always given to seeing things and most people thought that he'd made it up. But I've also spoken to sane and sensible people who've heard whisperings and voices around that old stile and nobody about. As I say, it has a very bad name on it in these parts." He sat back to take a drink and draw on his pipe.

"But what has this to do with Charlie Mangan?" I asked.

The doctor eyed me warily and then glanced at Mangan, who returned his gaze with a surly stare.

"I was coming to that," he replied.

It happened, they say, about thirty years ago *[went on the doctor]*. Charlie Mangan would be in his fifties now so that would be about right. At this time, his behaviour was more or less out of control, as we would say today. He was at the height of his powers as a hurler and he'd broken several hearts around the countryside, so I suppose he was feeling great with himself. And of course, the usual crowd was egging him on.

The other thing which Charlie liked was good fiddle music and in those days there was an old man living over near the fallen church that I told you about, called Moll Joe Rafferty. He had a great reputation as a fiddle player and he kept a céilí-house which ran 'til all hours, for Moll Joe had never married. They say he also ran a bit of a card-school and that this attracted young men from around the district to it. It was always packed 'til the early hours. Moll Joe would play and the young men would wager and there'd be girls there too. Of course, Moll Joe's dead now and the house is a ruin but it was a great place years ago. It was enough to draw Charlie Mangan and his cronies. In fact for a while Mangan almost lived there, drinking and gambling for days on end. In the end Moll Joe had to put him out in order to get some sleep. That's how bad it was.

On one particular night, the partying went on for most of the night. As well as being a grand fiddle-player, Moll Joe was an accomplished poteen-maker and according to tradition the spirit had been flowing all night and Charlie and his compatriots were all extremely drunk. They refused to go home but at last Moll Joe with much laughing got them out through the door and into the night.

"Go on home boys," says he. "We all need a night's sleep. I'll see ye all in the mornin'." But Charlie Mangan was not to be turned. He still had a bottle of the poteen about him and was in the mood to continue the céilí. Moll Joe, however, closed his door and left him and two or three of his companions on the road outside.

Charlie Mangan, however, didn't go home. He wanted a céilí and was determined to have one. He hammered for a while on Moll Joe's door but the old fiddler didn't open it. At last he tired.

"Come on," he said to his friends, "we'll go and take our céilí somewhere else." But the boys were not all that anxious to go with him.

"Maybe Moll Joe's right," said one of them, James Feeney. "It's a wee while to cock-crow and I could do with gettin' my head down. Maybe we should all just go home to bed."

But Charlie glowered at him. "You may want to go home," he said sharply. "But the night's still young an' I'm not tired. I'll party some more an' yous'll all come with me. We've still a lot more céilí-ing to do before the sun rises." And with that he led them off into the countryside. They looked at each other and shrugged; they were tired and wanted to get to their own beds, but they thought they might stick with him for a while.

They travelled through the district for an hour, along the banks of the Nore, lying silver under the moon, knocking at any door they could find and demanding to be let in. Most people, however, were in their beds and were in no mood for their antics. With all doors remaining closed to them, Charlie grew increasingly frustrated.

"If nobody wants to céilí with us," he declared, "we'll have our own céilí out here in the open. I've a mind to go up to that oul' ruined church in the fields beyond Moll Joe's and céilí there. Are you all with me?"

To hold a céilí in a church was the sort of outrageous and rebellious thing that appealed to Charlie and once he had set his mind to something, he was difficult to turn. However, the venture meant that they had to go along the old laneway from the road, over the haunted stile and up through the fields. None of his companions was particularly happy about that and, I suppose, neither was Charlie himself – only the drink-courage was on him and he had a kind of reputation to maintain amongst them all.

"Maybe we should go home, Charlie," said James Feeney again, "an' leave our céilí-ing for another night."

But Charlie angrily waved the suggestion away. "I'm ready to céilí until the clouds of the morning," he announced, "and I want my friends with me. We'll have a grand time up in that oul' place. Look, I still have a bottle of good poteen with me! An' if you're worried about the ghosts and fairies that are supposed to hang about down that laneway and around that stile, then you're all a bunch of oul' women!"

And with that he turned on his heel, took a swig on the bottle of poteen and made off down the road. Reluctantly the others followed and for a short while their good spirits returned. Many a local girl had their good name ridiculed as they passed along between the sleeping houses. But, as they neared the mouth of the old laneway, such frivolity began to fall away. Even Charlie himself appeared more sombre.

They reached the entrance to the lane and stopped on the roadside. Even though there was a full moon which lit up the countryside as though it were daytime, the lane seemed extremely dark and full of shadows that appeared to move all by themselves. A couple of the others made to turn back but Charlie, full of the poteen, stopped them.

"It's only an oul' laneway," he pointed out, "and the tall hedges make it appear ghostly. But there's nothing in it – nothing that can harm any one of us. An' ye'll have forgotten about it when we get up to the oul' church an' start our céilí." He spoke so positively that the men changed their minds. "Ye'll all laugh when ye have a drink behind the church walls. It's only oul' superstition, that's all it is." From somewhere away down the dark laneway came a sound that was somewhere between a cough and a throaty chuckle. They all heard it and one of the men stepped back. Charlie grabbed his arm, pulling him forward again, anxious to get going to the céilí.

"That's nothing," he snapped, "only the wind in the hedges. It'll take more than a fuff o' wind to turn Charlie

Mangan." And he marched into the mouth of the lane. The sound at the far end fell silent.

"See! That's all it was. A wee sound in the hedge an' ye're all imaginin' things." And with another swig from the poteen bottle he strode forward into the darkness.

The doctor paused for breath. There was a roar of laughter from farther along the bar where two farmers were sharing a joke, taken up by those around them. I looked at Charles Mangan but the brooding, bent man seemed lost in his own gloomy thoughts and gave no sign that he'd even heard them. His deformed face seemed drawn in a perpetual scowl which not even the laughter from the bar could penetrate. The doctor drew on his pipe and continued with the tale.

They all walked down the laneway well enough *[he went on]*, although it was very dark and the ground below their feet was very uneven. More than once one of them staggered into potholes and once James Feeney nearly fell his full length on the ground. Of course, being very drunk didn't help much either but they somehow managed to make their way along the length of the lane.

At the far end, the old stile lay, mysterious and shadowy under the dark branches of the overhanging trees, caught for a moment in a shaft of moonlight. Beyond, clear as day, lay the ruins on the crest of the low hill. The revellers halted and drew back, almost afraid to go any further, and Feeney later said that he would have turned back at this stage had it not been for Charlie Mangan.

"Come on," he shouted. "We're nearly there." At the sound of his voice something moved and rustled in the tree-branches above the stile and there was a noise like a low, throaty chuckle from somewhere near at hand. A couple of the men crossed themselves. Not Charlie, though, for the drink had made him reckless.

"It's only a bird in the hedge," he declared angrily, "and all these noises are no more than wee night creatures – bats or owls. We've nothing to be frightened of." But they sensed that he spoke more to reassure himself than anything else. As if in reply to his words, the branches of one of the trees above the stile seemed to move slightly as though something unseen had scuttled quickly along it. Feeney cried out and jumped back.

Charlie Mangan shook his head. "It's a trick of the moon," he murmured. He turned to the others. "That's all it is." He appeared to compose himself. "Let's get across the stile and over the field to that oul' church. Then we'll have our céilí and we can laugh at ourselves for our childishness." The others, however, still hung back, unsure. The sound like the low, dry laugh came again, this time from somewhere close at hand – almost beside them. It stirred Charlie into action.

"Well, if yous are all a bunch of oul' women, I'm not afraid!" he shouted, running towards the stile as if intending to jump it. The branches overhead moved again, but he didn't stop.

"Charlie!" shouted James Feeney warningly, but it was already too late. Something moved along the branch of the tree – those who were there said that it was no more than a shadow that was gone again when they looked at it directly – and seemed to drop down onto Charlie's shoulders as he passed below. The weight of it carried him face downwards to the ground, where he lay struggling against something that the others couldn't see. His entire body seemed to be covered in a mass of shadow but there was really nothing of substance there at all. Yet he seemed to be in pain and fighting against something.

"Get it off me!" he shouted. "It's killing me! I'm done for!" He writhed on the ground whilst the shadows moved around him, flowing between his flailing body and the earth below. The harsh dry cackle sounded again, this time from somewhere directly in front of them. "It's got its feet in my back and I can feel its arms round my throat!" screamed Charlie again. But though the others looked, they could see nothing. There was nothing else there, only Charlie Mangan writhing on the ground.

"What is it, Charlie?" choked Feeney, frightened to go any closer. "What is it that has you?"

Although he was obviously in terrible pain, Charlie answered him. "Dry, horrible arms round my neck," he wailed. "For God's sake, get it off!"

Another of the boys darted forward, poking at the air beside him with his hand. Later he would say that he felt nothing solid at all but that the air seemed very cold on his skin. Something unseen hissed and spat and he pulled back his hand in an instant, turning and running back along the lane as fast as he could. James Feeney and the other lad just stood there, too frightened to move.

"Help me!" shouted Charlie Mangan. "It's crushing the life out of me! Oh God!" It was then that Feeney had a flash of inspiration. This was something supernatural, something that they couldn't deal with by ordinary means. But he had a crucifix in his pocket – a symbol of the Holy Church – and *that* might work against something dark and unknowable. He drew it from his pocket and thrust it towards Mangan.

"Whoever or whatever you are!" he shouted. "In the Name of God, begone! Leave this man alone!"

Once again, the hissing and spitting of the unseen thing filled the laneway and Feeney felt something like naked talons lightly brush the back of his hand as if trying to make him drop the crucifix. But he held onto it tightly. "In God's Name, just go!" he shouted again.

There was a sudden movement which was sensed rather than seen – a ripple in the air – and something seemed to jump from Charlie Mangan's body and onto the low-hanging branch of a nearby tree. The branch sagged and moved as it scampered up and was gone. From somewhere overhead came that low, throaty cackle once again – and then nothing. The only thing that broke the silence of that lane was the groaning of Charlie Mangan as he lay where he'd fallen. In front of them was the old stile, caught in a shaft of moonlight, with the ruined church in the field beyond it.

The two boys lifted Charlie between them and carried him back along the road to Moll Joe Rafferty's. After much banging and shouting at the door, the old man finally got up and let them into the house. They laid Charlie on a low bed in the back room and called for me.

Here the doctor paused. "I treated him as best I could. I suggested trying to get him to a hospital, but he wouldn't hear of it. Even then I knew that something had tried to twist his spine and pulled his face a little to one side with considerable force, and that he would never be the same afterwards. I pleaded with him several times to go and see some sort of specialist – maybe up in Dublin – who might have been able to do something for him, but he always said that he wouldn't go. He seemed to look on this as some sort of punishment for his past life. Ever since that night, he has been the way you see him now – sullen, morose, hating the world, the exact opposite to what he used to be. His mother died a long number of years ago and he has lived alone, more or less shunning all human company. He took this job only recently to make himself a bit of money." He seemed to shiver and took another mouthful of his drink.

"I also treated James Feeney for some scratches on the back of his hand – scratches that looked as if they'd been made by some sort of claw. They took a long time to heal and, even yet, you can still see the small white marks of them on his skin."

There was more laughter from along the bar. A crowd had gathered at the far end and were exchanging jokes and humorous anecdotes. Many of them seemed very drunk. The doctor, however, didn't seem to share their merriment but sat there puffing on his pipe, looking into the middle distance in front of him.

"What do you think it was?" I asked at last.

His gaze never varied. "I don't know," he answered. "I heard the story that I've just told you from James Feeney who was there and he could make no sense of it either. There are people in this locality who'll put it down to ghosts and fairies. They say that the old lane and the stile at its end are bad places, that there are things there that come and go between this world and another and which will harm you if you come near them. And maybe they're right. Maybe there *are* things that share this world with us, just beyond the limits of our vision. We might catch a glimpse of them from time to time out of the corners of our eyes, but normally we don't see them at all. But they're there, lurking in certain places, watching us and what we do and if we venture too near them, they'll make their presence known. We call them fairies and sheehogues and refer to the places where they lurk as 'fairy places' but maybe there is *something* there – something that is not too friendly towards mankind. Our ancestors knew about such things and were afraid." He paused, drawing on his pipe once again and I detected a certain nervousness in his tone.

"You're a man of medicine, a rational man," I told him, "but you're beginning to sound like some sort of . . . oh, I don't know . . . superstitious backwoods peasant. What might have happened is that Charlie Mangan might simply have had some sort of stroke or something, brought on by years of céilí-ing and bad poteen. You said that he'd been drinking the stuff. The convulsions might have twisted his spine and pulled his face to one side. The scratches on James Feeney's hand might have been made by branches or brambles in the hedge along the laneway. There's a quite reasonable explanation for it all, I'm sure."

He thought for a moment and nodded slowly. "You're right," he said, "that *is* the rational man's explanation of things and, before seeing Charlie, I would have said exactly the same as you." He looked down the bar to where Mangan was wordlessly serving one of the farmers. "But that night they brought me in to tend him, I saw something that made me wonder. In order to get a better look at him, I had to take his shirt off and examine his crooked back. I only had an oil lamp to do so – Moll Joe had no electricity in his house at the time – but I was able to see the back quite clearly. And there was no mistake. Near the base of the spine were two small indentations surrounded by bruising, where considerable pressure had been applied. The outlines of the marks were very fresh and very clear. I tell you, they were the marks of *two small feet* and there was no doubt in my mind that they marked a place where someone or *something* had clung onto him for the express purpose of deliberately twisting his spine. Now what do you make of that?"

* * *

Note: Although the above story has been presented to the reader in a somewhat literary style and the names have been changed, the events detailed there are true. The place in question – a stile, overhung by dark trees, across a stone ditch and into a field – can still be seen today, as far as I know, and some of those involved may very well still be alive. The tale itself serves as a reminder to us that perhaps there are places scattered throughout the Irish countryside which are much better avoided by humans and left solely to the largely unseen forces that dwell there.

The Dark Art

14

THE CREEPING SHADOW

County Wexford

In the lore of many ancient cultures, including that of the early Celts, a man's shadow was highly significant. In many instances a man's shadow was believed to be somehow inextricably connected to his essence or soul. In fact, in some parts of the ancient world, it was believed that the shadow was an outward expression of the inner soul and that if it came to harm in some way, the person in question would die with no chance of salvation. Thus, to step on a shadow was thought to do unimaginable injury to its owner. Similarly, to allow an animal to run across one's shadow or to allow one's shadow to fall on a "brute beast" was supposed to have some form of supernatural repercussion. This might be "corruption" of the pure, immortal soul by animal contact and might even deny it a place in Heaven after death. It was therefore as well to protect one's image on the ground (as it was viewed by many ancient peoples) as best one could.

Conversely, however, the shadow of an evil man – as an extension of his evil soul – might bring evil to those that it fell across. In some places it was believed that black magicians, through their dark arts, might actually detach their shadows from their bodies and send them out to do mischief in the wider community. This was a common belief amongst the Vikings, who were often terrified of the shadows of evil men which, it was thought, could actually do them serious physical harm. In fact, some of these shadows were known in Viking folklore as "stranglers" because of the death which it was believed they could inflict on their victims at the behest of evil masters or mistresses.

Ireland was, of course, no different to many other ancient cultures with regard to shadows. Indeed, in some areas of the country, the belief that shadows were the adjuncts of the soul persisted throughout the nineteenth and even well into the twentieth centuries. I can personally remember, as late as the 1950s in some parts of the rural North, a common belief that to step on someone's shadow was to bring them "bad luck" or illness. Even in those more "enlightened" times, there was a deliberate avoidance of the shadows of those who were considered "suspect" within the community, due to the belief that these might confer sickness on those who stepped upon them. There was even still a tradition at this time which said that shadows might detach themselves from their owners in order to do harm in a community.

The following story is from County Wexford, which is said to boast a long Viking tradition, being originally a Viking settlement or "wintering station" (its name derives from the Viking "Weis Fjord" – inlet of the mud flats). It is not surprising, therefore, to find a number of old Norse beliefs integrated into the native Irish tradition in this part of the world. This story was told to me by an old man, Daniel Fanning, who lived in a rural area between Enniscorthy and Boolavogue. He, in turn, claimed to have heard it from his grandfather, whom, he said, knew many of the people concerned.

I'll tell you this. There was a man living not far from here before my grandfather's time and his name was Tom Foley. He was well known across the countryside and indeed his name lived after him, for he was, by all accounts, a black-hearted villain. He lived in the low end of a shebeen that had a very bad name about it, in the middle of the fields well away from the road. One end of the house was where he lived but the other end was a place that served drink and poteen and only the worst of people gathered there. Not that it was open very often, for Tom Foley was never a man that liked work much, nor was he on very good terms with his neighbours and he only opened the place when it suited him.

Little was known about his background, although it was believed that he'd come from another part of Wexford. There was also a story that one of his ancestors had been tied up in the bit of unpleasantness at Scullabogue House near Carrickbyrne Hill, New Ross, in the Risings of 1798 – the one where the barn was fired with prisoners in it. They said that one of Foley's forefathers had put a torch to the barn and that the family had a black curse on it. There were those, though, who said that this was nonsense and that the family might have come from County Mayo.

Nobody knew what he worked at, for he seemed to lie in his bed of a day and stayed close to his own place. He might have done a bit of farming, for he owned land round about, but if he did, it was very little. Yet he never seemed to be

227

short of any money; in fact, it was whispered about that Tom Foley was one of the richest men in the whole of Wexford, though you would never have thought it by the look of him.

He was a tall, sour-looking man, very dark and swarthy and with a long face that was always frowning. But it was the darkness of his eyes that frightened some people, for he could look at you with a stare that would have cut you in two. And, despite all his rumoured money, he always dressed in old clothes as he went about the countryside. Nor if he had money about him did he ever spend it on the house, for it was always dark and smoky, but maybe that was the way that he liked it. The thatch was always overgrown and there were nettles growing above the door frame. Tom Foley lived there all alone, for he'd never married – it was said that, for all his rumoured wealth, no woman would have him.

There was another thing about him too that made the people wary of him. He seemed to know all their business and maybe all the things that they didn't want knowing. He knew, for instance, when the schoolteacher went to England to have a baby and her not married; he knew who had raided the poor box at the chapel one year, although nobody was took up for it; and he is said to have known plenty of other things besides. Nobody was sure how he knew them although everybody guessed plenty. Some people said that he had a magic mirror somewhere in his shebeen in which he could see what went on in the countryside around; some people said that he went about the countryside either invisibly or in the shape of some animal or bird and learned all these things. And in all of these ideas, there was the notion that Tom Foley was well in with the Evil One, the

Enemy of all Mankind, or with the fairies. It was well noted that he never went to Mass on a Sunday morning and when the priest called round to see him and invited him to come, he actually chased the clergyman from his door.

"What brings you, peerin' an' peekin' about my house?" he shouted. "Get back to your mumblin' prayers an' reekin' incense an' leave me alone."

He would have hit the priest if the holy man hadn't hurried away. "Be about your own business," he shouted after him, "an' leave me to mine!" That was the way of him, and he was greatly feared by the local people. He seemed to enjoy the power that this gave him in the locality. From time to time, he would go up to people that he met – on the road or sometimes in the pub – and say things to them in a sort of knowing way. These would be things that nobody else would know about and it frightened the people greatly. Sometimes some of them stood up to him but it was said that something unpleasant always happened to them if they did. This only strengthened Foley's reputation as being a magician or, at the very least, well in with the fairies, and it was a reputation that he certainly seemed to enjoy.

One year there was a wonderful spell of weather in the middle of the summer. The sun shone all the time and the days and nights were very mild. It was so warm that the old people could get neither sleep nor rest but tossed and turned in their beds of a night and in the daytime. The dogs lay panting by the door because of the heat. There was not so much as a cat's fuff of wind for days and the country dreamed under the heat as the shadows on the ground lengthened from morn 'til dusk. In the countryside, there were one or two people that died – some said that it was because of the heat, but some said that it was something else, for all of those who died had crossed Tom Foley at some point. There were those who said that Foley himself had something to do with their deaths, but these thoughts were always spoken about in quiet tones, for they never knew if Foley himself might somehow be listening or if he knew what was being said in some way.

There was another man living in this part of the world too by the name of Jimmy Kavanagh, whose wife had a fearfully sharp tongue on her. Jimmy might well have been a relation of my own and was an easy-going sort of a man, but his wife was a terrible Tartar who took offence at the smallest thing. Once she got started, there was no stopping her. She took a spite against Tom Foley. I'm not sure what it was about – maybe it was because of his lazy ways, for she was a stickler for hard work, or maybe it was something else – but whenever she was near him, she was fairly bristling. And the tongue of her! Some said that she even walked all the way across the field to Foley's shebeen to give him a mouthful.

If she didn't like him at all, he liked her even less. On several occasions he had told her to her face that her bad tongue would be the worse for her, especially when she crossed him, but such warnings never seemed to worry her, although they would have frightened other people. She seemed to have no fear of him at all, and this seemed to annoy Tom Foley greatly. He threatened badness on her and her family as well. So the countryside waited to see what would happen. For a while, nothing did.

The summer weather grew hotter and hotter and there was never a day went past that the sun didn't shine. There were shadows everywhere – they were along the hedges and in the fields; down through the laneways and in the farmyards. Everywhere anything moved or something stood to block out the sun, there was a shadow. They thronged everywhere, seeming to move themselves with the changing light.

As I said, Jimmy Kavanagh and his wife had two small children, one of which was a baby in a crib – a little girl not a year old. She was a beautiful child and was the apple of her father's eye. Even her mother, for all her fierceness, loved the little child. Indeed, it was impossible not to like her, for she had such a pleasant way about her. She was always smiling and laughing and was quiet and peaceable for the greater part of the time – never crying or whining the way that some babies do. Manys the time she lay in her little cot at the cottage door taking advantage of the sun and the warm air, while her mother worked inside. When the sun was starting to turn, the mother would go out and bring her into the cool of the house. The child lay and smiled at the movements of clouds across the sky or the shadows of birds swooped across the yard beyond the cottage. This was the way of it for many days while the good weather lasted.

One day, just about twelve o'clock when the sun was about directly overhead, Jimmy Kavanagh and his wife were in their house. He had come home because it was too warm to work out in the open and he was waiting until the middle of the day had passed and the weather had started to cool again (that was an old way among some of the farming people). She was making him something to eat. The other child – a little boy – was playing close to the hearthstone at his father's feet. From outside the open door, the baby in the crib started to scream and scream loudly, crying sorely. Thinking that a dog or some other animal had wandered into the yard and was threatening their child, both parents ran out. There was nothing in the yard, although it was full of shadows. A big oak tree grew in one corner and in the sunlight, its branches threw shadows everywhere; there was the shadow of a gatepost and the shadow of birds coming and going in the sky overhead. But nothing tangible moved and the child still lay crying in its crib by the door. Her father looked up and down the sunny yard but he could see nothing. The parents went back into the house, the child in the crib went to sleep and there was no further trouble that day.

The next day was even hotter. The wife was doing some sewing in the cool of the cottage whilst the child dozed in its crib just outside the door. Suddenly and without warning, it began to scream and cry. The woman jumped up from the stool where she been sitting and ran out. Once again, the yard was empty, but this time she thought that something moved away very fast, although she wasn't sure what it was. She thought that it might be something long and dark, but it moved so quickly, she couldn't really see it. Anyway, the yard was full of shadows again and whatever it was seemed to have been mixed in among them. She told Jimmy about it when he came home that night but he said that she might have been dreaming about seeing it.

A while later in the day, Tom Foley came past her gate and looked into the yard with a long, strange stare. He walked very slowly as he passed by the gateway and he kept his eyes fixed on the crib by the door. Seeing him pass and thinking that he might be up to something, the woman came out to her door.

"Walk on, Foley," she called to him, "an' don't be hanging about in front of our house or I'll come and sort you out myself. I don't want you anywhere near us, for I know what people are sayin' about you – what a black and horrible creature y'are." Those were the sort of things that she said to people. She was frightened that he might put the evil eye on the house or that he might make some spell against those inside. Tom Foley just gave her a thin, cold and very sinister-looking smile.

"I'd look to that fine child of yours, Mrs Kavanagh," he said slowly and with a bit of an edge to his voice. "She's such a pretty little thing, I'm sure that it would be a great trouble to you if anything was to happen to her." For all her fierceness, his words sent a chill through Mrs Kavanagh's heart. She made to say something but Tom Foley had turned on his heel and was already walking away down the road. She told Jimmy Kavanagh when he came home that night but he told her not to worry and he thought that there was little that Tom Foley could do.

"He can frighten decent folks and that's about the height of it," he said. "Pay no heed to his threats." All the same, his wife was a little worried.

The next day, the sun was hotter than ever. Jimmy Kavanagh's wife had put the crib beside the door to give the child in it some air, but she kept her eye on it all the time as she worked inside the cottage. Still, about midday, she had gone to a cupboard at the far end of the room for something for the other child when she heard the infant screaming again. Dropping everything, she ran to the door. Again, there was nothing in the yard, but on the cottage wall, just above the crib, was a large shadow, spreading across the stonework in the sunshine. At first she thought that it was the shadow of the tree at the far end of the yard – the tips of its branches perhaps – but then she realised that it wasn't. It was very long, like a tall man with his arms outstretched, and it spread along the wall towards the corner of the building.

As she looked at it, she thought that it moved slightly in a sort of strange and awkward way, a bit like a man swimming underwater. And it seemed to be moving by itself! But when she looked at it again, it was only a shadow. She stood there for a minute looking at it, wondering what she'd seen, when all of a sudden, a sound from behind her made her jump and turn, but it was only a bird calling from a bush nearby. When she turned back, the shadow – or whatever it was – had gone and there was just the sun shining on the bare wall. She went back into the cottage wondering at it. In the end, she put the whole thing down to her own fancy and got on with her work about the house. She said nothing about it to Jimmy when he came home that evening, for she was a proud woman and didn't want him to think that she was foolish.

The next day was even warmer. People said that there was thunder in the air and that the evening would end with a heavy downpour. All the same, the sun streamed down on the countryside and the day was very heavy and still. In order to give her a breath of air, the child was put in her crib in the accustomed place by the door, where she lay chuckling to herself and watching the sky overhead. The other child played as he always did on the edge of the hearthstone and all was at peace.

By midday it was far too warm for men to work and so, as

234

before, Jimmy came home from the fields for a while until the heat had passed. They were both sitting in the cottage when the child by the door started to scream again. Both parents rushed out to find the yard empty but on the wall, just above the crib itself, the same strange shadow had spread itself out. This time it *did* look like a man but with very long arms, which it had spread out towards the infant itself, creeping slowly towards the crib. The thing rippled and moved on the wall as if it was alive.

Jimmy Kavanagh stood there in the yard for a minute, not terribly sure what he was looking at. Then he stepped forward to move the crib away from the wall and as he did this, the shadow seemed to move with him. He moved back and the shadow seemed to rear up as if it was following him in some way. Its very long arms looked as if they were moving towards him and he jumped back a bit. He grabbed the end of the crib and pulled it towards him but as he did so the shadow seemed to move forward, running from the wall like dark water and onto the ground towards him. Of a sudden, he felt something tighten about his throat – like hands it was, squeezing at his neck – though he could see nothing. He knew, however, that it was the shadow. The feeling only lasted for a couple of seconds and then the thing was gone, but Jimmy knew that he had felt it all right. He looked around him but the yard was filled with shadows from the bright midday sun and he couldn't follow where it had gone.

Jimmy and his wife were badly shaken by what had happened. Now both of them were sure that their child might be in danger and so they moved her from the doorway and into the house.

"This is some trick of that Tom Foley's," Mrs Kavanagh declared sharply, but Jimmy shook his head.

"There's no tellin' what it is," he answered. "It might be some plan of the fairies. Isn't there a fairy rath only a couple of fields away? And it's well know that the Good People'll steal away human babies if they can." However, he was really at a loss to explain the peculiar shadow, except to agree that it was dangerous.

"I'd go an' see the priest," replied his wife, "for if it's fairies or something like that, only the priest can deal with it."

But Jimmy shook his head. He wasn't sure what it was and he didn't want to drag the clergy in if he could help it. Once you let them in, it's difficult to get rid of them again and Jimmy had no great respect for the Church.

"Let's see what happens," he suggested to her, "for whatever it is, we might've scared it away."

But he was wrong, for the shadow-thing seemed to have grown bolder and as Jimmy's wife looked out of the window that night, she saw that it was back in the main yard in front of the house, waving and dancing in the moonlight. From time to time, it made a motion as if it was moving towards the house and then drew back again – but it seemed to be coming closer anyway. She guessed that it was only a matter of time before it would actually get into the house and then it might attack their child. Jimmy himself was worried but he was an easy-going man and liked very little trouble or upset.

"Go and see the priest!" his wife urged him, but Jimmy still hung back.

"We don't know what we're up against," he said with a great caution. "Maybe the priest will hound us and won't come. But there's a man I know – Yellow Daniel – who knows about these things and he might know what it is."

Yellow Daniel was the name the country people called Daniel Fallon who lived in a run-down house that was little more than a hut by the roadside over towards Enniscorthy. He was a wee man, lame in one foot, and was considered to be very wise. The name came from the fact that he'd once had very fair hair but it was very grey now and tucked up under a knitted black hat that he always wore. They said he had once been a priest himself but had been thrown out of Holy Orders for drinking. Even at this time, he was seldom sober. But everybody said that he knew a great deal about "things". Jimmy thought that he might know something about the shadow in his yard. Mrs Kavanagh wasn't all that keen on going to see him for, like most people in the countryside, she'd had sharp words for Yellow Daniel from time to time. But her worry about the child made her swallow her pride and go to see the old man.

In his dark and dirty house, Yellow Daniel listened very intently to what they told him about the strange shadow. Then he took a long draw on his pipe, poking it tight between his toothless gums.

"Has either one of you," and here he looked directly at Mrs. Kavanagh, "had bad words with Tom Foley? I've heard it said that he has . . . powers such as what you describe."

Jimmy Kavanagh's wife stared back at him. "What do you mean?" she asked him directly. "Speak plainly now." There was no mistaking the dislike that she had in her voice for the old man but then she had little time for any of her neighbours.

Yellow Daniel ignored her tone and took another long draw on his pipe. "They say that he has very old powers –

powers that the Vikings brought with them from the northern lands when they first came to Wexford. In those dark days it was believed that certain people could cut off their shadows and send them out to do their bidding, whatever that might be, and that this was done through darkest magic. It was said that witches living in Norway and away in the isles of the North could do it and that this power has been passed down to some people living in Wexford these days. Maybe Tom Foley is one of them."

"You think that this is Foley's shadow?" declared Mrs Kavanagh in surprise. "Will it harm my child? Surely not, for it's only a shadow after all."

But Yellow Daniel looked at her through his bleary, drink-clouded eyes. The reek of poteen from his clothes threatened to take her breath away. "Believe me, the shadow can do you as much harm as an ordinary man," he said. "The old Vikings used to send them out to kill people."

Jimmy nodded, for he had felt the shadow's "hands" about his own throat. "If what you're saying is true," he said slowly, "is there anything that can be done about it, for I think that the shadow is coming to do harm to our child?" His wife made to say something but he silenced her and let Yellow Daniel think.

"These things are very dangerous. They have a great power about them," the old man said at last.

Mrs Kavanagh turned on him angrily. "There! Didn't I tell you that we were wasting our time! I told you that we should've gone to the priest. He's the only one who can help us."

Yellow Daniel now faced her directly and there was a hint of anger in his bloodshot eyes. "They threw me out of the priesthood because I was too well in with the fairies," he said, "so I know what I'm talking about. These things can't be driven away easily and the local priests would be no use to you. Their mumbling prayers and all the reeking incense in the world wouldn't get rid of *that* Thing. It comes from a time before the Church had any power at all." His manner eased a little bit. "But I can give you something that'll probably help you and that has a bit of the Church in it as well." Going to a cupboard at the back of his house, he brought out a very small bottle that was made out of blue glass. "Here's something that might destroy what's been sent against you. It's holy water brought from the Church, but that on its own is not enough to defeat the Thing. I've added a few ingredients of my own to it in order to make it a bit more powerful against these forces. Here's what you must do. You must draw the shadow to you, out into the open, for it will always seek the shade where it's safe. Then just pour the stuff that's in this bottle directly into the heart of the shadow and see what happens. But remember, I can't give you any certainty that it'll be of use – this is very old magic, from the times of the Vikings that were in Ireland a thousand years ago."

Jimmy Kavanagh paid him for the bottle and brought it home, much to the disgust of his sharp-tongued wife.

"I wouldn't trust that dirty oul' creature," she told him, "for he's as bad as Tom Foley himself – worse, for he'd take the eye out of your head and tell you that you were better off without it. Throw whatever's in the bottle into the dunghill and let that be an end of it." But Jimmy kept the bottle close by him.

The next day, the sun blazed down again and there were shadows everywhere. That day, Jimmy didn't go to the fields but stayed at home in case the shadow should come back again. And so it did, slipping amongst the patterns of light under the trees until it reached the corner of the house. There it began to creep up the wall, moving to where the young child was lying in the shelter of the doorway. It seemed to be unaware that Jimmy Kavanagh was watching it from just inside the doorpost. It drew nearer and nearer, rippling and changing itself as it did. One time it was just a bunch of darkness and then it was long, like a very tall man crawling forwards. It moved with a sly, floating motion like a man swimming through a bog. It came forward all the time and Jimmy waited in the shadow of the doorway. As it approached the crib, he suddenly stepped out and moved the infant, making the shadow rear up as if in surprise.

"Give me Yellow Daniel's bottle! Quick!" he shouted to his wife, but she hung back. The shadow began to extend its long arms towards him. "For goodness sake, give me the bottle!"

But the wife was reluctant to do so. "It'll do no good," she shouted back. "Even Daniel himself said that it mightn't work."

Already Jimmy could feel a tightness about his throat as if a thumb were being pressed against his windpipe. He could almost feel fingers on the side of his neck, although he could see nothing at all, just the shadow in front of him. The Thing seemed to be crushing the life out of him. It was now very close, flowing like water from the cottage wall, reforming itself and almost towering over him, rearing up like a snake.

"In the Name of God, woman, give me the bottle!" he shouted. At the mention of the Holy Name, the tightness about his throat seemed to ease a little bit and, seeing his distress, his wife handed him the bottle which she'd opened. Jimmy threw the contents at the very centre of the Thing. There was a sizzling sound like bacon frying and the shadow seemed to fall in on itself, turning into a dark ball in the yard in front of his feet. From far away, both of them thought that they heard a scream like the shout of a man in great pain. Jimmy Kavanagh and his wife stared in astonishment as the shadow in front of them started to fizzle out on the ground and then was gone. He turned to see his infant daughter sleeping peacefully in her crib and he guessed that the danger was past.

When nobody had seen Tom Foley for a while and when his untidy shebeen remained closed for well over a week, people began to get concerned about him. He wasn't all that well liked, but his neighbours didn't like the idea that something might have happened to him. A group of men from the locality decided to break into the upper end of the building where Foley lived and they hammered down the door. When they got in they found Foley in a back room, lying on a flea-ridden mattress in the corner, his face twisted in an awful look of pain and fright. He was quite dead and, although nobody knew what had killed him, Jimmy Kavanagh and his wife were able to guess. Around him in the room, the men found some other things – very old things – that they were afraid to touch and wouldn't talk about. They sent for the priest, who took them away, and nobody knew what he did with them. There were some old books too that the Church ordered to be burned without anybody reading them. And that was the end of it.

Jimmy Kavanagh's daughter grew up to be a fine woman and married in the locality – her descendants still live in Wexford yet. Jimmy and his wife had other children and they spread throughout Ireland; I think some of them might even live as far away as the North. But ever after that, Jimmy and his wife were both frightened of exceptionally sunny days when the shadows were on the ground, and wouldn't venture all that far from their house in such weather. And sure, who could blame them?

* * *

Note: Although understandably stories of such creeping shadows appear in the main in County Wexford (which had a significant Viking influence in its early history), they sometimes appear in other areas of Ireland as well. Some of these do not have a particularly Norse connection and it is worth considering whether such a belief – that a man or woman might be able to detach him or herself from their shadows – was also a feature of Celtic culture as well. The idea of a stealthy shadow, out to create mischief or danger, of course adds a sinister touch to even the sunniest of days, so that even at the height of summer, the dark edge of the supernatural is never all that far away.

15

LANNIHAN'S PALE WIFE

COUNTY KERRY

In many rural areas, the coming of a stranger or someone from far away to live as a permanent resident was a cause for suspicion and alarm. Someone who came from far away, who maybe had strange ways about them and who might not fit in with the local community was, in rural eyes, bound to be up to no good. They might even actively be working towards the spread of evil in a locality – at least that was the thinking. Thus, in many instances those who took partners from far away were inviting danger and darkness into their own part of the countryside. In many country areas, then, those who were considered to be witches or who were "in with the fairies" usually tended to be the partners of somebody from within the local community. Usually, too, they tended to be women. Therefore, in some of the more remote rural communities, there appears to have been some sort of unspoken prohibition against marrying someone from relatively far away.

If marrying someone from a distance away was a problem, then marrying a tinker was even worse. Tinkers were travelling people and in their travels had supposedly picked up unfamiliar habits which didn't sit well amongst settled people. Tinker women especially were believed by the settled community to have odd and dangerous powers which could be used against a community if these women so chose. Therefore, the settled man who married a tinker woman – and there were some instances of this in Ireland – was sometimes as much of an outcast as the woman herself was. A tinker woman, it was also said, would never get on with her husband and would never settle with a family. This was because of her travelling nature and her attitude toward the stable community around her. And it is easy to see how simple personal disagreements might be amplified by such factors.

The following story comes from County Kerry and is reputedly associated with the Tullig area, which is on the edge if the Magillycuddy Reeks. Other versions have it located somewhere in the parish of Sneem, which also lies in the county. In fact, in the 1930s, Tim Murphy – a collector for the Irish Folklore Commission (his notes are archived in University College Dublin) – recorded a fragment of a similar story in that area, so the tale, in various forms, must be fairly common in the Kerry region. This version of the story was told to me by Patrick Sullivan, an old man who claimed connection with the area. He, in turn, had heard it from Father Hugh Cahane, who was the parish priest directly involved in the matter. This, he assured me, meant that the tale was authentic.

It should also be said that this is a very old tale and reflects the perceptions and prejudices of previous generations. It is typical of the sorts of stories which settled folk told about tinkers and reflects the unease which many communities felt towards them in former times. In these more enlightened days, we take a much different approach and so, although after a great deal of thought I have included the story in its original form, it in no way reflects the reality of the tinkers or of the travelling community either then or now.

There was a man living one time in a very remote mountain parish and his name was Paddy Lannihan. He was a civil and decent enough man, although he was prone to be a bit headstrong and a bit full of himself at times. At the time I'm speaking of, he was a man of about thirty or thirty-five years of age and he was a mountain farmer. Now he should have been a grand catch for any woman, for he owned acres of good mountain land with neither brother nor sister to share it with, for he lived on his own, and he was well connected to the clergy, being a cousin or a second cousin of Father Michael Hayes, who was a great priest in County Mayo – Ballintubber or Crossmolina or somewhere like that. You would have thought that the women would come to him in droves. But no, when it came to getting a husband, they married his neighbours – them that were available – and left him alone. It's difficult to say why, for he was a personable enough looking fellow. Maybe it was because he was very headstrong and set in his ways. And maybe it was that, for some reason, he never fitted in with the community. There was a kind of oddness about him and nobody could really say what it was. It was always remarked that, despite his isolation and on the face of it, he seemed happy enough. But deep down he was lonely, although he never told anybody about it.

Well below his house, on a stretch of bare mountain, was a small glen with a river and a road running through it. In its very centre was a small bridge with a stand of low trees at its end, sheltered from the wind by the mountains above. It was a beautiful place that caught the sun on good days and it was very peaceful and still. At certain times, tinkers would come and camp there, as they had done for long years before. As the autumn drew on, the smoke from their open fires would rise up from the shelter of the trees into the cooling mountain air and the smell of their cooking would waft across the slopes. They came about the same time every year and they came in wooden caravans, pulled by horses, several families of them, to camp out close to the trees at the end of the bridge where the road ran across the river. Local people didn't mind them for they were fairly quiet and peaceable in their ways and were usually gone after a week was out. It was usually the same families that came – and the people round about knew them – but sometimes others would come, just as autumn was easing its grip on the mountains and before the winter took hold properly. They were a much more secretive people who only stayed for a couple of days but used the campsites that the others had left. There were only a couple of families – maybe no more than one – but they didn't mix with local people or have much to do with the countryside around them. Locals often gave them a wide berth. They seemed to come and go at night; they would be there one evening and gone the next morning and that was all that would be seen of them for the year.

From where he lived, Paddy Lannihan could hear the tinkers in the glen below his house. In the autumn months he could hear their fiddles and the laughter around their fires and maybe this made him feel all the more lonely. He knew that he could go down and join in their sport – and he would probably have been made most welcome – but he didn't like to. So he left them alone and they did likewise.

In the winter, he could sometimes hear the rumble of iron cart-wheels coming and going as the other tinkers arrived and left. There was no music or dancing or laughter and when he went to the door of his house he could only know that they were there by the red glow of their fires down in the glen. Again, he never bothered them and they never bothered much with him. That is, until something happened one morning.

At the back of Lannihan's house, on the very edge of a large field that came up almost to his back door, was a well. It was separated from his back kitchen by a low stone wall through which there was a small gate. It was supposedly one of the best wells in the countryside for miles – the water from it was sweet and cool and very pure. Some local people used it – Lannihan used it himself – but he also allowed both sets of tinkers – those that came in the autumn and those that came later – to come up and draw their water from it. They usually did this early in the morning or last thing at night and Lannihan never bothered much with them except to say "Good morning" or "Good evening" when he occasionally saw one of them.

On a morning late in October, he rose early and went to the back door. On the other side of the wall, a tinker woman was filling a bucket from the well, stooping down as she did so. She was a young woman – hardly beyond her teens – with a narrow face, a band of sun-freckles across the bridge of her nose; her hair was russet-red and tied back in a bun on her neck, which was white and slender like that of a swan. She was quite possibly the prettiest girl that Lannihan had ever seen. She had been bending over the well filling a bucket, but when Lannihan came to the back door she straightened up as if she'd been caught in some furtive and illegal action. The morning sun caught her russet red hair as she did so and lit up her face, making her look even more perfect. Paddy Lannihan was smitten. The girl went to move back, like some wild animal startled when drinking, but Lannihan held up his hand to show her that he meant no harm.

"Good morning!" he called out. "Isn't that a grand morning? Are you getting some water from the well?" The girl eyed him warily, almost like a forest creature. He noticed that, in the morning light, her skin was very pale, made all the more white by her red hair. "Do you need a hand to carry it?" he enquired hopefully.

"I can fetch it well enough myself," she answered him, speaking for the first time. Her voice was low but there was a harshness to it that he found odd. It was like the voice of a moorland bird, heard at a distance, pleasant enough but with a wild edge to it. "I've carried water for my father and my brothers ever since I was a child." As if to show him, she lifted two buckets quickly. Even so, some water slopped out over the rim of one of them.

"Here!" he said, walking across to the low gate. "You're spilling it. Let me give you a hand, for those buckets are very full." She stood back and he lifted one of the heavy buckets and walked down with her towards the glen, where the first smoke of the tinkers' fires was already starting to rise into the still morning air. She followed him slowly, carrying the other bucket.

"Do you have a name?" he asked her as they walked.

"Aoife," she told him. "It was my mother's name when she was alive and I was called for her." She would say no more.

There were only a handful of tinkers in the camp – a couple of thin, oldish women and three or four young men working with the horses. They had lit a fire in the shadow of the stand of trees and an old man in a grimy, grey, ragged coat was sitting in front of it, poking at the edges of it with a stick. He had a shapeless old hat perched on his head, the brim of it pulled down a bit as if to shield his face.

"Is that Aoife back with water?" he asked in a rather high-pitched, creaky voice, without turning round or looking up.

"It is, father," replied the girl. The old man coughed and spat into the fire.

"Then go and give Donal a hand with the horses. We're to be away by tonight and we're heading north. I'll be glad to see the back of this cold place, girl." He spoke as if he was unaware of Lannihan's presence close by. Paddy moved a little and the old man started. "Ah, I don't recognise that footfall or the smell of whoever comes. Have ye brought somebody with ye, girl?"

"Somebody to carry the water, father," answered Aoife. "A man from the farm beyond – beside the well. He helped me down with one o' the buckets."

The old man turned his face towards Lannihan, letting the sun fall full on it and Paddy saw how evil it looked – pinched and withered, narrow and furtive, and the eyes . . .

249

the eyes were huge, white and sightless, standing out against the shrivelled, weathered skin like two great pale eggs.

"Then we are in your debt, sir, and I thank you for the kindness," he said; but there was something in his tone that was almost dismissive. It was as if now that Lannihan had brought the water down to the camp, he wanted to be rid of him as quickly as possible.

"There's no bother, sir," he replied. "I'll be glad to do it any time. I think that your daughter will struggle with the heavy buckets." The old man laughed like the shrill, wild cry of a bird. Paddy thought it an unpleasant sound, but he said nothing.

"Aoife needs no help carrying the water," replied the tinker, "for she's been carrying for us since her mother died. She is a good worker, my daughter, and better still, she knows her place." And he laughed again, just as unpleasantly. Out of the corner of one eye, Paddy could see that a couple of the younger tinkers had moved away from their horses and were turning in his direction. They looked very aggressive and Lannihan suddenly felt uncomfortable. He wished the old man a good day and retreated up towards his house with the two younger men looking up the glen after him. That, he thought, would be the end of it. But that's not the way that things worked out.

Late that night, Lannihan lay awake in his bed, listening for the rumble of iron cartwheels disappearing off into the night, but none came. The next morning when he opened his back door, there was Aoife, filling her buckets from the well on the other side of the low stone wall.

"Good morning," said he. "I thought that you were leaving last night?"

She straightened up and looked at him directly with those deep blue eyes and he thought that she looked very beautiful.

"My father took a wee turn late in the evening," she answered. "He sometimes does; it's a weakness that he has. We'll stay here for another few days while he rests. But we have to be away to the north before the winter begins to set in."

Lannihan nodded. "I'm rightly sorry to hear about your father," he said. "Do you want me to give you a hand to carry the water down to your camp?" For a moment she hesitated, considering the offer. "Ah, now let me, for with a sick father I'm sure you're hard pressed."

Again she seemed to pause. "My brothers are about and they don't mix too well with settled folk," she warned him. "They have very rough and wild ways about them and only my father can control them. I've little power over them myself." She paused. "But I wouldn't mind it if you carried one of the buckets down for me. They are very heavy but your water is good." Coming over the wall, Lannihan walked down the slope of the field with her to the glen below.

The old man was gathered together in front of the fire, wrapped in a long, torn army greatcoat while the young men worked at the wheel of a wagon below the trees. Aoife's father was still poking at the fire with a stick and Paddy thought that he looked even older, thinner and more evil. He lifted his head as the two of them approached as though he sensed them in some way.

"You are back with the water, girl," he said, "and you've brought the settled man with you, I think. Be careful of her, sir, for she has a bad name about her – Aoife was a witch-woman." And he gave another of his shrill laughs. Paddy knew that already, for it was the witch Aoife who had turned the four children of Lir into swans in the old story.

"I'm sure that there's little of the witch about her," he replied. The boys had stopped working at the cart and were moving a little ways towards him. He watched them out of the corner of his eye.

"Her mother had . . . powers," went on the old man, his eyes wide and white, "and sometimes I think so has she. So I'd be careful how close you got to her, sir." There was a kind of warning tone in his voice that made Paddy feel a wee bit uneasy. But he looked across at Aoife and she still looked very beautiful. The two boys had moved a little closer and the old man seemed to sense that as well. "Donal! Diarmuid! Get on with your work!" he commanded, just as somebody would speak to a dog. They turned away and went back to work at the cart-wheel again. The old man settled back again, pulling the greatcoat even more tightly about his skinny body. "We're in your debt again, sir. We'll not be here for much longer, so we thank you now."

"Stay as long as you want," said Lannihan, glancing in the direction of Aoife. He was badly smitten now.

The old man shook his head. "The winter's nearly upon us," he said, "and we have to be on the road to the north before the worst of it. So we'll not be here all that much longer – just 'til I get my breath back. But thank you very much for your offer, sir."

And that's the way that it was left. For the next few mornings Lannihan helped Aoife with her buckets of water down to the camp and in that time, she seemed to soften towards him. As for himself, he was as excited as a young boy again, drooling over his first girlfriend. They seemed to be drawing closer and closer and Lannihan noticed with some satisfaction that the old man seemed to be getting no better and that he seemed to have accepted the situation.

Then one night, almost a week later, Lannihan wakened out of his sleep to hear the sound of iron wheels on the road coming up from the glen. They were past his house and gone before he even got to the window in order to look out but he knew that the tinkers were gone north. And he was right, for Aoife didn't come for her buckets of water the following morning and when he walked down to the trees at the foot of the glen there was no trace of any of them – only the ring of ashes that marked the fire where the old man had sat. Lannihan felt his heart sink within him but she was gone and he had to make the best of it.

For almost a year, he tried his best, but she had smitten him very deeply. He found himself thinking about her day after day and as the seasons turned, the longing in his heart grew worse. As the autumn came within touching distance, the pale, red-headed tinker woman was never far from his mind.

The early days of September brought the first set of tinkers to the glen. Late into the evening Lannihan could hear their fiddles and their laughter down amongst the trees but although several young men and children – who all greeted him cheerily enough – came up to the well for water, he never bothered much with them. Soon they were gone as the darker, cooler days of October approached.

Several nights after they had departed Lannihan awoke

253

to hear the sound of the iron wheels on the road below and he knew that the others had now arrived. He hoped that Aoife was with them. And indeed she was, for when he hurried down and opened his back door the following morning, there she was on the other side of the wall, filling her buckets as before.

A year had barely changed her, although he thought that she looked slightly paler than she had done. He talked to her over the low stone wall – telling her, like a schoolboy, how much he'd missed her – and once again he offered to carry the water down to the camp for her. In the back of his mind, however, he'd made a decision – this time he wasn't going to let her go with her family away to the north. This time he was going to ask her to marry him.

The old man was seated at the fire, poking at it with a crutch or a stick, just as he'd been doing a year before. The morning was dark and the shadows didn't make him look any less evil. The two boys were working with the horses a little way away – they took no notice of Lannihan as he came down with the water. Aoife's father raised his head slightly as he approached, turning his great white eyes in his direction.

"The seasons have turned and we've come again," he said in the same creaky voice. "And I believe that you are as interested in my daughter as you ever were." Ignoring the two brothers, Lannihan sat down opposite him on the edge of the fire and told him what was in his heart, for the old man seemed to know it anyway. Aoife stood back, as was sometimes the way of the women in Kerry, and let the men do the talking. Surprisingly, for he was a close man, Paddy told the tinker his plans about marrying his daughter and the old man seemed to nod. When it was done, the tinker turned his sightless face towards Aoife.

"What d'ye think, girl?" he asked her in that harsh voice of his. "Would ye take this man if he asked ye? D'ye like him?"

Her pale skin reddened a bit. "I like him well enough," she replied, "and I suppose that I'd take him if he were to ask me. But he hasn't asked me yet."

The old man laughed high and long, making the boys working at the horses turn their heads towards them. "There ye are," he said to Lannihan. "There's yer answer. If ye ask her, she's yours, for neither me nor my sons will raise any objection." He leaned forward towards the farmer. "But if she takes ye, she must be married in the old way. Not in any church or religious buildin' but in the open air an' under the trees. We were never ones for settled people's places o' worship. We have our own ways an' our own customs. D'ye understand that, sir? You must give me yer word that no priest or cleric o' the church will come near her. I can marry her myself for I am a leader among our people. If ye abide by all of that, ye can ask her to marry ye."

It was a strange request and a difficult one for Paddy Lannihan, who had relatives in the priesthood, but he looked across at Aoife and he knew that she was what he wanted more than anything. So he agreed. Then he turned to Aoife and asked her to marry him.

"Don't think too long or hard about such a proposal," advised the blind man from the fire, "for it's made well an' this is a grand farmin' man – a settled man. I know that he's not of our kind – but then our kind is vanishin' off the roads as snow falls from a ditch in the spring. There are very few

255

of us left for you to take up with. I'm old and not long for this world an' yer brothers will go their own way when I'm gone – that's the sort o' them. So don't take too long over yer answer."

Aoife said that she would marry Lannihan and so it was settled. But as Lannihan himself turned away, the old man hauled himself up. Aoife had already gone to carry the water-buckets over to the caravan under the trees.

"A minute if ye would, sir," said the blind man, hobbling forward. He caught Lannihan by the shoulder with a bony claw. "I'd have a word with ye. If ye're bent on marryin' my daughter there are some things ye should take account of." He leant closer. "She is not like other women; she has a bad name, her mother's name . . . and she has . . . ways about her as well. She can be strange sometimes and headstrong. An' she never says much, for she's a close woman. She goes about her business in her own way. And if ye ask her, she won't tell you. It's just the way of her. But if ye can overlook these things, she will make ye a fine wife. Just be good to her an' be tolerant of her ways and the pair o' ye will get on fine." And without another word, he let go of Lannihan's shoulder and went back to his fire. The farmer made to follow him but he saw the two sons move away from the cart and thought the better of it.

And that was the way it turned out. Paddy Lannihan took the tinker woman for his wife and where they were married nobody knew, for it was in no church. And who officiated and who was present there nobody knew, for Lannihan never said – he was always a close man who kept his business as his own. And when the iron wheels of the tinker's cart rumbled away through the darkness of the night, Aoife stayed with him in the farm above the glen.

Of course, there was great talk throughout the countryside. For a farmer to marry a tinker woman was a bad and unusual thing and set local tongues wagging. And the manner of the wedding was a subject of great conversation as well – one minute Lannihan was a single man, the next he had a wife living with him and none knew why or where they had been married. Is it any wonder that there was gossip? But Lannihan paid them no heed. He was greatly taken by his new wife, who seemed to be as good to him as any wife could be. She cleaned for him and cooked for him and lay in the bed beside him at night and that was all that he wanted, for he'd grown tired of his own company.

There were things about her that were strange. For instance, as her father had said, she was not a great talker. At night when he came in from the field, she would have his meal on the table for him and when he was finished, she would sit down in front of the fire with him and get on with some sewing and give him hardly a word. If he asked her a question she would sometimes reply with a grunt and sometimes not at all. Sometimes she would only reply in two or three words and then fall silent again. She never said very much.

The second curious thing about her was that he never saw her eat anything. Certainly, she cooked him a dinner every night (and she was a passable enough cook) but she never sat with him at the table and he never saw her eat a morsel. She always said that she wasn't feeling hungry or that she wasn't feeling the best or that she would eat later. But she never ate at any of the mealtimes, no matter how good the food appeared to be.

And just to add a further curiosity, there were times when he awoke during the night to find himself alone in the bed. Where his wife had gone, he had no idea, for whenever he got up, she didn't seem to be anywhere in the house. So he went back to bed and, shortly afterwards, she would come into the room and get into bed herself. In the morning, she would never speak about where she'd been or even mention that she hadn't been in bed at all.

There was something else too. Since she'd come to live with Lannihan, he'd heard that some of his neighbours had become sick with some sort of mysterious disease. Indeed, it had been so bad that a couple of children had died of it, away up the glen, and another couple had been forced to go to the doctor's surgery. But there was no explanation for it; the doctor just scratched his head and admitted that he didn't know. There were some who said that the sickness was supernatural – that it had come from the fairies or the Devil. There was some talk that it was witchcraft and that, seeing how it had started when Lannihan's wife had come to the district, she was somehow responsible for it. Lannihan himself ignored all this, but sometimes when he was alone in the fields, he wondered about it.

As time wore on, Aoife seemed to withdraw more and more into herself. When Lannihan came in of a night and sat down to the meal that she'd cooked for him, seldom a word passed between them. It was the same when he rose from the table. She would get on with her sewing and some sort of housework, while he would read the paper and all was silence in the house. When he was away working in the fields, she would take herself out to wander along the old roadways and amongst the old raths and mounds that were to be found about the countryside, so that if he came in for tea in the middle of the day, there was nobody there to welcome him. He knew that this was the case, for he'd spoken to neighbours who had seen her amongst the old ringforts or in groves of trees away from the road, seemingly talking to herself or maybe to somebody that no other could see.

Now Lannihan was a fairly smart man and he put this down to his wife's makeup. She was a tinker, after all, and perhaps she missed the life on the open road with her father and brothers. Maybe she was resentful towards him for taking her away from it. But still, there were many questions that nagged away at the corner of his mind. Why didn't she eat? Where did she go when she got up in the middle of the night, when she thought that he was asleep? There were some nights when he lay awake until it was almost light and she still hadn't come back – slipping into the bed as soon as the sun came over the horizon. What was she doing? He recalled the words of her old blind father, that she had a bad name on her – a witch-woman's name – and that she wasn't like other women. Did this have some sort of significance, maybe? He resolved to find out. He would pretend to be asleep and when she rose from the bed and went out, he would follow her and see where she went.

And that was the way of it. One night, he lay down in bed with her and pretended to fall into a deep, sound sleep. When he seemed to be snoring, she stirred and rose, slipping out of the house and into the night outside. Lannihan opened an eye and then he too rose from the bed and followed her.

All around him the countryside was plain for miles about. By the light of a big ball of a moon, he could see the dark shape of her ahead of him as she hurried down their lane and along the road, climbing a gate and into the fields beyond. Everywhere she went, Lannihan followed her, staying well behind her, but always keeping her in view. He followed her across fields and along narrow lanes, over ditches and hedges, through drains and gullies, and he never once lost sight of her. It was the paleness of her skin, you see, which showed white in the strong moonlight.

One of the lanes that she followed led down to an old ruined church with a graveyard beside it, standing on the edge of a bog. The place had a very bad name about it and many locals stayed away from it. But there were some burials in the cemetery beside it – not many, but a few, which were carried out in family plots and suchlike. It was surrounded by a low stone wall overhung with dark trees and bushes. It was here that Aoife made for, climbing over the mossy wall and into the churchyard beyond.

In the very centre of the old cemetery was a grave, all set about with rusty railings through which laurel bushes grew. It belonged to a grand family in the area and from time to time burials were still carried out there. There was a great iron gate set into the railings, with a large padlock on it. Even as he watched her, Lannihan saw Aoife touch the padlock and it fell away, allowing her to open the gate and go in. Dropping down on her knees, he saw her scrabble like an animal amongst the loose soil at the foot of a bush, just inside the railings. To his horror, she seemed to lift the arm of a corpse from the earth, sinking her teeth into its most fleshy bit. All the while, she seemed to be muttering something like a spell to herself. He moved forward to get a better look; as he did so, a twig snapped under his foot with a loud crack. The witch-woman paused in what she was doing and turned a little way in his direction.

"I know that you are there," she said in a voice that was cold, harsh and old beyond her years, "for I've sensed you following me. Come out and show yourself, husband of mine – or are you too afraid?" Lannihan stepped out into a shaft of moonlight where his wife could clearly see him.

"Now I know why you never ate the good meat that you cooked for me," he said, "for I can see that this sort of meat is more to your taste. What manner of creature are you that has to gnaw on the flesh of corpses like a wild animal?" She rose from the grave and he saw that her face looked deathly pale, made even paler by the redness of her lips.

"My father told you that I was different from other women," she answered in that same cold, ancient voice, "but you didn't heed him. Now you see how different I am. I am one of an old race of women that once walked these lands. They were witches and conjurers that held great sway over ancient kings. They guided and advised these old monarchs and led them into many bloody wars, for we live off carnage and misery and death. That's why I feast here amongst these rotting corpses, from which I draw my sustenance. *This* is the woman that you married!"

Lannihan fell back, with a cry rising in the back of his throat, for his mind could barely grasp what she was saying.

The witch-woman laughed – a low, unpleasant sound. "And now you think that you'll expose me and tell the world about me, but you'll do nothing of the kind, for our powers have ensured that we've walked amongst humankind for centuries. I have the power to stop you telling anyone about me with a simple act of will. Look deep into my eyes, Paddy Lannihan!"

Desperately, Lannihan tried to turn his eyes away from her stare, but he kept being drawn back with a dangerous fascination. He felt all the will drain out of him as he looked deep into those hypnotic pools that gazed back at him.

"Now I have the power to still your tongue when you go to speak of what you have seen this night," the witch went on. "If you try to tell any other about me, words will fail you and you will be tongue-tied. And you will continue to live with me as your wife and nobody will suspect who or what I am."

Lannihan tried to speak, tried to curse her for the devil that she was, but the words tripped over each other and came out jumbled. He made no sense at all.

"Now," went on Aoife, "go home again and let me get on with my feast. I will be with you in the morning and I will be certain that you will tell nobody about me." He would have rushed her then and there and tried to kill her, but he was terribly frightened. He didn't truly know what sort of creature she was and what sort of powers that she might have. He decided to do what she said for the present and to bide his time. So he turned and went home.

During the next couple of days, Paddy Lannihan tried to speak to a number of people about his pale wife and what she was, but each time he did so, the words got mixed up and he embarrassed himself by talking nonsense. He could certainly talk about her in general terms but once he began to mention her witchcraft or how she ate corpses, the words ran away with him and he made no sense. It was the witch-woman's spell on him. He was now greatly afraid of his wife. He was afraid of the way that she watched him when he was about the house and the way that she followed him about when he was out in the yard or in the fields. He tried to stay out of her way but it wasn't easy. In the night he would waken and he'd be alone in the bed and he knew that she was out on her rambles. God knew what she was up to.

The sicknesses in the area grew worse. There was some sort of fever that went from farm to farm in the locality, affecting young and old alike and taking away the weak and elderly. There seemed to be no cure for it and the doctors and healers were badly stumped. With each death, Lannihan's wife seemed more sprightly and went about smiling to herself. Lannihan wondered to himself if she had something to do with the awful disease but he dared not ask her. Nor could he have done so even if he had wanted to.

But Paddy Lannihan was a clever man – far cleverer than the witch had given him credit for – and he soon found a way to talk about his wife and about what she really was. He went to the priest, an elderly, kindly man, Father Hugh Cahane who came from County Clare but had been the clergyman in the countryside for many years. Father Hugh, he reasoned, was protected by his holy office and might be able to lift the spell that his pale wife had cast on him. So he went to the old priest.

"Ask me a question and ask it in the Name of God," he said to the astonished clergyman. "Ask me about my wife." Father Hugh was a bit taken aback, but he had heard some of the stories that were going about the countryside concerning Lannihan's wife and about the disease that was affecting local people and he thought that there might be something to his odd request. So he asked him to speak about his wife in the Name of God. Once the Holy Name is uttered, no dark spell has any power at all and Lannihan was able to tell the priest about what had happened in the ruined churchyard.

Father Cahane listened intently, nodding occasionally. He was an old, wise man who had seen many things in the course of his ministry.

"I've heard of such creatures," he said, "for I once knew a great priest who was an exorcist and who knew the dark ways very well. I had a suspicion that your wife might be one of them, but I never liked to say. These things are very old and can trace their ancestry back to Lilith, the witch that was Adam's first wife and the Mother of all Evils. But they are scattered all over the world and can only be driven out by the pure light of God. They have to be exorcised in their darkest form, when they are practising their foul witchcraft. Therefore we must capture her at night and put an end to her badness." He spoke with a kind of certainty that Lannihan found very reassuring.

That night, the priest waited at the end of Paddy Lannihan's lane. He stayed there until he saw the dark shadowy figure of the pale wife pass him by on her nightly rambles. Shortly after her came Paddy himself, who had wakened in the bed to find his wife gone and knew what she was about. Once again the moon was big and the countryside was lit up as if it was daytime. The two men – the priest in his dark coat and Lannihan dressed in his ordinary clothes – hurried along the narrow roads and cart-tracks, through ditches and over hedges, following the witch-woman. They passed by sleeping houses and through the grounds of dreaming churches, farther and farther into the countryside.

At last they came to an old place, no more than a hill in a field, that was walled off by a low stone wall and unmarked. This was a *caldreah*, a graveyard that was used for burying suicides, unbaptised children and those who had died outside the Church. There were a number of graves there, but none of them had any headstone or memorial about them and the site was greatly avoided by the country people.

"Such bodies are of great interest to witches and the like," said the priest softly, "for they don't have the Church's blessing about them. They can be used in spells and charms and are of great interest to them that practise the dark arts. I'm not surprised that she came here." He watched the pale wife climb over the low wall and into the *caldreach*. "Now we must go and face her while she's up to her badness." Lannihan hung back for a moment but the priest laid a comforting hand on his shoulder. "We have the power of Our Lord with us. No evil thing can harm us," he whispered.

Together the two men followed the witch into the unblessed cemetery. In the moonlight, they could see her, little more than a dark hunched shape, at the top of the hill. She had fallen on her knees and appeared to be drawing something up out of the earth.

"She is feeding in the way of her kind," went on the priest. "She has an appetite for dead flesh. Maybe now's the time to confront her whilst she's busy." So saying, he stepped out into the moonlight, holding out his crucifix in front of him like a weapon. At his movement, the witch-woman turned and Lannihan saw what she held in her hands. It was the body of a small baby, recently dead and still wrapped in its shawl, its tiny arm hanging limply down. Aoife looked directly at the two approaching men with a stare that was a mixture of both anger and alarm. There was a ring of old blood around her mouth and her eyes flashed with hellish fire. Lannihan wondered how he had ever seen any beauty in that terrible face – she had cast some sort of spell on him, he reasoned.

"Priest!" she said, and her words sounded like a hiss. "Leave this place. This is none of your business." Father Cahane, however, held his ground, although Lannihan noticed that his face had gone deathly pale in the moonlight. The moon glinted brightly on the crucifix that he held in his outstretched hand.

"Witch-woman," he said softly, "I know your sort, for they have been around for centuries. You speak truly. I have no business with you, but Our Lord whom I serve wishes to make you His." The moon suddenly flashed on the crucifix and the witch stumbled backwards as if shielding herself against its light, dropping the bundle as she did so. Lannihan cried out in terror but stayed where he was behind Father Cahane.

"Take that thing away!" she cried. "I'm only a poor woman." Much of the venom seemed to have gone from her voice and Lannihan glimpsed, only for a moment, the beauty that he'd first seen in Aoife when she'd come to draw the water from his well. "You have my husband with you. He will tell you."

Father Cahane was unmoved. "Don't mock me, witch!" he said sternly. "For I know that you're descended from the Mother of Lies. You now face the power of the Risen Christ, who instructs you to quit this place and go to that which has been appointed for you. Leave this man and this parish alone! It is the power of Christ that commands you!"

The witch shrank back but still seemed defiant. "Do you think that I am frightened of your words, priest?" she spat, although Lannihan and the priest thought they heard an uncertainty in her voice. "Your God is dead and hanging upon a tree. What have I to fear from *Him*?" Father Cahane's jaw tightened, although Paddy saw that the hand which held up the crucifix was trembling a little.

"Blaspheme all you want, witch!" he answered her. "But the power of the Risen Christ will always triumph over such as you!" And he thrust the crucifix towards her, making her fall back all the more. The cross glowed with a silvery light, a reflection of the moon that was now overhead, and the brilliance from it struck the witch woman. She gave a loud cry and suddenly the *caldreach* was filled with a cacophony of sounds. There were children crying, men talking, people shouting from far away. But above all of these there was the sound of iron cart-wheels on a hard road, moving away into the distance. Lannihan turned around but could see nothing, only the empty hillside, and yet the sounds seemed to grow louder, all except the sound of the cart-wheels, which appeared to be fading away. Father Cahane stood like a tree, the glowing crucifix stretched out in front of him.

"What is it, Father?" cried Lannihan. "What is all that noise?"

Father Cahane's face was very grim. "It's the sound of the dead," he replied, "and the sound of evil. Our Lord is at His work. Look away now, man, and remember your wife as she was when you loved her. You do not wish to remember the witch that she is now." Lannihan did as he was told and the sounds of the dead began to lessen. When he turned his head back, Aoife was gone and the sound of the cart-wheels had all but faded away into the dark.

Father Cahane wiped the sweat from his brow, for it had been an ordeal for him as well. "Go home, Paddy," he told Lannihan. "Go home and give thanks for your escape. It is few men that marry such beings and very few of those who do survive to talk about it. It was the power of Christ that saved you just in time."

Still shaking from the experience, Paddy did what the priest had told him, although he jumped at every shadow that moved in the hedges. Even so, when he got back to his own place, he half-expected to find Aoife waiting for him, as lovely as she'd been when he first saw her, but the house was empty.

The next morning, Father Cahane called to see if he was all right. The priest still looked very pale.

"You've had a very narrow escape," he told Lannihan. "This is what comes of consorting with tinkers. The tinker people are not as settled as we are, either in their ways or in their beliefs, and this makes them especially vulnerable to creatures of that sort. Do not neglect your Mass, Paddy, for you've the taint of those things upon you and it can always draw more of them. But have no more to do with the tinker kind – that's my advice to you."

And that was the way of it. For the rest of his days, Lannihan lived alone in the house above the glen, going about quietly and never neglecting Mass. But, from then on, he tended to keep people at a distance – never mixing too freely with them – and many thought that he was lonely. And maybe he was, for he went about the house and the fields as if he was looking for somebody. Despite all her wickedness, maybe some part of him still missed Aoife.

The first set of tinkers came back and camped in the glen as soon as September came round. The sound of their fiddles and their laughter drifted up to Lannihan's house, but he never bothered with them. And when they came up for water at his well, he stayed indoors with the blinds drawn and never went out. Soon they were gone and the long winter days set in. No more tinkers arrived in the glen – neither the old blind man nor his fierce-looking sons. Nor did they come back to the glen at all and many were glad to see them go. But, it is thought, on many nights Lannihan lay awake in his bed, listening for the sound of iron cart-wheels on the road below, the hunger for company in his heart and the loneliness devouring him. Although she had been defeated, the witch-woman had still left him with a terrible curse.

* * *

Note: The idea of settled folk shunning tinkers and of tinker-people turning into something else in order to work mischief is a quite common one in Irish folklore. In many cases tinkers, like witches, can change themselves into animals, according to these traditions, in order to carry out their supposed wickedness – to steal items from the household, to break things or even to smother children in their cradles. Guises which they particularly favoured, it was said, were those of cats or stoats and these animals were to be driven away from the house, since they could be tinkers who might revert to human shape and abduct children. There are therefore a number of cautionary tales in several counties, both north and south, of which the tale of Lannihan and his wife is one.

16

THE DUMB SUPPER
County Offaly

In many remote country areas of Ireland, it was difficult for men and women to meet socially and perhaps form relationships, with a view to marriage. Houses tended to be scattered and although some céilís or dances did go on, they tended to be rather sporadic in isolated areas. Many girls and boys often relied upon parish events organised by the Church in order to meet each other. These too tended to be very sporadic and were usually strictly controlled by the parish priests. In remote areas, therefore, there was little chance for any form of close fraternisation between the sexes.

This, of course, did not prevent young people from thinking or dreaming about love. In general folk tales, it seems to have been mostly girls who did so and it may be that in male-dominated, remote rural societies, females felt especially isolated. Unlike today, perhaps many of the young girls considered that their future lay in finding and marrying a husband and raising a family. Marriage had become a function, something set for the rest of one's life and perhaps something to be anticipated. Consequently, many young girls wanted to know in advance whom they would marry (if they married at all), where they would live after marriage and how many children they would have.

There were many "spells" and "charms" to find out such information. They could, for example, collect water in a basin under a new moon; looking into it, they would see the face of their prospective husband looking back at them. If they saw their own face, it meant that they wouldn't be married. The first snail of the morning, placed on a dish of flour, would trace out the initial of the Christian name of a future partner, whilst if impaled on a thorn and its skin placed under a pillow, the sleeper would dream of the possible husband or wife. Another "charm" was a bit more risqué. A girl might wash a chemise in her own urine and hang it up to dry in front of the fire. On the stroke of midnight, the shape of her future husband would come in and turn the chemise so that it dried.

On the face of it, such practices may seem harmless enough – the dreams and imaginings of lonely girls. To the Church, however, they were suggestive of the darkest witchcraft. Local priests sometimes raged against them and those who practised them from the pulpit. Only God alone should know the course of a person's life and it was not for silly girls to try to see what lay in store for them, they thundered. But there was yet another side to such notions.

How could the affections of a loved one be secured? As someone who grew up in a remote country area I know full well the shyness that was often felt by country people with regard to the opposite sex. It was one thing to dream about such things, but how could one turn them into a reality, especially if one felt shy and awkward? Or what could one do if the person in question seemed attracted to someone else? Again there were charms and spells that could be used but they reeked of darkest witchcraft and were outlawed and abhorred by the Church. One of these was the Dumb Supper.

When I was growing up on the edge of the Mourne Mountains in County Down, there was a girl living quite close to us who was excommunicated from the Church for having practised the Dumb Supper in order to draw a man to her. She lived in a very isolated part of the mountains and had little chance of meeting someone. I suppose it all eventually got to her. I heard the following story too in the lower reaches of the Slieve Bloom Mountains in County Offaly and I have adapted it to demonstrate the loneliness and at times desperation of some of the country people.

From where she stood at the cottage door, Bridget could see all the way down the slope and into the narrow valley below. It was late summer and the Slieve Bloom was looking at its best: the changing hues of the heather; the sparkle of a distant waterfall; the subtle shadows slowly moving across the mountainsides. Away across the shoulder of the land, she could see the thin trail of blue smoke rising from a neighbour's chimney – very far away. It would take over an hour's good walk to reach Dan Quilly's door and he was the nearest house to them.

The Slieve Bloom was very beautiful, to be sure, but it was also very isolated. People lived in scattered houses, maybe miles apart, and saw each other only infrequently. Life in these breathtaking mountains could be very lonely and that loneliness was all that Bridget had ever known. And yet she knew that it wasn't like that everywhere. Mrs Reardon from down in the glen had brought her some old torn and creased magazines one time. How Mrs Reardon

273

had got her hands on them, she didn't know, but when the neighbour woman had given them to her – "Take them, I'm finished with them" – Bridget had pored over them intently. She ignored the text – she had never been a great reader anyway – and concentrated on the pictures. They were full of pictures – photos of busy streets, of people – and advertisements with glossy illustrations. In one or two of these, men and women sat together, over coffee, looking fondly into each other's eyes; walked together hand-in-hand in parks; or huddled together on benches to demonstrate the warmth of a sweater. It was all very glamorous and very loving; all very different from her own life. She looked out across the bare mountain to where Dan Quilly's smoke still curled over the lip of the land.

"Bridie!" The voice was high and querulous – an old man's voice, from inside the house. "Bridie, are ye there girl? I need the privy!"

Her father had been bedridden with a bad stroke for almost three years now and never ventured far beyond the narrow back room of the cottage. A small, thin, weaselly man, he seemed to have become more demanding since Bridget's mother had died over a year before. Sometimes she thought that he was far better than he said he was. And she knew that he could get about far better than he said he could. When he thought that she wasn't looking, she'd seen him get up from a chair by the fire to get a cup of tea from the kitchen table. But it suited him to lie in bed, pretending he was poorly, to be waited on hand and foot by his daughter and to carp and complain about how life had treated him badly. Sometimes she thought of running away and leaving him to his own devices; but where could she go?

There had been four children living in that cottage when her mother was alive, three girls and a boy. One of her sisters had gone to Dublin – just got up and left one morning – whilst the other had followed shortly after and was now somewhere in London. Both of them were married now and had families of their own. Her brother had gone to America and though she only heard from him infrequently, she knew that he was happy and, although not married, he had a steady girlfriend. She, however, had stayed on, unwilling to leave her mother alone with her demanding father. She had planned to leave at some point, as the rest of her family had done, but somehow she'd never got round to it. As her mother's health had deteriorated – worn out by her father's constant whining – the possibility had moved further and further away. When her mother had died, she had been left in the cottage with her father whom none of the others wanted. The possibility of leaving now seemed to be gone.

"Bridie! Come on, girl! I need the privy. Quick! Before I wet meself an' ye'll have t'change the bed!" With a sigh, Bridget turned away from the door and went to see to him. Was this to be the pattern of her life from now on?

After she had lifted the moaning and complaining bag of bones that was her father out of his bed and onto the commode and back to bed again, she walked back to the door and looked out once more. It had grown cloudier, darker, with a kind of gloom rolling in from the west. The Slieve Bloom, however, still looked beautiful and as she stood at the door, Bridget knew that she'd miss the peace and tranquillity of the place if she were to leave. But what was the alternative? A life of continual drudgery with her whining father? And when he eventually died, living up

275

here on this isolated farm? But there was another way: Thomas Connolly.

Bridget had loved Thomas Connolly for a number of years now, ever since he'd come across the valley to put in some posts around the edge of the cottage to keep wandering sheep out. If she stood on her tip-toes, she could just about see the gable of his own cottage just beyond the shoulder of the hill above which Dan Quilley's chimney-smoke hung in the air. He was in his thirties – the same age as herself – and was dark and good-looking, with a rugged jaw and smouldering eyes that promised much. She dreamed about him almost every night as she lay alone in her own narrow bed. At times she thought that she could reach out and feel his bare skin beside her in the bed. She wished it were so.

There were problems with her loving dreams, however. First, whilst he had been courteous and pleasant to her, he had not taken any great notice of her. True, he had laughed and joked with her when he'd been working around the place, but she suspected that he'd all but forgotten her as soon as he struck out for home across the mountain. The second thing was even more serious: Thomas Connolly already had a wife and two small children.

Bridget didn't know his wife but she'd seen her at a distance a number of times – a tall, pleasant-faced woman, with long, tumbling, dark hair. Thomas was obviously very fond of her. And yet, Bridget loved him with a passion that only a lonely woman can muster. In her dreams, she wished that he would somehow leave his wife and come across the mountain to her, taking her away from the lonely cottage. Someone else would look after his wife and family, but they would go and live together, maybe nearer the town. This was her dream although, deep in her heart, she knew that it was impossible. Thomas Connolly would never come striding across the mountain to take her away with him. It was all just a fantasy. Or was it?

"Bridie! Get me something to eat!" her father's voice called from the bedroom. "I'm near faintin' in here with hunger. Would ye have me die here for want of food, ye ungrateful girl?" Again she turned with a heavy sigh and made her way into the kitchen to fetch him something.

That night, as her father lay snoring in his bed, worn out by all his whining and complaining, she sat in front of the fire and leafed through one of the magazines that Mrs Reardon had brought her. There seemed to be pictures of loving couples scattered everywhere through it. It was all very romantic and it seemed to taunt her. She would never know love like that – not from Thomas anyway. All she would have was her father's constant carping, and loneliness after he was gone. And yet there *might* be a way to win Thomas's heart – but it was a dark and dangerous path.

As a child Bridget had heard of spells and charms that could make someone fall in love. However, these were of the darkest form of witchcraft, or so the Church taught, and no Christian person should have anything to do with them. To be involved in such practices, the priest said, was to damn one's immortal soul and consign it to Hell. And yet, could Hell be any worse than the loneliness and oppression that she felt looking after her father in this lonely cottage?

Away at the throat of the valley, there was a woman living called Mary Kenny. She was an old woman, narrow-faced, small and thin, with her hair grey and tied back in a bun at the nape of her neck. Bridget had seen her sometimes up among the old fairy forts on the upper slopes above her house, always dressed in a thin old red coat and grey woollen stockings. Nobody knew what age Mary Kenny might be but many said that she was very old – their fathers and even their grandfathers remembered her living there. And yet, despite her advanced years and withered appearance, Mary could still draw men to her – even young men. It was said that any man she cast her watery eyes at would eventually make their way to her falling cottage to lie with her in her filthy bed. That was what the neighbours said anyway.

How could an old, withered, raddled woman achieve this? Well, it was also said that Mary Kenny was a witch and that she used the Dark Arts to accomplish it. Long ago, Bridget had heard how the old woman – she was old even then – had been able to cure conditions like ringworm and warts, bad stomachs, headaches and toothache. She could banish a bad burn and stop a flow of blood from a wound. But she had other powers as well – older, darker, more pagan powers – and these she used to her own advantage. It was said that she could stir love in the coldest breast and prepare a charm which would bring even the most unwilling to a person's bed.

As she sat there, turning the pages of the magazine in the glow of the firelight, a plan began to form in Bridget's mind. Maybe, she imagined, Mary Kenny might be able to help her win Thomas Connolly's heart for her own.

Mary Kenny's house was hidden away in an isolated stand of dark trees just below the entrance to the glen. It was a tumble-down affair with loose, hanging slates on the roof and a yellowing wash on the walls. The door and windows were dirty and narrow, overhung with weeds and grass that grew down from the roof. The path which led up to it snaked between the trees which hung their branches down as if to bar the way. It was evening and already a late gloom was stealing across the Slieve Bloom, but the faint brilliance of an oil lamp burned in Mary Kenny's window.

Bridget approached warily. She could see the ruddy light from the window glinting through the dark tree-foliage and around the edge of the half-open door. Mary Kenny was at home. She walked on, ducking under the branch of a tree. Something cracked beneath her foot, starting up a bird in the tree – a slate fallen from the roof and half hidden amongst the long grasses. Then she was at the cottage door.

"Who's there?" came a thin, quavering voice from inside the house. "Who's coming to torment a lone woman at this late hour of the evening?"

Bridget swallowed. "It's only me, Mary. Bridget Fagan, from up the valley!" The voice paused.

"Paddy's daughter? I know ye, surely. Well come in, child, an' tell me your business." Bridget stepped across the threshold and into the low, cluttered interior.

Directly in front of her was the large open hearth with the bellows to one side at which Mary Kenny sat. The fire looked as if it had burned down to ashes but there was still a fair heat in the room. To her right was a large wooden table cluttered with bits and pieces – an old clock, a statue of the Virgin, dirty dishes and a crock of milk. Above the table were a couple of shelves which were cluttered with jars and bottles, some obviously holding jam but others containing other substances.

Hanging from a nail on the end of one were several muslin bags. Goodness knows what they might contain.

It had been a while since she'd last seen Mary Kenny, but the old woman was even smaller and more frail than she remembered. She sat in a large armchair, the sides of which were split and from which the stuffing spilled out onto the stone-flagged floor. She had her thin legs spread out towards the dying embers of the fire and Bridget saw that they were swathed in grey woollen socks. Mary was also wearing her red coat, gathered around her like a shawl – despite the residual heat of the cottage, she obviously felt the evening cold!

"Come forward girl!" the little woman beckoned. "It's been a while since I've had a look at you. I'm an old woman and I can't see all that well." She turned her narrow face and red-rimmed narrow eyes toward her visitor. Leaning forward in the big chair, she appeared to be straining to see and Bridget wondered how a drained old creature like this could get any man she wanted. "How's Paddy? I haven't seen or heard of him lately. Of course, I don't get out as much now."

"He has a bad stomach," said Bridget timidly. "That's why I'm here." She told herself not to be frightened of the old woman – she probably wasn't as big a witch as the people said – but her senses wouldn't heed her. "For a powder or somethin'." The old woman nodded.

"Paddy was always bad with his stomach," she agreed. "Too much drink. Too much poteen." She cackled, a shrill old woman's laugh. A bird called back from somewhere in the gathering darkness outside. "But I'm sure that we've somethin' for him." She motioned with a skinny hand in the direction of the shelves above the table. "Have a look in that red jar up there. There should be a handful of powder in it. There's a twist of paper to the side of it – just fill it up but take no more. Too much is as bad as too little. I can't be bothered gettin' up." Bridget helped herself. "Give it to Paddy in some water before he lies down in bed. It'll settle his stomach an' help him sleep. Tell him that it's nothin' more than powdered roots and herbs that I found up by the Ghost Road in the Slieve Bloom." Bridget asked how much she owed and Mary Kenny named her price. Bridget left the money on the edge of the wooden table as the old woman asked. She turned to go, then thought the better of it. Her father's stomach powders were not the only reason she had come to see Mary Kenny.

"Th-There was something else," began Bridget timidly. The old woman stirred again. Something moved suddenly in the gloom at her feet – a black cat. Bridget almost cried out.

"I thought there might be," said Mary Kenny. "What is it? Are you with child, maybe?"

Bridget snorted. "No, I am not!" she replied hotly.

"But there is a man involved," went on Mary Kenny knowingly. "There's *always* a man involved with a woman like yourself. Maybe it's somebody you want that you can't have. That's always the way of it." The cat moved along the hearth, seeking the last heat of the fire. "Is that it?"

"There is a man that I'd want to want me," stuttered Bridget, embarrassed that she was even *saying* these things. The small woman in the chair nodded slowly.

"And he doesn't?" Bridget blushed and hoped that Mary Kenny didn't see her do so in the poor light.

"No," she replied softly. "But I want him to." The old woman sighed and moved in the chair.

"And why do you come to me?" she asked. "I'm just a poor old woman with neither chick nor child near me. I've never been married and am past the age now. What makes you think that I would know how to get a man, Bridget Fagan?"

Bridget hesitated, unsure as to whether or not to reveal to the old lady what local people were saying about her – although she probably knew anyway.

"They say that you have powers – that you can bring men to you as you wish," she said warily, fearful of Mary Kenny's anger. "I wish that I had that power!"

The old woman laughed, high and shrill, and the bird in the trees outside answered her once again.

"They say many's a thing in these mountains," replied Mary Kenny. "I may not have as much power as you think, girl. But I do know some things. Up along the Ghost Road that runs through the mountains when I'm gathering herbs for my cures, I can hear the spirits and fairies whispering to each other and I learn things from it. They tell me things – dark things that would damn your soul if you knew them. Unless you are set on this man and willing to damn yourself to Hell, I would go home and forget about the way you're asking about. No good might come of it, either for yourself or for him that you want. That's my advice to you."

"And if I don't take it?" Seeing her option slip away, Bridget suddenly found the courage to confront the little woman in her chair. "What if I want this man above all else and what if I'm willing to chance everything for him? What then?"

For a moment, Mary Kenny didn't answer. "Then he must be a very special man," she said then, "and you must want him very badly. If you're heart is set on this road, then I will tell you what I know. But I can give you nothing; this must be all of your own doing, for I'll not have the damnation of your soul on my conscience. Is that agreed?"

Bridget sighed. "It's agreed." She had hoped for a powder or a potion but if Mary Kenny were to give her some arcane knowledge to draw Thomas to her then that would work just as well. The old woman leaned further forward and her cat scuttled away into the shadows.

"There are a number of ways in which you can bring this man to you, to win his heart, though the love he will give you will be born out of the Dark Arts and will not be true love. Will you settle for that?" Bridget nodded. "Very well, then. There is a charm called the burrough-boos, which is a length of skin, taken in a single strip from the crown to the heel of a fresh corpse. It is a very old charm and there are few who practise it now. I do not know much about it myself – nor could I prepare it – and I know of no-one in this country that does."

"So we can forget about that," said Bridget. "But you said that there were other ways."

Mary Kenny nodded. "I hear the need in your voice," she answered. "There is always the Dumb Supper, which can be done by anyone and will be just as effective – and as dangerous as the burrough-boos. Is that the one you want to try, Bridget Fagan?"

"Tell me how it's done?" whispered Bridget eagerly.

Mary Kenny raised a warning hand. "The spell must be cast in total silence," she said. "There must be no sound, not even the tick of a clock. All of the clocks in your house must be stopped. No word must be spoken, no human sound uttered – not even a sneeze or a cough, or all will be undone and your soul will be damned for nothing. Everything must be put out of the house – all animals or birds, for if they make the slightest sound, everything will come to naught. Can you do this, Bridget?"

"I'll try," replied Bridget.

"Trying is not enough," answered Mary Kenny, "for this will affect not only your own soul but the very life of the man that you're dreaming of. The house must be as silent as the tomb. And it must be swept clean before you begin. You must prepare then for baking, for you must bake a loaf of bread in total silence – stirring it up and making it ready for the oven for baking. This must all be done between the hours of eleven and midnight and the loaf must be ready and presented on the table before twelve o'clock. It must be placed in the very centre of the table and with an iron knife across it. Everything must be done in silence – as if you and the whole house were dumb. Then, on the very stroke of midnight, there will come a rap on the door. You will go and open it. There, the shape of him that you most desire will be standing, waiting. You must motion him in without speaking and the Shape will come in and go to the table and the loaf. He will lift the knife and cut the loaf, taking a slice and offering it to you. Once you have taken the slice, he is yours and nothing can come between you both. He is yours forever, although as the priest will tell you, you have damned your immortal soul through witchcraft. But I warn you, if there is so much as a sound until you accept the bread, the man that you desire will be lost to you forever and you will have damned your soul for nothing. Is that the sort of road that you wish to go down, Bridget Fagan?"

Again Bridget hesitated – this certainly smacked of black witchcraft and for an instant she was frightened. But the thought of the lonely years which probably lay ahead made up her mind.

"What about my father?" she asked. "He's old and bedridden and might make some sound when I've started the spell."

Mary Kenny considered. "For the Dumb Supper, it's always best that you clear the house and that you are alone, so that there's no sound," she said slowly. "But I would think that with Paddy, that's not possible?" Bridget shook her head. "Then I must give you something that'll make him sleep like a baby." She cackled. "But it'll cost you a wee bit extra." Bridget said that she would pay it – now that she'd committed herself, she could do little else.

"There! It's done!" said the old woman with a certain finality in her voice. "Now, take one of those bags from the end of the shelf. There, at the very end – it has a sleeping draught in it that *should* work on your father – give it to him in the heel of a cup of water and he should be asleep shortly after. But be careful, for these things are never certain. Now leave my money and go, for I'm tired. I'm an old woman an' all this talk about men has wearied me." And she made a dismissive motion in the air with a long finger.

Bridget left the money and turned away, unsure of the road on which she had now set herself. As she made her way back along the twisting path through the gloomy trees an owl called mournfully after her.

All the way home across the mountain slope, she wondered if she was doing the right thing. This was her immortal soul, after all, and from what Mary Kenny had said, she might threaten the life of Thomas Connolly and consign his soul to Hell as well. Was this worth it? Those doubts were still there when she reached the door of her cottage and slid the key into the lock. She turned it and pushed the door open.

"Bridie? Is that you, girl? I need the privy. Quick now, girl, for I'm near bustin'!" The voice drifted to her from the back bedroom, thin and demanding, summoning her even before she'd crossed the threshold. And, as she walked across the narrow kitchen, she knew that she'd taken the right path.

It was a week after she had visited Mary Kenny. It was also late at night, just before eleven o'clock. She had given her father the old woman's sleeping draught and about five minutes later she heard him snoring. She cleaned the cottage scrupulously as Mary Kenny had instructed, made sure that there wasn't a dog, a cat or a hen anywhere near it, and then stopped all the clocks. Going in to her father's bedroom, she turned the old man on his side so that he wouldn't snore. He murmured a bit but soon fell silent. As soon as the place was completely quiet, she began to make preparations for baking the loaf of bread, gathering together the flour, the salt and the milk as silently as possible. Then she began to bake, striving hard not to make a sound. And in the back bedroom where her father lay, all was quiet. In the back of her mind, she remembered that Mary Kenny had told her that the powder was uncertain and she prayed that the old man wouldn't wake up and destroy the spell.

The bread was baked and, though all the clocks in the room were stopped, she knew instinctively that it was somewhere near midnight. Placing the freshly baked loaf in the centre of the table, she put the iron knife diagonally across its crust. Then she waited. Minutes passed. Maybe the Dumb Supper had failed her. Then suddenly there was the sound of someone striking the door. Rising from her chair, Bridget crossed the kitchen and opened it. It was dark outside but there was a large and high moon which threw a silvery light across part of the mountain and by its brilliance, she could see the dark figure that stood there. It was Thomas Connolly – or at least his likeness. The Shape was dressed in the working clothes that he'd worn when he'd come to work for her father and the moonlight from the mountain made his skin look unnaturally pale against the darkness of the jacket and jumper. He stood there as if waiting for her. Wordlessly, she beckoned him in and he crossed the threshold without making a sound. Without pausing, the Shape walked across the kitchen towards the table. Bridget's heart stalled within her – the spell was almost complete now. Thomas Connolly was almost hers.

The Shape moved slowly, stiffly, like an old man crippled with pains, but it reached the table. Lifting the knife, it began to cut the loaf.

"Almost there!" thought Bridget. Whatever stood in front of her started to lift a piece of cut bread and made to offer it to her. She stretched out her hand to take the offered bread.

"Bridie!" the voice rang out from the back bedroom as the old man stirred. "Bridie! Where are ye, girl? I need the privy!"

The thing on the other side of the table staggered back, flickering in and out of reality as it did so, its mouth opening in a scream that crackled and echoed all around the tiny cottage, but Bridget was aware that only she could hear it.

Then it was gone, almost like a puff of smoke, and she was alone in the kitchen once more.

"Bridie! Are ye not comin', girl? I know ye're there! I need the privy!"

The sun spread across the mountain slope, driving whatever dark shadows were there before it as it went. Standing at the cottage door, Bridget could see the faint trace of smoke from Dan Quilly's chimney, curling up over the lip of a hill to be lost in the air, somewhere high above. It had been over a week since she'd practised the Dumb Supper, but the memory of that terrible evening was burned indelibly into her mind. The day was beautiful once again but her mind was dark and gloomy.

The day after she cast the spell, Mrs Reardon had called by on her way up from the valley. She brought very grave news – Thomas Connolly from farther down the mountain had been found dead in his bed that morning. Nobody knew why – he'd gone to bed hale and healthy the night before, but around midnight, he appeared to have taken some sort of seizure and had died almost at once. Maybe something to do with the heart, Mrs Reardon had said.

"It's awful, so it is. His poor wife an' wee children left behind. Terrible! Terrible!" and the woman shook her head wonderingly. She didn't know, but Bridget did.

"If the spell fails, then the man that you desire will be lost to you forever." Isn't that what Mary Kenny had said? And it had come true. There was no way that she'd have Thomas Connolly now. Her lonely life stretched out before her – and after that, the torments of Hell. This was her fate now. No matter how lovely the Slieve Bloom looked, its beauty was now absorbed by the darkness of her heart.

"Bridie? Are ye there? Is there anything t'eat? I'm fair starvin' back here'. The voice held the familiar whine. With a sigh, Bridget turned away from the doorpost.

"Coming, father!" she called back wearily.

* * *

Note: Although this story has been somewhat amended and stylised, it is based on a number of actual slightly more generalised stories – including one from the Slieve Bloom – told to me by a variety of people from several remote areas of Ireland. Perhaps at one time, the practice of the Dumb Supper may have been more widespread amongst lonely people in very isolated communities than is generally suspected. Not only this, but I've also heard similar stories in the Ozark Mountains of America, where the charm seems even more common, so maybe some Irish "witchcraft" has transferred itself to the United States!

A personal Tale

17

THE GATE HOUSE

COUNTY LONGFORD

Several years ago, I visited a lady whom I knew very well, in her new house which she had built inside part of a fairy rath. She complained bitterly about the problems she was having – the doors wouldn't hang properly, her new cellar flooded, the plumbing was suspect, the electricity was sometimes sporadic, cutting off without warning and without explanation. The very building seemed to be liable to subsidence, she said. I could have told her that no good would come from building a house in or near a rath.

All over Ireland, it was widely believed that supernatural powers concentrated within certain points in the landscape. These might include ringforts, mounds, raths and tumuli from former years. These were places to be avoided, for their influence was considerable and often malignant. Furthermore, it was also believed that these sites might be the abodes of primal forces, once worshipped as gods by the ancient Celts, which were still aware and which might exercise a malign power over those who came close. These "powers" were invisible but they were there and were still

293

watchful, wary of the humans who crossed or loitered on what they considered to be their own domain. Their vengeance over those who trespassed upon their lands could be swift and terrible and was often designed to show the superiority of these ancient powers over rash but fragile mortals. Such forces were often specific to the one site.

Houses built in such places never seemed to have any luck about them. In fact, in some instances, old stories claimed that they were "possessed" by the spirit that inhabited the land – the genius loci *itself. It might manifest itself perhaps in the form of a ghostly presence – there are several stories about it in this aspect from various areas of Ireland – or in poltergeist activity – and there are even more tales concerning this aspect. Each aspect, however, seems to have followed one particular purpose: to drive the human inhabitants out. According to many stories, such activity was often successful.*

In some cases, large houses and their attendant buildings were built on the lands occupied by such forces, giving rise to many local legends about ghosts and sheehogues. Whether true or not, many such tales are attached to some of the grand Irish families and their homes. Perhaps the origins of such stories lie in the acquisition of land by such families during the various Irish plantations and the resentment which it engendered amongst their tenantry.

The following tale comes from County Longford, which I visited a little while ago. I came upon the story almost by accident and it refers to an area between Granard and Edgeworthstown where, I was told, a house was built on a site occupied by one of these sheehogues or genius loci.

I've always considered Longford to be a rather strange and eerie county. My general memories of it usually consist of driving along endless empty roads, with gloomy fields on either side and between small and dreaming hamlets. Here and there are certainly larger towns, bustling and very much alive, but it's the lonely roads and the shadowy fields which stick in my mind and which I always associate with the county. Here too are the remnants of large estates, some dating back to the seventeenth century and the Irish Plantations. There have been great houses there too, most of which have nowadays been turned to other uses – hotels, care homes, administrative buildings – often diminishing their former grandeur. And yet perhaps something still remains from former times, something that was probably there long before the house and its attendant buildings were erected, something that might still have an influence, even into the present day. . . .

"I can tell you that it's a bad place," said the old man without looking up. He stirred the edges of the open fire a little with the end of his stick. In the background, the old woman was pulling the neck of a bird into a tin bucket. It struggled and squawked and flapped its wings but she held it firmly, her fingers tightening steadily around its throat.

"But all them oul' houses are," her husband went on. "The place itself was a ruin even when I was a boy and places like that always draw ghosts and things to them."

"Was it a big house?" I asked.

He spat at the coals, his spittle falling short and sizzling on the warm hearthstone. "Big enough," he said. "Not the biggest in these parts but big enough. Built by the Forbes family, maybe for a daughter or something. Big enough to have a bit of a drive up to it and a gate house at the end. The house is near gone completely now, but the gate house is still there – beside what's left of the gates."

The bird struggled once again with a kind of a croak but its movements seemed weaker now. Its captor held it very firmly.

"Some people round about here say that the old house was badly haunted, but I know for a fact that the gate house is . . ." he looked for the word ". . . disturbed. Aye, an' maybe by somethin' more than a ghost." He looked at me pointedly. "There are things about in this countryside that are sometimes far worse than ghosts."

"What do you mean?" I asked him. I had been visiting County Longford in order to find out something about the Forbes family, the Earls of Granard, who also held lands around Edgeworthstown, home of the famous Maria Edgeworth, author of *Castle Rackrent*. In the course of my travels I had been directed to this old couple who, I was told, knew a bit about an old house, believed to have once been owned by the Forbeses, which allegedly lay between Granard and Edgeworthstown but of which no trace now remained. I had found the old man and the old woman extremely welcoming; they had brought me into their cluttered and claustrophobic cottage and offered to answer my questions as best they could. I took it from their attitude that they would tell me only those things that they wished to. But I was grateful for any information, so I sat back and just let them talk. It was the old man who was the most forward of the couple. He had worked on the lands around the ruined house, which had been owned not by the Forbeses but by a series of local landowners. All the same, his stories were both amusing and enlightening, even if they told me very little about the house that had once stood there. I suspected that the old man knew very little about it himself.

"The old house might've been haunted, for people said that it was always a sad oul' place, but it was the gate house that was dangerous. I heard my grandfather say that he'd heard when he was a boy that it had been built on an oul' mound that was supposed to be sacred away back in some time long past. My grandfather never minded the mound, for the gate house was there in his time too – and it was never lived in – but he minded the oul' people talkin' about it. It was always considered to be a bad place. Buildin' in them oul' places is always a bad thing."

"A bad thing," repeated the old woman like an echo. "A very bad thing." She had pulled the fowl's neck and the blood ran red between her fingers. Its body hung limp across her aproned lap. "There are things that live in them sorts o' places that never go away." The old man gave her a knowing glance.

"What sort of things?" I enquired.

The old couple looked at me as if considering between themselves whether to elaborate any further.

"There's things that have lived in this land since the old times," said the old man at last. "Those raths and mounds were built to keep them in but at one time they moved about all over the countryside. They're not as powerful as they used to be but there's still some of them about. People sometimes mistake them for ghosts and fairies, but they're not – they might be far older, for they were here when men first came to Ireland."

"And you think that this gate lodge that served the old Forbes house has one of these things about it?" I asked.

He looked at me as if I'd taken leave of my senses. "Sure, didn't I tell you that it had?" he demanded. "Even though the oul' mound was tumbled, the thing stayed on and became part of that house. The people told the Forbeses not to pull it down – that no good would come outa it – but they wouldn't listen. They pulled down the oul' mound and built the house an' the thing in it. *That's* why nobody lives there now an' why every family that's tried to has had to leave it."

"All of them had to go," said the old woman, rising from her chair, the dead bird half-tucked under her arm. Its neck hung limp, running blood. "It wouldn't let any of them stay. That's the way of them oul' things." She spoke in a matter-of-fact tone and might as well have been talking about the weather.

"And is there a story about the place?" I pressed him. He seemed to be thinking. The old woman had gone out into a back scullery to pluck the fowl but had left the connecting door open and appeared to be listening.

"Not really," he replied eventually. "There was an oul' tale that a miser lived there at one time, just after the Forbeses had given the place up. They say that he hanged himself from one of the rafters in the place but nobody minds who he was or where he came from. It's only an oul' ghost story to explain things away. All oul' houses have stories like that about them. If it was no more than ghosts they could be dealt with. The thing that is in that house is far older than any ghost. It's been there since the oul' mound was there."

"Far older," said the wife from the scullery, her voice sounding eerie against the stonework of the tiny room.

The old man looked into the open fire. He appeared to be thinking of something in the past. "I mind a man livin' there a long number of years ago. He was one of the last that I mind there – though there *might've* been others that I've forgot. But he was a man like yourself from the North. He was a clergyman – Church of Ireland, I think he was – but retired. He came to live in the house – a friend o' his had bought the place on a time an' had rented it out to him. What was his name now? . . . It was an unusual one for this part of the world, as I remember, Valance or Vance or maybe Vane or something like that – not the sort that you would hear too often." He laughed a little. "He was writin' a book on church history or somethin', I think. Thought the place would be quiet for him to work. But he was wrong."

"Very wrong," the old woman added. "The oul' thing was there. He wasn't there on his own. It was there an' waitin' for him."

The old man nodded. "It was indeed. He didn't stay there long. I mind him well, for he was a very decent man. But he had to leave." He leaned forward almost confidentially. "There were sounds, y'see, an' things were moved about. An' there was a sort of . . . *feelin'* . . . about the place. A sort of heaviness, as if somebody was watchin' ye all the time. I've felt it myself about that place. It's not a good feelin' an' I know that the clergyman felt it too. Aye, an' he heard things too." He shifted his chair slightly, making its wooden legs shriek against the flagstones of the cottage floor. "I mind one time I went down to see him there – I did some work about the place, though I never stayed there

299

after six o'clock in the evenin'. Anyway, this evenin' he turns to me.

"'John,' says he, 'are you a good whistler?' It was a strange question and I don't know what he was askin' me for. I couldn't whistle to save my life – never could. Even when I was wee I couldn't do it – I'd just purse my lips and blow air. And that's what I told him. He seemed to frown very deeply.

"'If it's not you, then who is it?' he asked me, speaking almost to himself. 'I sometimes hear somebody whistling round the back of the house. A very strong whistle, but tuneless – no real melody to it. I've gone out to the back door and looked but there's never anybody there and as soon as I step out, the whistling stops. For some reason, John, I thought that it might be you. It's all very strange.'

"I know too that there was a kind of strange feeling in the house – a sort of *heaviness* – and that the clergyman felt it too, although he never really said. He would say things like: 'Do you find it *close* in here, John? Very oppressive.' Or 'Do you think there'll be thunder today, John? It's very close. Very heavy.' That was how that house felt and you always got the notion that there was somebody else there with you – that if you turned suddenly, somebody would jump back or go through a door behind you. But there'd never be anybody there.

"Then one time he said to me, 'Will you take a look at the drains, John? There's an awful *smell* about the place. I know that the drains here are very' – what did he call them? – '*primitive,* so maybe it's something simple. Maybe something's blocked them up.' I looked but there was nothing, though I could smell the thing as well – a heavy, rotten, sickening stink, like something that had died. Indeed, that's what the clergyman thought that it was. 'Something's crawled in, John, and got stuck and has starved to death.' But no matter how hard I looked, I could find nothin'. And then there were times when there was no smell at all. He couldn't understand it."

"It was the smells and things that drove that family out of the place as well," the old woman called from the back door of the scullery. "They were hardly there at all and got settled 'til they were away again."

"That's right," said the old man. "There was a family – a man, a woman and a couple of children – came to live there one time but I can't remember what their name was. They were there no time. Didn't like the place and they moved to Dublin or somewhere. Mind you, I think that they might have *seen* things about it. The house was a great place for shadows and suchlike. You never knew what you might see in the half-light. You were never sure – it was that sort of a place. I think the woman might have been badly scared, or maybe I only thought that."

"And have you ever seen anything yourself?" I asked. The old man shot a furtive glance towards the scullery where his wife was still working, plucking the fowl.

"Ah no, sir. I've seen nothing about the place; but I've smelt the stench. Like something dead. And I've never heard the whistling that the reverend gentleman spoke of. They say it was ghosts but it was the Thing that's still there." He stopped for a moment as if an idea had occurred to him. "Would you like to see the place? I can take you there and I've a key. I never use it much but it's there."

"The key to the gate lodge, you mean?" I asked.

He nodded. "There's nothing to see of the house where the Forbeses lived, just a few stones and the stump of an old wall. But you can look at the gate lodge if you want before it gets dark." He made to get up and I followed. In the back scullery, the old woman continued to pluck the dead bird.

We walked down the narrow country road. On either side the fields swept down to the roadside, narrow and filled with shadows as the late evening sun began to go down. Even so, the evening was quite warm and mild. A car passed us heading towards Edgeworthstown but there seemed to be little traffic.

"I didn't like to say, sir," he half-turned to me. "I didn't like to say in front of the wife. She can be a . . . nervous . . . woman and things sometimes annoy her. But you asked me if I'd ever *seen* anything and I didn't like to say yes. I've surely seen things an' not only at the gate lodge. There was one time I was workin' near an oul' rath in the fields beyond and it was late in the evenin'. I was sure that I saw the shape of a man standin' under the trees deep inside the rath and watchin' me as I was workin'. That's the truth. But when I looked again, the shape or whatever it was was gone. You might say that it was a trick of the light but I was sure it had been there. The landscape all around here is full of those old things in raths and forts and such stuff from the old times."

"And you saw something at the gate house?" I asked.

"Yes, more than once. I mind when the old clergyman lived there, I was coming down to see him late one evening. I sometimes came down to see him of a night, to smoke a pipe with him and maybe have a glass of whiskey before he went to bed. As I was coming down, I saw the shape of a man walking down to the end of the garden. I had a clear view of it from the road. It stood at the gate for a minute and I was feared to come forward. It was like nobody that I knew – a low-set man with a hat of some sort and dressed very oddly in an old-looking coat. Then the thing turned and walked up into the house and as it did it started to fade away like smoke or rain in the sun, and there was nothing there. It walked in a funny, almost jumping way that didn't look like a human walk at all. When it was gone, I went up and saw the clergyman but the house seemed very close. I never told him what I'd seen but that was one of the nights that he heard the whistling."

I made to say something but he hadn't finished. Now that he had a listener, he seemed anxious to unburden himself about the place.

"There was another time, much later when there was nobody living there. I had a fancy to walk up late one afternoon past the oul' house to see a man that lived beyond it. The light was starting to go down as I drew level with the oul' place and as I came forward on the road I thought that there was a man standing at the door. I say it was a man but it was no more than a shape – more like a shadow. It was bending down at the door as if it was trying to put a key into the lock. And as I came a wee bit closer I didn't think it was human. I stood my ground, not sure what to do, and then it seemed to give a wee jerk forwards and was gone into the house. There was nothing there at all but I knew that I'd seen it and I quickened my step to walk past the house. As I did this I was sure that there was somebody or something watching me from behind one of the windows. I never liked to go too close to it after that. It might've been no more than my own imagining, o' course, but I always had a bad feeling whenever I went by it. Here we are now!"

We had rounded a bend in the road and in front of me I saw what looked like an overgrown entrance to a fairly grand driveway. There were the remnants of two pillars, one on either side of a mess of weeds and briars which showed where the gateposts had once been. There were the ruins of a rusty spiked iron fence too and part of an old wall, most of which seemed to be gone. A little way from the road, beside what must once have been the drive, stood the gate house, half-masked behind high bushes and trees.

It was much smaller than I had imagined it to be – a longish, hunched building made of dark stone, with low and beetling eaves which gave it a slightly sinister appearance. Narrow windows stared out towards the road like watchful eyes, the dying sun catching their edges and giving the glass a jaundiced glow. In many respects it was no different from many of the gate lodges and porter houses that I'd seen elsewhere – and yet there was something *different* about it. Despite the balminess of the late evening, it seemed to exude a coldness and a distinct air of menace as we approached. There was something that was *unnatural* about it that made it appear almost *alive*. Of course, I reasoned that such an impression – and it was no more than an impression – was probably down to the tales the old couple had told me about the place. I realised that the old man had suddenly stopped on the road beside me.

"There it is," he said. "I'll go no farther. You can go up yourself an' take a closer look if you want. I'll wait here for ye. You can even go in if you want, for I've a key." I stayed where I was, unsure of whether I wanted to go any closer, let alone go in. He handed me a large, old-fashioned, awkward-looking key. "You can try it if you want. An educated Northern man like you shouldn't be afraid of a few oul' ghosts."

I went up to the door. It was painted green and had badly peeled. The coldness, however, didn't diminish and I was in two minds about whether to try the key in the lock or not. The old man had stayed slightly farther back on the road, though he seemed to have come a little closer. Standing on the weed-grown doorstep, I tried the key in the lock and began to turn it. It stuck for a moment and then began to move, albeit stiffly and uncertainly. I heard a faint click and put my hand to the door, pushing it gently inwards. It opened in front of me, emitting a rush of stale air that smelt like the belch from a foul stomach. The door opened slowly, but it opened.

Beyond was a narrow hall which seemed to lead down into the gloomy back of the house. From where I stood I could see dirty white-painted doors leading off to either side. Between them, peeling wallpaper hung from the walls in great torn sheets, threatening to come down completely at the slightest touch. The hall itself was almost impassable because of the rubbish and debris that was piled there – boxes, old newspapers and magazines, what looked like post and circulars, and packing cartons. I thought that I even saw the ruins of an old pram pushed up against one of the white doors. At the far end another door lay open into what looked like a small kitchen with a window, through which I could see the moon, starting to emerge from behind some distant clouds. That was all.

I wondered if I should take a step in. The place held the acrid smell of being closed up and damp. I took a step across the threshold, then another. A strange feeling came over me; it was the feeling of *oppression*, as if a great fist had closed around me. I went on, picking my way carefully up the hall, hearing hidden glass crack under my footfall.

The place genuinely was smaller than I had thought. In no time, even walking slowly, I was at the end of the hall and peering into the kitchen. There was nothing there – just the marks on the wall where an old cooker and several cupboards appeared to have been. An old sink, stained and cracked, with brass taps close to the window, faced me directly and there were several old benches and work surfaces, all thick with dust and cobwebs. A spider's web hung from the window in front of me.

The whole place had the air of dereliction and abandonment about it. And yet somehow I was convinced that I was not alone – that something watched me from the shadows of the hallway. I half-expected to see a shape peering at me through a chink in one of the doors off to the side. Walking backwards with some difficulty, I touched one of them and pushed it open. What seemed to have been once a bedroom lay beyond. Like everything else in the house, it was a mess. Floral wallpaper sagged and hung in great swathes. What still clung precariously to the wall was badly stained with damp. In the far corner, by an uncurtained window, an old armchair with the stuffing hanging out of it had been pushed tight against the wall. There was no trace of a bed but in the centre of the room, an old mattress, torn and badly stained, had been folded over on itself and now lay in a heap. There was the broken end of an old crate and several empty bottles lying beside it. As I watched, something crawled from the base of the old mattress – a huge, shiny, black beetle.

The sense of dereliction was almost overwhelming but then so was the sense of watchfulness. I made to turn around and make my way back to the outer door when I was sure that I felt that something pushed past me. I looked around but there was nothing there – just the cluttered hallway, filled with rubbish. However, I had received the distinct impression that, just for a second, someone, or *something* had physically pushed against me in an effort to get past – or perhaps even to do me harm – and had passed on down the hallway again. The sensation was extremely unsettling. I might have been mistaken – it might have been no more than an exposed nail momentarily catching the end of my coat – but it felt as if there was something there and in the closeness of that grim house the feeling was most unsettling. It was as if something had touched me and moved on. With the sense of oppression increasing, I moved out into the daylight, pulling the door of the house after me.

"It's a grim place," said the old man, waiting for me on the road. "I haven't been in it since the old reverend gentleman was there and I wouldn't go into it again if you paid me a fortune. There's *somethin'* there. You'd think the whole house was alive with it." And as I handed him back the old key, I suspected that he was right.

In the days afterward, I tried to rationalise it all away. The old couple's stories and the close atmosphere of the house itself had made me imagine all sorts of things. A bit of loose wood or a nail had caught me, making me imagine that something had touched me. The stink and the miasma of the place had made me imagine things. And yet, over the years I have come to believe that there are at least some places in this world which are not particularly welcoming to Humankind and where men should not go. It's a personal belief but I hold fast to it. Perhaps the old man was right; perhaps the gate house, being built on the site of some ancient prehistoric mound, was one of those places. Maybe once disturbed, whatever lurked there had become active once more and would not go away. But these are only thoughts. Would I go back there and venture into that narrow hall once more in an attempt to confront my own fear? I seriously doubt it. Some houses *are* perhaps better left untenanted – at least by humans.

* * *

Note: This is my own personal story, which has been slightly adapted. However, the location does *exist – or at least it did. About a year ago I had occasion to pass through that area of Longford on my way south to Athlone and I took a minor detour to see if it was still there. There was now no trace of it on that lonely back road and where I remembered it to be was now surrounded by a high builder's fence and was marked for development – although what was being built there I have no idea. Even the house where the old couple had lived appeared to be gone. Of course, my memory may be faulty and I might have been on the wrong road, but I wondered: if building is going on there, has the strange Thing which was supposed to inhabit the site moved on, or is it still there in the ground like a disease, waiting for the next people to come along? Who can say?*